The CODE for LOVE and HEARTBREAK

The CODE for LOVE and HEARTBREAK

JILLIAN CANTOR

ISBN-13: 978-1-335-09059-1

Recycling programs for this product may not exist in your area.

The Code for Love and Heartbreak

This edition published by arrangement with Harlequin Books S.A.

For questions and comments about the quality of this book, please contact us at CustomerService@Harlequin.com.

Inkyard Press
22 Adelaide St. West, 40th Floor
Toronto, Ontario M5H 4E3, Canada
www.InkyardPress.com

Printed in U.S.A.

For B and O: Always trust that feeling deep in your gut.

It was foolish, it was wrong,
to take so active a part in
bringing any two people together.

—EMMA WOODHOUSE,
IN JANE AUSTEN'S *EMMA*

PROLOGUE

I've always loved numbers a whole lot more than I love people. For one thing, I can make numbers behave any way I want them to. No arguments, no questions. I write a line of code, and my computer performs a specific and very regulated task. Numbers don't play games or hide behind some nuance I've missed. I write an equation, then formulate a definitive and absolutely correct answer.

And maybe most importantly, numbers never leave me.

I tell this to Izzy as she's sitting on her suitcase, trying to force it closed, having just packed the last of her closet before leaving for her freshman year at UCLA, which is exactly 2,764 miles from our house in Highbury, New Jersey. A number which seems insurmountable, and which makes me think that after this day, Izzy's last one at home until Christmas break, we'll be more like two strangers floating across a continent from one another than sisters.

"Numbers," I say to Izzy now, "are much better than people."

"You're such a nerd, Em," Izzy says, but she stops what she's doing and squeezes my arm affectionately, before finally getting the suitcase to zip. She's a nerd, too, but not for numbers like me—for books. Izzy is running 2,764 miles away from New Jersey *to read*, to major in English at UCLA. Which is ridiculous, given she could've done the same at Rutgers, or the College of New Jersey, or almost any one of the other sixty-two colleges in our state, any of which would've been within driving distance so we could've seen each other on weekends. Izzy says she's going to California for the sunshine, but Dad and I both know the real reason is that her boyfriend, John, decided to go to UCLA to study film. Izzy chose John over me, and that part stings the most.

"I can't believe you're actually going," I say, and not for the first time. I've been saying this to Izzy all summer, hoping she might change her mind. But now that her suitcase is zipped, it feels like she's really leaving, and my eyes start to well up. I do love numbers more than people. Most people.

Izzy and I are only seventeen months apart, and our mom died when we were both toddlers. Dad works a lot, and Izzy and I have barely been apart for more than a night in as long as I can remember, much less *months*.

She stops messing with her suitcase now, walks over to where I'm sitting on her bed and puts her arm around me. I lean my head on her shoulder, and breathe in the comforting scent of her strawberry shampoo, one last time. "I'm going to miss you, too, Em," she says. "But you're going to have a great senior year." She says it emphatically, her voice filled with enthusiasm that I don't believe or even understand.

"You really could stay," I say. "You got into two colleges in New Jersey." This has been my argument to her all summer. I keep thinking if I say it enough she really will change her mind. But even as I say it, I know it's probably too late for her to change anything for fall semester now, no matter how much I might want her to. And she just looks back at me with worry all over her face.

"Em, you know I can't."

"Can't or won't?" I wipe my nose with the back of my hand, pulling away from her.

She leaves me on her bed, and goes back to her suitcase. She shifts it around, props it upright and then looks back at me. "You know what you need?" she says, breathing hard from managing the weight of her entire life, crammed inside this giant suitcase. "To get out there this year. Be more social. Get some friends. Maybe even a boyfriend."

"A boyfriend?" I half laugh, half sniffle at the ridiculousness of it.

"If you keep busy, you won't even notice I'm gone." She speaks quickly, excitedly. There's nothing Izzy likes more than a good plan, but this sounds terrible to me. "Christmas will be here before you know it—" she's still talking "—then next year, you'll be off to college, too."

Maybe that would be true for her, if I were the one leaving, and if she were staying here. If I were the older one, leaving for California first, Izzy would stay here, spend the year with John and barely even notice my absence. Which is what

I guess she's about to do at UCLA. But I've always needed Izzy much more than she's needed me.

"I hate being social. And I don't want a boyfriend," I say. "And anyway, you know what the boys are like at our high school. No thanks." Mostly, they're intimidated by me and my penchant for math, and I find their intimidation so annoying that I can barely even stand to have a conversation with them, much less a date. And the few that aren't? Well, the one that isn't—George—is my equal and co-president of coding club. He also happens to be John's younger brother. We're something like friends, George and I. Or maybe not, because we don't really hang out outside of family stuff, school or coding club, and I guess in a way we're supposed to be rivals. One of us will for certain be valedictorian of our class this year. The other will be salutatorian. And knowing George, he's going to be more than a little bit annoyed when he's staring at my back during graduation.

"You love numbers so much and you're so good at coding," Izzy says now with a flip of her blond curls over her shoulder. She wheels the suitcase toward her bedroom door and stops and looks back at me. "You could always code yourself a boyfriend." She shrugs, then laughs a little, trying to make this moment lighter.

I don't even crack a smile. "That's a really ridiculous thing to say," I tell her. "Thank God you're going to be an English major."

But later, after it all fell apart, I would blame her. I'd say that it was all Izzy's fault, that she started the unraveling of everything with her one stupid offhand comment on the morning that she left me.

CHAPTER 1

"Okay," George says, tapping his fingers against the edge of his laptop in that annoying way he always does when I'm trying to think. "We need to come up with something really good to win the state competition this year."

It's after school on the first Friday of the year, and it's still way too hot outside even though it's almost mid-September. We're all sweating inside Highbury High, which was constructed of solid brick and sadly built long before central air. But coding club is my favorite thing about school—partly because I'm co-president this year, along with George. And partly because last year we came in third in the state coding competition, and this year I really believe we can come in first. I also want to come up with something that will look good on my Stanford application. That's right, if Izzy can go to California for college, then I can, too. And not for a boy, either.

I blow at my bangs in an attempt to lift them from my sweaty forehead and circulate some air. They're damp and barely move.

George fans himself with the paper that has the deadlines for this year's competition. The air movement pushes his sandy blond curls up, causing him to look more disheveled and overheated, not less. But George doesn't notice, or care—he keeps on fanning himself. "We just need to solve global warming," he says. "Should be easy enough."

A girl, whose name I haven't learned yet, giggles a little, and I shoot her a look to say: *George is not funny. Don't encourage him.* We have only four weeks to submit the application with our idea and proposal, and then get it ready for the regional competition in November. I don't want to waste any time. She's small, I'm assuming a freshman, and she's all curly red hair, which nearly covers her face more than frames it. She gives me a little shrug, and then glances back down at the competition guidelines, so all that's visible is her hair.

Coding club meets every Friday, even this very first one, and I'm excited to be back here, heat and all. The first week of school has felt interminably long and lonely without Izzy, and I've been looking forward to this meeting and starting our project. George, evidenced by the tapping of his fingers, is excited to be back, too. Ms. Taylor, our faculty adviser, not so much. She's staring out the window, somewhere between bored, exhausted and sweaty, and not paying much attention to us at all.

We're a relatively small club, but we're dedicated. We've lost some members—a few graduated last year. And we've had a little attrition, too. Phillip decided to run cross-country instead this year, which really is fine by me, since he spent more time messing around on YouTube than working on code last year, anyway.

I look down at the list of members in front of me and determine, by process of elimination, that the red-haired freshman must be *Hannah Smith*, as I already know the other girl on the list—Jane Fairfax—a junior who is sitting to my right and who always and un-ironically wears a lab coat as a fashion accessory. She's wearing one now, even though it is way too hot to wear any kind of coat. There are two boy names aside from George on the list and I don't recognize either—Robert Martin and Franklin Churchill. Though, glancing around the table, one is clearly a very small, very nervous-looking freshman. The other looks older, and…maybe new to the school? He has olive skin, dark wavy hair and bright green eyes that catch mine. Then he smiles.

I look away. "Ms. Taylor," I say, clearing my throat. "Should we do introductions for new members first?" I remember now, probably ten minutes later than I should've, that this is my duty as a senior and president of the club. To make sure everyone knows one another before we jump in.

Ms. Taylor has her gaze fixed out the window and doesn't seem to hear a word I'm saying to her.

I stand and walk to the window, to see what she's looking at. The only thing I see in the parking lot is my calculus teacher, Mr. Weston, sitting on the hood of a bright red Prius, talking on his phone. "Ms. Taylor," I say her name again, a little louder.

"What?" She snaps her head around, seems to see and hear me for the first time. "Oh, yes, right, Emma. State competition."

"Introductions first, though," George says kindly. She smiles at him and nods, and it's like no one even remembers that I've already said this. Sometimes it's frustrating to watch the way that George seems to be just naturally better with people than I am.

"Of course," she says now, her gaze trailing back out the window again.

George raises his eyebrows at me and shrugs.

"Okay, I'll go first," I say. I tell them only the basics, that I'm Emma Woodhouse, a senior, club president. That I expect them all to treat this club with the utmost seriousness, and that my first choice for college is Stanford. Green Eyes whistles lightly under his breath, like I've impressed him, and I'm annoyed to feel my face turning hot. I fan myself with the paper now, in case anyone notices and thinks it's any more than this heat. Honestly, it's not. "You next," I say, meeting his eyes.

He smiles again, and it feels like it's just at me, which makes my face feel even hotter. "I'm Franklin Churchill the third, which is the world's most pretentious name, I know. And though I'm sure that's what it says on the sheet there, my middle name is Samuel and everyone calls me Sam." I glance at George, who has gone back to fanning himself and looks bored, hot and unimpressed. "I just moved here, and I was in coding club at my old school. But we mainly messed around. Never entered any state competitions or anything like that."

"Welcome," George says, and I realize too late that I should have said that first. Then George jumps in and starts talking about himself. He mentions how his goal in life is to use technology to change the world, and I've heard it from him before. George is noble, maybe; much too idealistic, definitely. And I stop listening to him, turning my focus back to Sam. He looks away from George, smiles at me again. For some reason, I think about what Izzy said to me before she left, that part of what I need to make it through this year without her is a boyfriend. But it's a ridiculous thought.

What I need is a brilliant idea for our state competition project, something amazing enough that will get us first place and help me get into Stanford. Numbers are better than people, and my senior year is going to be all about how numbers are going to help me ensure my future after high school.

After the meeting ends, I drive George home. His parents let John take their third car out to LA. My dad, on the other hand, told Izzy she'd have to make it through at least her freshman year in California without the car, so I could use our second car for my last year of high school. Really, he doesn't have time to drive me around, and he knows Izzy has John out there. And though we never really sat down and discussed it, everyone seemed to assume that I could just drive George to and from school this year, and it would be fine. George likes to talk, and I don't, and I was worried that driving him would annoy me. But so far, it hasn't. The nice thing about George, I've come to notice, is he doesn't talk just to hear the sound of his own voice. He usually only talks when he has something to say.

"Sam seems smart," George says to me now.

"Mmm," I murmur, like I didn't notice Sam. "I hope so."

"And he has experience," he says. "Hannah and Robert will hopefully be quick learners. And we still have Jane, who really is amazing working with servers."

Jane is never very friendly to me, and she always annoyingly acts like she's so much smarter and better than I am. But George is right about her. I'm good with algorithms, George with animation. Jane is amazing with the back end, and I'm glad we have her for that.

I pull into George's empty driveway, and his two-story brick colonial is pretty similar to mine, which is in a nearly identical subdivision five minutes farther from school, down Highbury Pike. The blinds are all pulled shut tightly, and I imagine the house is dark and empty inside. It's after five, but his parents both work in Manhattan and probably won't be home for hours. Dad only works twenty minutes away in Princeton, but he rarely ever makes it home before eight. My house is similarly dark and empty, and I sigh a little, thinking about Izzy on another coast, basking in her sunshine. With the three-hour time difference, I wonder if she's even had lunch yet.

"You want to come in?" George asks, as if he's contemplating the same thing I am. "We can order a pizza. Brainstorm some more."

I'm about to say no, because George and I don't usually hang out outside of school. Last year I would've gone home on Friday night after coding club, boiled pasta with Izzy and argued over what to watch on Netflix until Dad got home and then Izzy and John would go out to see a movie and I'd go up to my room to work on coding or homework. Until this year, Izzy was not only my sister, but also my friend, my escape and my best excuse. I never had to worry about who to talk to or what to do or where to go on weekends, because I had her. I didn't need anyone else.

But this first week of school, going home every night to a dark, empty house—the quiet has unnerved me, and even working through my calculus equations and practicing piano hasn't calmed me down. I wonder if George has felt it, too? I wonder if, unlike me, he has other friends, other people he hangs out with aside from John. But maybe that's not the same? And now, with our siblings on another coast and our workaholic parents always at work, George and I have something besides school and coding club in common: we're both stranded here in Highbury for one more year, just waiting for our real lives to begin.

"Yeah, sure. Why not?" I finally say. "I like pizza." And I turn off the car and follow George inside his house.

I've only been inside George's house a few other times before, most recently for John's graduation party last June, which Izzy forced me to attend with her. Then, the house was packed with people I either didn't know or didn't like, and they all talked so much and so loud it made my head hurt.

I'd told Izzy I was getting a migraine and had taken the car and left after an hour.

But now, the inside is so quiet I can hear the dull buzz of the refrigerator, and hum of the A/C unit as I step inside. It reminds me oddly of the art museum in here: there's a large antique grandfather clock in the entryway, a formal glass dining set to my right and, to my left, a very formal living room with a large oriental rug, and expensive-looking velour-lined couches. In contrast, our house is what Dad refers to as "lived-in." We still have the same blue reclining couch and love seat in our living room that Mom picked out before she died, and even though they're worn, I don't think Dad will ever get rid of them. Which is fine with me.

I'm afraid to touch anything, and I stand very still as George takes out his phone and orders a large pizza from Giuseppe's: half mushroom and olive for me, half pepperoni for him. He knows my pizza preference without asking, from all the times we stayed late at coding club last year and ordered pizza in, and he never fails to make a face when he orders it, or comment on how mushrooms and olives only *ruin a good pizza*, while his pepperoni *enhances* it. He does it now, too. I shrug, and say, "Agree to disagree, George. Agree to disagree." He shakes his head and shoots me a funny smile. I've been a vegetarian since sixth grade when I accidentally watched a documentary on slaughterhouses on the Discovery channel, and that happened to be the year George and I first met, too, the first year of middle school.

George finishes ordering and offers me a seat at the kitchen table, which is slightly less formal than the rest of the house:

just a plain oak table, much like the one in our kitchen at home. He gets us two glasses of water and hands one to me. I gulp mine down, not even realizing how thirsty I was. George refills it for me at the fridge, and then sits down at the table with me.

"It really is way too hot today. And I was only half kidding about solving global warming," George says, pausing to drink his own water.

"I know you want to save the world, George. But we have *four weeks* to get a proposal together for this project. If you could figure out a way to solve global warming in four weeks, I think you'd win a Nobel Prize. And then who cares about the state competition—you would get a full ride to any college you want."

He smiles, relenting that my logic has won over his ideals, for now. And then his whole face relaxes, making him look younger again, like the George I remember from sixth grade when we first met, when his family moved to Highbury and he joined my middle school mathlete team. He was shorter and skinnier than I was back then, and pretty quiet, too. So when he first joined the team as this small, slight new kid, I saw him as no threat at all. Until he beat me out on the state level for the championship, and I realized, for the first time, that when it came to numbers, I finally had a worthy opponent. Of course, now he's half a foot taller than I am, and he's not at all quiet anymore. He's still a worthy opponent. But ever since sixth grade, I've known to take him seriously. He hasn't beat me at anything since.

"We could always build another robot," he says now.

That was our project last year—the brainchild of Brian and Daniel, the two seniors on our team. We built a robot and programmed her to play basketball on a twelve-by-twelve replica of a court. Two of the presentation judges thought we were brilliant—the third judge said you can't really play basketball alone, not even if you're a robot. But to me, it seemed like a beautiful design, to figure out a way to play a team sport, all alone. And it was pretty amazing to watch her roll down the court and shoot a basket, and to realize that we had programmed her to do that. We'd ended up in third place, and I'm not sure we'd do any better this year, even if we programmed her to play a more solo sport. Besides, the robot was Brian and Daniel's. I want something that's mine, now that I'm a senior and club president. Well, mine and George's.

"We should do our own thing," I say. "I just have to think of something no one else will think to do." George gets a half smile on his face, looks at me funny, then looks away. "What?" I say. He shakes his head. "No, what?"

He puts his hand on my arm, and my first thought is that his fingers are warm, and my skin is cool now that we're inside and the A/C is on. And my second is that I should pull away, because George and I aren't the kind of friends who touch each other's arms or hug or anything like that. Except for some reason, I don't move.

"It's nothing," he finally says. "It's just that…you're not like anyone else, Emma. Of course you're going to think of something no one else will."

I try to decide if that's an insult or a compliment, or maybe somewhere in between: just a solid fact. Then the doorbell rings, and George pulls his hand away quickly, jumping up.

"Our pizza," he says.

And as he runs to get it, I feel something weird in my stomach. Not hunger exactly, and not the loneliness I've been feeling all week missing Izzy, but something else. Something I'm not sure I quite have the words to describe.

CHAPTER 2

First thing Monday morning, I'm in Ms. Taylor's counseling office, having signed up for her first available appointment to discuss my college applications. Going to Stanford next year is something I've wanted since I learned to code in fifth grade. Stanford is the leader in tech and right there in the middle of Silicon Valley. Not only would their coursework be the best for my future career in coding, but it would also practically ensure my place in that world after college. Palo Alto is where I belong.

My desire for Stanford has only been tempered slightly these past few months by the fact that Izzy, last minute, and completely on what felt like a whim, decided on UCLA. I always assumed she'd stay nearby for college. But now I feel a little pang in my chest at the thought of Dad, stranded out here in New Jersey all alone, with only his work. Who will make sure he eats and who will do the laundry, and who will remind him to make dentist appointments every six months? I know he's a respected attorney, and he's perfectly capable of being an adult. But part of me also believes that he's been like a Jenga tower all these years since Mom died, moving ever so carefully around life, lest one small piece fall away, and everything that's left of him comes crashing down. What if that one small piece is me?

I don't tell any of this to Ms. Taylor, though. What I tell her is that Stanford is basically my first and only choice. That I will do anything—*anything*—she says to get in. Though, yes, of course I will apply to some backup schools, too. But they're not what I want. And not where I will be happy.

"You'll be successful anywhere you go, Emma," Ms. Taylor says kindly. "And Stanford would be lucky to have you." She's been my guidance counselor since freshman year, and as our coding club adviser, she's also seen me work harder than maybe any other adult at Highbury High. Still, I bask for a few seconds in her compliment. It's nice to be believed in, even if it's only by Ms. Taylor. She pushes her glasses up a little on the bridge of her nose. "But you know Stanford has an extremely rigorous admissions process. You could do everything right and still not get in."

I do know the statistics: last year over 47,000 students applied to Stanford and only 2,700 got accepted. Less than six percent. But I'm ranked first in my class of 106 students (tied with George) and I got a perfect score on my SATs. I'm president of coding club and treasurer of NHS. Why can't I be in that six percent?

I say all that out loud to Ms. Taylor and she laughs. "I do love your confidence," she says. She looks over my academic records, then back at me and she frowns a little. "But you know what you need to add to all this, a little something social to spice it up."

"Social?" I shake my head, not even quite sure what she means. She sounds like Izzy, but she can't possibly be telling me to get a boyfriend to get into Stanford.

"I don't know…join the committee to plan the fall formal. Or throw your hat in the ring for homecoming court. Or try out for the dance team this year."

"Are you kidding?" I'm pretty sure she is because I don't have the skills to make the dance team even if I wanted to. Or campaign for *homecoming court*? That sounds absolutely horrifying—trying to convince all the people I don't know and don't talk to at my school to like me? No thanks. "I play piano," I remind her. Since it's not through school, it's probably not in my academic record. But I've been studying since I was little, lessons once a week with Mrs. Howard, and I play a recital and compete at least once a year. "I won the New Jersey Music Teachers Association competition in my age group last year for solo performance," I tell her.

"Yes, *solo*," she emphasizes.

"I guess I could enter a duet this year."

She laughs a little and shakes her head. "Just think about it," she says. "It's your senior year. Shake it up a little bit, Emma.

Show Stanford you're not just another math brain in a very large pile of math brains."

I tell her I'll think about it, but as I walk out of her office I feel a rare sliver of doubt about my capabilities, my future—a fleeting heartbeat in my throat, wondering if she's right. I don't have a social bone in my body. Maybe to Stanford I will be just another number, in a very large pile of applications.

Sam spots me in the cafeteria at lunch as I'm paying for my cheese hoagie and shouts my name. "Hey! Emma Woodhouse. Over here." He's pretty loud for being new to our school, and also for being a junior. But even in the awful fluorescent cafeteria light, he's also really pleasant to look at. Plus, last year I used to eat with Izzy and her friends, and now they're all gone. Even George has B lunch and isn't here. All last week, I ate alone, and the twenty-three minutes in lunch period that had seemed too short last year suddenly felt much longer, interminable. I make my way over to Sam's table.

"Sorry," he says as I plop my tray down. "I don't know too many people yet, and I got a little overexcited when I saw you. Hope it wasn't too embarrassing."

"I don't get embarrassed easily," I say, and I think about what Ms. Taylor said, that I need to work on being more social to get Stanford to accept me. Maybe I'm supposed to get embarrassed more. I'm definitely supposed to be making new friends. Or, I guess, any friends, now that Izzy is gone.

As I take a bite of my sandwich, I consider what to say to Sam. What are you supposed to say in these situations? I don't want to go back to eating lunch alone tomorrow. So I don't say anything at first.

Sam has brought a lunch from home, in an insulated lunch box. Which I find both weird and endearing. There's something about him that feels comfortable and safe—he called out for me in the cafeteria and now he's pulling out his oddly elementary-school-like lunch. He doesn't care what he looks like, what other people think of him. I watch him pull out a bag of sliced carrots and a small tub of hummus from his lunch box.

"Vegetarian?" I blurt out as he dips a carrot into the hummus and takes a bite.

"What?"

Obviously, I've already said the wrong thing. "I saw your lunch…and…I'm a vegetarian. Are you?"

"No," he says. "I'm not a vegetarian, but that's cool. I just like carrots. And hummus. And my mom was working all weekend, I don't have my license here yet and it was all we had in the fridge this morning when I packed my lunch."

"Your mom works a lot?" I ask, realizing only now, too late, that asking about his parents would've been a more apt first question.

But Sam doesn't seem bothered by my awkwardness. He nods and keeps eating his lunch. "My parents got divorced last spring," he says. "My mom's an ER nurse and she got a job out here, so she could live closer to my aunt in Philly. But now she's the new one on staff, so she's always working. And weird hours, too."

"My dad works a lot, too," I tell him. "And I used to do

everything with my older sister, Izzy, but she decided to go to UCLA for college this year."

He smiles at me. In the cafeteria light, his eyes are more blue than green, but the colors have mixed in a weird and pretty way that I've never quite noticed on anyone else before. "I was happy to join coding club," Sam is saying now. "Thanks for making me feel welcome the other day."

I made him feel welcome? Maybe I am better with people than I, or Ms. Taylor, believes. "Where'd you go to school last year?" I ask him. There's a rhythm to our conversation now that feels easier. Like when I'm playing the piano, the way my fingers always feel like they're sighing in the slow second movement of a sonata.

"Phoenix," he says. "My dad's still there." His voice breaks a little.

"You miss him?"

"Yeah, well, he works a lot, too, and he's getting remarried, so everyone thought it would be better for me to move out here to finish school." He pauses and finishes off his carrots. Then reseals the tub of hummus and puts it in his lunch box. "Can I tell you something I haven't told anyone else?"

I nod, but I wonder what it means to be the keeper of a person's secrets, if that person is someone you barely know.

"I lied to both my parents. I told my dad that I'd definitely come back to Phoenix for college. It's why he let my mom take me across the country to begin with. But I promised my mom I'd stay out here near her for college."

"What do you want to do?" I ask him.

He shrugs. "I don't know. All my friends are in Phoenix. But college is two years away. That's a long time..."

"We can be friends," I say quickly—maybe too quickly—and after I say it, I think that it's probably not something Izzy would've said in this situation. "I mean, if you want to." Then I add, for good measure: "But I'm not going to be here next year when you're a senior. I'm planning to go to Stanford."

"Yeah, you told us. At the coding club meeting." He smiles again. "You've got lofty goals, don't you, Emma Woodhouse?"

"Well," I say, rolling my napkin up into a ball, my fingers trembling a little. "I'll tell you a secret, too. I don't think Ms. Taylor believes I can get into Stanford. She thinks I'm not social enough. And she's probably right. And even if I do get in...I don't know what'll happen to my dad if both my sister and I are so far away in California."

He nods like he understands, like we're both somewhat the same, and maybe a little bit, we are.

The bell rings, and I stand up to throw away my trash. "Hey, Emma," Sam calls after me. I turn back and look at him. "We should hang out sometime, after school."

"We should," I say, and then for some reason, I can't stop myself from smiling, all the way through calculus.

CHAPTER 3

I'm still thinking about my lunch with Sam after school, and I'm not really listening to what George is talking about as we get in the car, until I hear him mention Ms. Taylor's name. "What?" I ask him.

"I said, I think Mr. Weston likes Ms. Taylor."

"Mr. Weston?" I make a right out of the parking lot, and keep my eyes on the line of traffic, all students flooding Highbury Pike, anxious to drive home.

Out of the corner of my eye, I see George nodding. "He was pacing outside her office when I went to my college appointment with her this morning." Of course, George made one of the first appointments with her, too, just like I did. He really wants to get into one of the top animation programs, either at USC or UCLA. "He was wringing his hands all weird." George is still talking about Mr. Weston. "Like he wanted to go in and talk to her. But then he saw me and changed his mind."

I remember Ms. Taylor's gaze, fixed out the window at coding club on Friday, Mr. Weston sitting on top of his Prius, talking on his cell phone. Ms. Taylor seems young for a counselor. I would guess in her late twenties. And this is Mr. Weston's first year teaching at our school. He's finishing up his PhD at Princeton and teaching us to earn extra money in the meantime. They might be about the same age. "Do you think they both like each other?" I ask him.

George shrugs. And then neither one of us say anything for a little while. The silence feels nice, and it's easy, too.

Last year, when Izzy drove me home after school, she would always have a story to tell me, something that happened during the day. Laela got caught cheating on her physics test, or Max and Ellie broke up, got back together, had a shouting match in between third and fourth periods by her locker, broke up again. Though I knew all her friends, they weren't *my* friends, and when she told me her stories, I sometimes felt like she was just recounting an episode of some show she binged on Netflix without me. She tried really hard; she wanted me to love it just as much as she did. But the truth was, I didn't care about all that stuff, and sometimes it just made my head hurt. In a weird way, I feel much more relaxed this year, driving home after school with George.

George fiddles with the radio now, until NPR comes on. They're doing a fluff story on dating apps today, and I'm about to reach over and turn it off when I remember again that silly thing that Izzy said to me, right before she left, about *coding* myself a boyfriend. I still don't want, or need, a boyfriend. But now I'm thinking about what George just said, too, about Mr. Weston and Ms. Taylor. What if there's a way to show them mathematically, in a way they'll both understand, that they're right for each other? What if there's an algorithm for love and I could figure out a way to write it? And even better: What if this could be our coding club project and also fit Ms. Taylor's suggestion for me to do something *more social* to get into Stanford? In a sea of math brains, could this make me stand out?

"I have an idea," I say to George as I turn into his driveway.

He's still focused on NPR, and he points at the radio. "These people that use these dating apps are so superficial." He shakes his head. "Swiping yes or no, just because of someone's photo. And I bet the photos aren't even real at least half the time."

"Okay, that's a made-up statistic." George knows that irritates me more than almost anything: numbers are facts, right and wrong. I can't tolerate it when people just make up statistics for emphasis. He shrugs a little, and I push my annoyance aside to tell him my idea. "What if we make our own?" I say. "For coding club."

He laughs, unbuckles his seat belt and grabs his bag. "You're joking, right?"

"No, I mean it. But not a dating app, necessarily. More... a *matching* app. We could figure out the algorithm for falling in love. Who's supposed to be dating at our school and who shouldn't be, based on a mathematical equation. And we start with Ms. Taylor and Mr. Weston."

He opens the car door. "Okay, now you're being ridiculous."

"But remember when you said I would come up with a unique idea because *I'm me.* Maybe this is it?"

"This is definitely not it." He gets out, shuts the door and waves goodbye before he walks up the driveway. He either thinks I'm joking or just plain crazy. My face burns bright red with annoyance, or is it embarrassment now? *Definitely not it.* What does he know?

As I watch him walk inside his house and shut the door, the idea bellows bigger in my head: loud and important and exciting. I feel a thrumming in my chest, and maybe the heat on my cheeks isn't annoyance at all, but excitement.

This, I think, as I drive toward my dark, empty house, could be the answer to everything.

Since Izzy left, dinner has been up to me. It's not that Dad expects me to cook for him or even that he asks me to. It's just that when I don't, we end up eating cereal or frozen pizzas for dinner, and there are only so many nights in a row you can exist on that stuff. Dad needs healthy food, too. His weight has crept up in the last few years, and I don't even want to know what he orders for lunch at work, so I don't ask. I worry a lot about what he'll eat next year when I'm gone.

But tonight, I just resign myself to a frozen pizza later with Dad. As soon as I get home, I go up to my room and sit on my bed with my laptop. George's words about me being *ri-*

diculous echo in my head. But I push them away. When have I ever cared what anyone has thought? Why should I start now?

What makes two people compatible? I type at the top of a blank document, and then I watch the cursor blink at me for a little while, not really sure of the answer.

I've never had a boyfriend. I've only had one kiss, at the fall dance in tenth grade when I let Izzy talk me into going with Richard Hall, one of her friends from drama club. Richard and I had slow-danced, and at the end of the song, and much to my surprise, he'd leaned down and kissed me on the lips. But Richard's kiss hadn't made me feel anything, other than the urge to count in my head how many seconds it was lasting, how many microbes might live in his saliva, how fast they might multiply in my mouth and also how long it would be until I could make it home and swish with Listerine. Izzy told me that was only because Richard wasn't the right guy for me.

She and John started dating after they were cast as Romeo and Juliet in the school play when they were in eleventh grade. It wouldn't surprise me if someday they got married, even though statistically that is very rare for couples who meet so young. But Izzy and John are special. They just...work. *Why?*

They both love movies, and not the new ones, either, which John calls sellouts, but those crackly black-and-white ones that they'd go see at film festivals in Brooklyn or they'd curl up and watch on AMC on our couch. Sometimes I'd sit on the love seat to watch with them; I'd fallen asleep more Sunday afternoons than I could remember, Izzy and John's voices buzzing with excitement in the background as they would discuss what they loved about the movie afterward.

Common interests/hobbies, I type at the top of my brainstorming document.

But then I feel stuck, so I do a Google search and find that there have been scientific studies that show people are attracted to people who look like themselves. Izzy and John are about the same height and they do both have blond hair. And maybe that's what those dating apps George was making fun of on NPR are thinking, too.

Physical features, I type.

Then: *Location/proximity. Belief system/religion. Background. Values. Age. Political affiliation. Sexual preference/orientation...*

And there it is, methodical as can be. I'll code an app to pull all this data, and then I'll match who belongs with whom at our high school. Just like that, I'm going to write the code for falling in love.

CHAPTER 4

By Friday, at our second meeting of coding club, I have a rudimentary mock-up and prototype of my app, which I'm tentatively calling 1-Factor, the mathematical term for a perfect match in graph theory. I haven't mentioned my idea to George again, so when I pull out my thumb drive, and pull everything I've been working on up on my screen at our meeting, George's eyes widen. First, with surprise, and then with either hurt or annoyance, I'm not sure. I look away, ignoring the flicker of remorse in my stomach for not including him. *He didn't want to be included*, I remind myself.

"What's this?" Ms. Taylor hovers over my screen, pulls down her glasses and squints a little.

"An idea I've been playing around with," I say, and I tell

them all how I've made a list of factors important to falling in love and assigned them all a value. To actually create an app that would match everyone in the school correctly, we'd have to create a database, get Jane to skim socials or set up some kind of survey to gather the data. But for now, on my prototype, I've done a sample match of Ms. Taylor and Mr. Weston, pulling relevant data about them on my own from what I could find in Google searches, their social media profiles and the school website. Knowing that they both already liked each other, I used this to create my algorithm. I also invited Mr. Weston to join our meeting today. He walks in now, just as everyone is staring at my screen and I'm explaining what I've been working on.

"Cool," Hannah says, pushing her red curls back from her face, gathering them in a mock-ponytail with her hands, so for the first time I see her face clearly. She has small cheekbones, big sea-glass eyes, and I wonder if by the time she's a senior, she'll grow into her hair and become a force.

"Not cool," George mutters under his breath, his eyes trained on Mr. Weston, his words aimed at me. He's upset I went behind his back and created the prototype without him, but he'll come around once he sees it.

I demonstrate for everyone how, based on all the data points I entered, Ms. Taylor and Mr. Weston come to a ninety-six percent likability match. In order to come up with this, I had to weight *age*, *background (they both did their undergrad at Rutgers)* and *common physical features* (they are both medium height with black hair and glasses) the highest. And in order to truly make this accurate on a larger scale, we'll have to do more research and collect a lot of data on what variables really should be weighted more than others, what really does lead to a perfect match. But for now, I offer them this example.

I look back up from the screen, and Ms. Taylor's face is bright red. Mr. Weston's staring very hard at his scuffed black shoes.

"This is just…just…" Ms. Taylor stops talking, then lets out a strange high-pitched laugh, and I cringe. I never meant for this to be so awkward. It had felt straightforward, and mathematical, and right, in my head last night. But now that it's all out here and we're all staring at each other, I regret inviting Mr. Weston. I thought I was helping them both, that they would be excited and grateful. But neither one of them look anything close to excited.

"Well," Mr. Weston finally says, looking up, after a moment of silence that feels like way longer than sixty seconds. But I check my watch—it hasn't been. "I have to go home and, um, let my dog out. I'll let you all get back to your meeting."

"Yes, of course," Ms. Taylor murmurs.

"Ms. Taylor." He smiles at her, and his eyes crinkle a little behind his glasses, so I don't think he's angry or upset. Is he interested? "I'm glad to know we're a statistical match."

He walks out and Ms. Taylor puts her head in her hands. George is glaring at me; Sam shrugs and offers me a small smile. Hannah is wide-eyed, and either in awe of or ashamed of me. Robert Martin doodles on his notebook, indifferent, and Jane, dressed today in her signature lab coat, is raising her hand wildly, waiting for Ms. Taylor to stop being mortified enough to notice her.

"Yes, Jane," Ms. Taylor finally looks up and says.

"I'm just going to state the obvious and say this is absolutely ridiculous."

"Yes, Jane." She shakes her head, sounding more resigned this time.

"I don't think it's ridiculous at all," Sam says. My face warms with the compliment and I shoot him a grateful smile.

"There are a million dating apps out there already," George cuts him off. "The world doesn't need another one."

"A *million*?" I fume. Is he deliberately speaking in hyperbole just to make me angry?

"Yeah, but this is different," Sam says. "It will tell you who you *should* date at *our* school. And teachers should be off-limits," he adds.

"And those *million* other apps aren't for us," I say, still feeling angry and defensive now, too. "Most of us aren't even old enough to use them. Our app will only connect people at Highbury High, so everyone can find their best match who also goes to our school. If we get it right, this could even become a model for high schools all over the country."

Ms. Taylor sighs. Her face has finally gone back to a normal color. Maybe it wasn't the best idea to use her in my prototype. But she seems to be considering my points now, too.

George turns to look at me and Sam and frowns. "Why would we waste our time on something so silly, when we could actually try and do something important?"

"And you can't just mess with people's lives like this," Jane adds emphatically, twisting her fingers around the sleeves of her coat. It's making me hot just to look at her in that thing. Seriously it's still in the 80s today. Why on earth does she feel the need to accessorize with a lab coat?

"I volunteer." Hannah raises her hand in the air. Jane shoots her an icy stare. "I mean…I just…" She looks away from Jane, and looks directly at me. "You're not messing with someone's life if she wants it to be messed with, right? I want a match. I volunteer to be the test subject."

"All right, everyone." Ms. Taylor waves her hand in the air. "That's enough for today. Why don't we call the meeting? Jane, George, if you want to come up with other prototypes to share with us next week, then we'll have some options, okay? In the meantime, Emma—" She shoots me a weird contorted look, and I can't tell whether she hates me or loves me right now. "Let's leave people's love lives alone, okay?"

George gathers up his things and walks toward the parking lot, ahead of me. I run to catch up. "George, wait," I call out. "I didn't mean to leave you out. I just thought you wouldn't take this idea seriously unless you saw it in action first. We could go back to my house and work on the prototype more together now."

He stops walking, turns around to face me. "Emma…" He shakes his head. "I thought you were better than this."

"I know the coding is still rudimentary, but it's only a prototype."

"I'm not talking about the coding," he says, and before I can ask him what he means, Jane walks up behind us.

"You need a ride?" she says to George, pulling her car keys out of the pocket of her lab coat.

"I'm giving him a ride," I say. Jane doesn't react or even turn to acknowledge me. It's like I'm invisible, and she doesn't see or hear me.

"Yeah, thanks," George says, turning away from me. "I would love a ride, Jane." His words sting, and I flinch a little.

I watch the two of them walk away together, thinking I should call after George, or apologize. But I don't know what I'm supposed to say or what I have to apologize for. It's not my fault he doesn't like my idea. George is being stubborn.

"I could use a ride," Hannah says. I was so focused on George I hadn't even realized she'd walked up next to me, until I hear her voice. "I mean, if you don't mind? I can text my mom to get me if it's a problem."

I turn, and Sam stands next to her. He's still watching George and Jane walk away. They both are. But then Sam turns to me and shrugs, as if to say I shouldn't let it bother me that George just ditched me to ride home with Jane. And it *shouldn't* bother me. I didn't even want to drive George this year in the first place. But for some reason, it does.

"Yeah, I can give you a ride," I finally say to Hannah. "You need a ride, too?" I ask Sam.

He says his mom got off work early for once and she's already waiting for him the parking lot. But we exchange numbers, and say we'll text over the weekend.

"And, Emma," he says as he walks away, then turns back and flashes me a smile, revealing his perfect straight white teeth. "Don't let them get to you. I think your idea is pretty brilliant."

★★★

"Sam is so nice," Hannah says as he gets in his mom's car and we walk toward mine.

"Yeah, he is," I say nonchalantly. She gives me directions to where to drop her off—apartments on the other side of town. And I nod, though Sam's word—*brilliant*—bounces around inside my head, and makes me feel warm. Or maybe it's just that it's so hot inside my car, from having sat outside in the sun all day. And anyway, I don't mention to Hannah that I'm kind of hoping Sam and I do text over the weekend, that maybe we make plans to hang out. I miss my sister and now George is mad at me, too. And it turns out I really don't like quiet as much as I always thought.

"So, I'm thinking," I realize Hannah is saying now. "That maybe I *match* with Rob."

"Rob? Robert Martin?" She nods enthusiastically. "No… We can't just match up in coding club. We have to think bigger. It has to be the whole school."

"Rob and I have a lot in common," she says. "And I swim with his older sister. She's really nice. We've actually been friends for years."

"But you're missing the point," I tell her. "Our algorithm can examine your likes and dislikes against every guy's in the whole school. Maybe there's someone else who you don't even know yet. You've just started at Highbury. There's 400 students. Maybe you would even match a junior or a senior?"

I don't say this out loud to her, but I also know that in order for me to win this little argument with George and Jane over our project, I'm going to have to do something bigger, a grand gesture. If I can get other people at school interested, outside of coding club, I could expand my *social horizons* as Ms. Taylor mentioned. And if I get the school excited, then coding club will be forced to do my project for the state competition. I think about Jane and George probably eating pepperoni pizza at his house right now and brainstorming other ideas, and for some reason, it makes me really annoyed.

"Hey," I say as I stop at the light across the street from her apartments. "How about you come over to my house now instead of me taking you home, and we can get to work on this together?"

"Now?" she asks, sounding surprised. I nod. "But I don't really know much about coding yet. I did a summer camp once in middle school, but that's it."

"Well, I'll teach you," I say quickly. That's my job as a senior and president of club, isn't it? To mentor.

She nods and her red hair bobs in front of her face, but even with her mess of hair, I can tell she's smiling. For once it feels like I've said exactly the right thing.

CHAPTER 5

Izzy FaceTimes me later that night, just after I've gotten into bed. My eyes are closed but I hear the chimes, the ringtone I set just for her, and I jump out of bed to grab my phone. It's midnight here, but only nine p.m. in California.

I pick up, and Izzy's pretty face fills my screen. Her cheeks look pinker than they used to—she's gotten too much sun already. I put my finger up to touch them on the screen. She's so far away but she's right here.

"Oh my gosh," she says, her voice bursting. Izzy has one speed, fast and excited. Seeing her again on my screen, I remember how exhausting it used to be sometimes to keep up with her last year. But then I feel an ache in my chest, missing it all the same. "You're in your pajamas," she's saying now. "It's late there. I keep forgetting about the time. Em, I'm sorry. Did I wake you?" She's texted me a bunch of times the past few weeks when I've been sleeping, then I've texted back when I wake up and she's sleeping. Three hours doesn't sound very far apart, and yet, it's been oddly unmanageable.

"It's okay," I yawn. "I just got into bed."

Hannah was here awhile, working on entering data from the yearbook with me so we could begin to form a database, and I finally drove her home and picked up Chipotle for me and Dad at nine, right around when he got home from work. We ate our black bean burritos at the kitchen table, while Dad scrolled through notes on his phone and I studied the algorithm I'd used to match Ms. Taylor and Mr. Weston, considering my next move in figuring out how to rank each data point.

Just before ten, Dad had put his phone down, then lowered the lid on my laptop. "You look so far away, Emma. And it's Friday night. Why are you studying so hard?" It was like he confused me and Izzy for a second, because I never went out on Friday nights the way she always had.

"I'm not studying," I said. "Just thinking about an algorithm for our coding club project."

He shook his head and laughed, like he didn't really understand the difference. Then he stood up, ruffled my hair and told me not to think too hard. "Even geniuses need a night off sometimes." Not that he should talk, because he was doing work on his phone, too. He kissed the top of my head. "I'm off to bed. Don't stay up too late."

I opened my laptop again, stared at all the data points and

weights I had up on my screen. "Hey, Dad," I called after him. "What made you fall in love with Mom?"

He stopped walking, turned to look at me. For a second he looked sad, but then he smiled, as if caught up in a memory he hadn't thought to recall in so long. "Her eyes," he said. "Your mother had the most intense blue eyes. She didn't even have to say a word and you could know exactly what she was feeling. She sat next to me in Torts—it took me a few weeks to work up the courage to talk to her, and before I did, I used to hope she'd turn and look at me just so I could see those eyes."

After he went up to bed, I sat there and stared at my screen awhile longer, wondering what I was supposed to do with that in my data points. Finally, I'd written *Eyes?* before going upstairs to get ready for bed.

"Em, are you listening to me?" Izzy is practically yelling at me through FaceTime now.

"Uh-huh," I lie, having no idea what she was just saying. I take my phone and get back into bed, pulling the covers up and holding the phone above my pillow so she can only see my face. I remember that it's Friday night, and still early there. Izzy likes to *do* things. She should be out with John. Why is she in her room, FaceTiming me? "What's going on, Iz? Everything okay with you?"

"Me?" she laughs. "I'm good. John's right over here." She flips the camera to show him lying on the futon across her dorm room, looking on his iPad, and when I see him again, I remember how much he looks like George, except he has contacts, gels his dark blond curls and wears trendier clothes. So he's like a prettier, shinier George. He waves now, and she flips the camera back to herself. "Are *you* okay?" she asks me, and I shake my head, confused. "George texted John that you've lost your mind. That's why I FaceTimed you."

George. I roll my eyes. Of course he did. What right does he have? George should mind his own business.

"You're trying to set up your teachers?" Izzy is still talking. Our connection freezes for a second, her pretty face locks in on a scrunched-up frown. "...doesn't even sound like you," she pops back. "Since when do you care who's dating? And why would you mess with the teachers' social lives?"

"It's a project for coding club. I'm trying to think outside the box and actually win this year, that's all. And the teachers were just for the prototype. We're going to match students." Izzy frowns again and twirls a blond curl around her finger. "Maybe George is the one who lost his mind?" I retort.

"My brother is way too nerdy to lose his mind." I hear John from across the room.

"Yeah, well, so is she." Izzy turns, so I know she's talking more to John than to me.

"Uh, thanks, Iz. I'm still here."

She turns back. "Yeah, I know," she says. "Sorry." But she doesn't sound sorry. "George is worried about you. And now we are, too."

I don't think John gives me a second thought, and George is jealous that I came up with this idea without him. Or annoyed with me, that I don't want to do something to try and save the world with our senior year co-presidency. Which is not the same as *worried*. But Izzy, she might genuinely be worried. I want to tell her that if there's any reason to worry, it's all her fault, for abandoning me in the first place. But instead I reassure her that I'm fine, that George is just jealous and that I have everything in coding club completely under control.

"But you've never even had a boyfriend. How are you going to tell people who they should fall in love with? This could be a social disaster for you," Izzy says, lowering her voice, casting her eyes downward.

"Iz, this has nothing to do with love," I tell her in my most emphatic voice. "This is all about numbers. Writing an algorithm to match people. And besides, didn't you tell me to be *more social* before you left?"

"Come on, Izzy. We're gonna be late. She'll be fine." I hear John's voice again, in the background. But Izzy doesn't answer him. She stares at me through the screen, her eyes open wide. The picture is too blurry for me to see how deeply blue they are, but I know the color of my sister's eyes by heart. I can't remember our mother's eyes, but I think about what our father said earlier, and I imagine now that they were something like Izzy's.

Finally she blinks, looks down and, even across all these miles and through my tiny blurry screen, I can tell she feels guilty, like maybe for the first time she regrets leaving me. But not because she misses me, the way I miss her, but because she's worried I'm not capable of navigating life on my own, without her.

I can't sleep after Izzy and I hang up, and I watch my fan make shadows across the ceiling, counting the rotations of the four blades: *four, eight, twelve, sixteen...* Patterns soothe and relax me.

I was only three when Mom died, and by the time I was five, in kindergarten, Dad grew concerned about me. I didn't have any friends, mainly, my kindergarten teacher Mrs. Jennings told Dad, because I refused to play with anyone. I was too busy, off by myself, memorizing the times tables on her math flash cards.

After Dad attended our spring conferences, he worried that maybe I wasn't at the right school. He wanted to move me to a private school where class size is smaller, but Highbury Prep is so expensive, and his practice was just getting off the ground. There were bills from Mom's death, and he couldn't afford to do it.

But it wasn't ever the public school that was the problem. What both Dad and Izzy never really got is that numbers are just so easy for me to understand. Mom's death I could never comprehend. I still can't. Even now. No matter how you look at it, it doesn't make sense that a healthy thirty-three-year-old woman can go to sleep one night, and then not wake up ever again. Numbers behave the way you ask them to. Numbers have always made sense to me. People don't.

"Maybe next year I can afford private school, Emma," Dad had said to me after he got home from his conferences that spring. We were all sitting down on Mom's new blue couches, Dad and me and Izzy. Izzy's conference had, of course, gone off spectacularly. Izzy was a model student and every other child in first grade just adored her. Dad hugged us both tightly to him, then pulled back to look at us.

His eyes started watering, and he rubbed them behind his thick glasses. Izzy reached out and put her tiny hand on his shoulder. "It's all right, Dad," she told him then. "I'm going to take care of Emma at school. I promise. You don't have to worry about paying for private school."

And Izzy took that promise to heart, for years. She sat with me at lunch; she made sure I had a date for that dance. Izzy still spent nights and weekends with me even after she started dating John. Izzy had a lot of friends, and she always included me: to sit with them, to go to movies with them, to drive to school with them.

But her friends were never my friends. Her activities weren't my activities. It was just me, tagging along. I think about John, hurrying her to get off FaceTime so they wouldn't be late for whatever they had planned for their Friday night. And for the first time, it occurs to me that maybe *I'm* the reason Izzy went to UCLA.

Did Izzy need to put 2,764 miles between us just so she could finally feel free to break her promise to Dad? So she could exist without me?

And then, suddenly, it is very hard for me to breathe. I watch the fan turn and turn, and I count the rotations in my head, but it is impossible to fall asleep.

CHAPTER 6

I wake up early the next morning, having barely slept at all. I kept tossing and turning all night, half dreaming that Izzy was here, telling me I know nothing about love. At six a.m., I finally just get out of bed, still annoyed by my conversations with dream-Izzy, and my FaceTime late last night with real-Izzy.

I put on a pot of coffee for Dad, who I know will be up soon—he's always an early riser, even on the weekends. I wait for the coffee to brew, take a cup for myself, filling it only halfway. I add milk for the other half and pour in a packet of powdered hot chocolate, stirring it with a spoon until it's something like a mocha. Then I take it up to my room and sip it in my bed with my laptop, populating the rest of the database that Hannah and I started on last night.

It's tedious work, going line by line, person by person, through the high school yearbook and Hannah's old middle school yearbook (for the freshmen), entering all their clubs and interests, and any background, defining features or likes and dislikes I can gather, but a few hours, and two mochas, later, I have enough data in to run a test match for Hannah through my algorithm. Phillip Elton's name comes back a few seconds later, at a ninety-six percent match, blinking on my screen in bold, a little like it's taunting me.

Phillip is a senior, like me, and though we're not in any classes together, I know him a little from the last two years when he was in coding club. He's tall and orange-haired with freckles, an easy smile and a muscular build. He's the kind of guy who cares way more about sports than math, but he's also smart enough to realize he needed to balance his academic and athletic pursuits to get into a good college. As soon as junior year was over he dropped out of coding club, saying he wanted to focus on cross-country for senior year. George and I had rolled our eyes at each other when Ms. Taylor mentioned why he said he wouldn't be coming back. We both knew he'd only joined the club to put it on his college application for those crucial junior year activities. But we hadn't cared all that much to lose him, either—he'd contributed very little to the club, other than, last year, helping to build the basketball court for our robot, and researching famous basketball plays to program our robot to repeat. Mostly he pretended to code while watching YouTube videos at our meetings.

But I don't necessarily dislike Phillip. When we came in third place at the state competition last year, he'd been genuinely upset like the rest of us at the loss. *I really thought we'd take it*, he said to me on the bus on the way back to Highbury from Rutgers.

He'd been sitting in the seat across from me, and he'd leaned across the aisle, looking pretty glum. I was sitting in a seat by myself, listening to an old Steve Jobs TED Talk, to try and calm myself down after our loss. I'd pulled an earbud out of my ear to talk to him for a second. "We'll win next year," I told him with a confidence I hadn't yet felt.

"Yeah," he'd said, leaning his head on the seat in front of him. "Maybe."

I'd put my earbud back in, and I'd forgotten all about that conversation until right now. But maybe it's a good thing that Hannah matches him? Phillip might be willing to help me, to help us, given his past history with coding club. Even though he's no longer part of the club, I do think he'll genuinely want us to win. That he might be willing to be my first test subject.

"Which one is Phillip?" Hannah asks as soon as I pick her up Monday morning to go to school. I'd texted her about my results yesterday, but she was at a swim meet all day and couldn't come over. Now I hand her my yearbook from last year, before pulling out of the parking lot of her apartment complex and driving toward school.

Phillip's face is flagged with a sticky note, so she finds him quickly. "He's cute," she says, sounding excited.

"Yeah, I guess so." Phillip's *cuteness* is beside the point. They're a statistical match, perfectly suited to date one another. But when I glance at her again, she's still staring at his picture, smiling a little.

I'd texted Phillip last night and asked him if he'd meet me in the courtyard before school this morning. He texted back that he really didn't have time for coding club anymore. I told him that was fine, that this was about something else, and then he had agreed to meet me. And that wasn't exactly a lie. I don't need or want him back in the club. I just need him to listen and give my algorithm a chance.

I'd texted George last night, too, asking him if he needed a ride to school this morning, hoping maybe he'd come with us, see my work in action and change his mind. All I got back was one word: *nope.* But he can't stay mad at me forever. As co-presidents, we're going to have to work together to submit our application for the state competition, and once I get Phillip on board, and maybe get a few more people interested in matches, George will come around. He'll have to.

Phillip is sitting in the courtyard, just like he'd promised. And I sigh with relief when I spot him there. It's not that I'd expected him to stand us up exactly, but I also wasn't sure whether he'd remember or care enough to actually show up, either.

"Hey, Em," he says, looking up as we approach. It annoys me, the way he calls me *Em*, like we're old friends. *We're not.* Em is reserved for people who really know me, who love me. Everyone calls me Emma, except for Izzy and sometimes Dad. But I bite my tongue, offer him a wave and a forced smile. His eyes move from me to Hannah, and he opens his mouth a little, like he wants to say something else, but then closes it, saying nothing at all.

I gently take Hannah by the shoulders, sit her down on the bench next to Phillip and stand in front of them, looking at them for a second. His orange hair is still just a little wet from the shower and curling up above his ears, and Hannah's red curls are also a little damp and flatter than usual, revealing more of her heart-shaped face and bright green eyes.

"Phillip," I say. "This is Hannah. She's a freshman, new in coding club this year. Hannah, this is Phillip." Hannah turns and rigidly holds out her arm, offering one of her tiny hands to shake. But Phillip cocks his head to the side, smiles at her. He picks her hand up, but instead of shaking, just holds on to it for a second, before she pulls away, her cheeks burning as red as her hair.

"I'm confused. What's so important that you guys needed to see me before school?" Phillip asks, turning back to me.

I take a deep breath and tell him about my matching app, not sure what to expect after the way things went horribly awry on Friday with Ms. Taylor and Mr. Weston. Once I finish explaining to Phillip about how I ran Hannah through my algorithm and how he matches her, he stares at me for another second, and then he bursts out laughing. I was not expecting that, and I frown. "Wait..." He's still laughing. "*You're* going to tell me who...I should...date, Em?" He can barely choke his sentence out, he's laughing so hard.

"Not me," I say, putting my hands on my hips. "Math. And stop calling me Em. *Emma.*"

Hannah stands up. Her cheeks are so red she looks sunburned, and her eyes have turned glassy. "I'm gonna go," she says, her voice trembling. "Nice to meet you, Phillip."

"No, Hannah, wait." Phillip stops laughing, stands and grabs her arm. "I wasn't laughing at you, I swear. I'm sorry if you thought that. It's just…Em…er, Emma, *setting me up*." He swallows back another laugh.

"It's not me," I say again, unable to keep my annoyance out of my voice. "Hannah and I wrote an algorithm—"

"Yeah, yeah, math," he cuts me off. And none of us say anything for a minute. I'm wondering what I'm supposed to do, if I should walk away. We could try and match someone other than Hannah to start. Or should I try and convince him some more? I bite my lip, really not sure.

He's not laughing any longer, but he looks at Hannah and smiles a little. He looks back at me. Then back at Hannah again. I can't tell at all what he's thinking. "All right," he finally says. "I actually need a date for the fall formal, anyway. Hannah, would you like to go with me?"

"I…" Hannah opens her mouth to speak but can't seem to form a coherent sentence.

"Yes. She would love to," I answer for her. I'm somewhere between relieved that my idea is *actually working* right now and giddy that I'm proving George and Izzy and John wrong about me. So it doesn't occur to me to question why he's gone from laughing at me to helping me in the span of a few minutes.

But it does occur to Hannah. "Why would you want to go to the formal…with me?" she blurts out.

"Why not?" Phillip says quickly. "If *Emma* says that math makes us a good match, who am I to deny that?"

"Exactly," I say, hoping Hannah will stop talking. Things are going better than I'd hoped—why does she need to question it?

Phillip gets Hannah's number and promises to text her so they can figure out the details about the dance and maybe meet up for coffee or a movie before then. The first bell rings, and we all gather up our things to get to class, and just as Phillip starts to walk away, I have an idea. "Hey, Phillip," I call after him. "If anyone else on the cross-country team wants a date for the dance, text me, okay? I'll run them through my algorithm, too."

He turns back to look at me, and for a second, I think he might laugh at me again. But instead he shoots me a thumbs-up, smiles and walks to class.

I turn to Hannah, and she doesn't look as happy as I would expect. But she doesn't look upset anymore, either, more like confused. "What?" I say. "This is a good thing. This is what we wanted."

"Okay, he's a senior, one. And two, I've never been to a formal," she says. "I don't even have a dress."

Izzy has dresses, half a rack in her closet that she'd left behind at home, saying she wouldn't have much use for all her formal wear in LA. She'd made a point of telling me I could borrow them anytime I liked, and I'd rolled my eyes at the suggestion. I measure up Hannah silently with my eyes now. She's about Izzy's size, maybe an inch shorter. That should be close enough. "I can help you figure out a dress," I tell her. "And anyway, why are you worried about that? You *match* him. It doesn't matter what you wear. You're going to be perfect together."

★★★

I spot Sam at lunch, and make a quick beeline to his table. I sit down across from him and update him on what happened this morning with Phillip and Hannah. He's peeling an orange with his thumbs, and I'm curious what else he has in that insulated lunch box of his, what else his mom managed to keep in the fridge over the weekend. He pulls out a canister of soup, and then I remember that his mom had picked him up Friday after coding club. Maybe she'd had the weekend off?

"Can you show me the app?" Sam asks in between spoonfuls of soup. "I want to try it."

"It's not an app...yet," I say. "So far, it's just an algorithm pulling from a database I created on my computer. To make it into an app, we'd need the whole club. I'd have to create it in Xcode and then we'd need Jane to put the database on a server and George to design the UI/UX and animation and..." My voice trails off on that thought, as I remember again that George is mad at me and that he has no interest in animating this app. "Anyway, we're a long way from that. And," I add, "you're not even in my database. Since you're new to the school, I didn't have any yearbook data for you. And I couldn't find you on social media."

He caps his soup canister and puts it back inside his insulated lunch box, turns to me and shrugs. "I'm not on social media. But I could tell you my info. We could input it, right?" His eyes are really green, brightened by the fluorescent cafeteria lights. And they're filled with kindness. He's not laughing at me like Phillip was, not angry with me like

George is. "I want to go to the fall formal, and I barely know anyone at school yet."

"You know me," I say quickly. And I put my hand to my mouth, realizing as soon as the words are out how it sounded, like I want to go to the fall formal with him. I quickly clarify: "I mean, thank goodness you know me, so I can find a match for you."

"Yeah." Sam flashes me that smile of his that makes me feel warm and happy. "Thank goodness I know you."

CHAPTER 7

On Friday, George and Jane walk into coding club carrying a huge chart on a bright green poster board. George has made a cute drawing of a recycling can with googly eyes that I assume he would bring to life with animation in whatever this world-saving idea of his is.

"What's this?" Ms. Taylor asks, smiling at George.

"We have our own prototype," Jane says with a smirk in my direction, and I want to roll my eyes so bad, but normally the person I'd roll them at in this situation would be George, and he won't even look at me.

I hold my thumb drive in my hand, clasping it hard against my palm. I'd come prepared with my new database to show off, and my update about Hannah and Phillip. Phillip also texted me last night saying he has a friend, Jason, on cross-country who wants a match, and Sam still wants a match, too. He plans to come over this weekend so we can input his data. But Jane is still going on about her prototype—hers *and George's*—and I bite my lip and let them talk.

"Basically it's an app to track your recycling," George is saying now. "You can connect with your friends and compete to see who recycles the most in any given week."

Sam catches my eye across the room, and gives me a half smile, a shrug, as if to say what I'm already thinking: *our matching app is so much more original and interesting.*

"I don't get it," Robert interrupts, surprising all of us. I think it's the first time he's spoken up at any of our meetings. His voice is deeper and more confident than I would've expected. Jane shoots him an icy stare, but he keeps talking. "What do you get if you win? What's the point?"

"You get *karma points,*" George says.

"Karma points?" Hannah pipes up, sounding skeptical.

"You collect them in the app," Jane says. "And then when you get a lot, you feel good about yourself."

And George texted John to complain about me? Maybe I should text Izzy and tell her John needs to worry about George's animated trash can and his *karma points.*

"I don't think that would make me feel good about myself," Sam is saying now. "I like Emma's idea better."

I shoot him a grateful smile, unclasp my thumb drive and put it into my laptop, bringing my Excel file and algorithm flowchart up on the screen. I update everyone about Hannah and Phillip, and also how I plan to work on new matches this weekend for Jason from cross-country and our very own Sam. At the mention of his name, Jane turns her icy gaze toward him, and Sam shrugs a little in response.

"Ms. Taylor," Jane complains. "I thought we all agreed that this dating app was a terrible idea."

"We did not agree on anything like that," I say quickly.

"Well..." Ms. Taylor's voice falters a little. She shoots me a half smile, then does the same thing to Jane. "I think these are both very interesting ideas and we should take the next week or so to think things over. We still have ten days to submit our application—we'll decide at next week's meeting. Let's take our time and make our idea the best we can before we send it in."

An hour later, Izzy FaceTimes me. I pick up, and her face is covered in a green gooey face mask. "You look like a swamp monster," I say. "Are you calling just to scare me?"

"I miss you, too, Em," she shoots back. "I'm going out tonight and I wanted to call you earlier so I didn't wake you up this week. How's it going?"

We haven't FaceTimed since last Friday night, and the truth is, I'm still a little annoyed with her. We'd texted during this past week a few times, but not as much as we had the week before and not about anything serious. I haven't updated her on my matches, and I'm not sure I should now, either. So all I say is, "It's going fine, Iz."

"Yeah?" She raises her eyebrows, and her green face looks even more ridiculous.

"Where are you going tonight? You said you're going out?"

I honestly don't care where she's going, but I'd much rather talk about that than have her bug me about my project, or my social life, or lack thereof, again.

"John and I are going to this film festival in Hollywood. It's all films from the '20s and you have to dress like the era. I got this really cute flapper dress..."

She's still talking but I'm not really listening. At the mention of her flapper dress, I remember again about all the dresses she left here in her closet and Hannah needing one for the dance. "Hey," I interrupt her. "Speaking of dresses. Is it okay if Hannah borrows one of yours for the fall formal?"

"Okay, wait. Back up. One, who's Hannah? And two, YOU ARE GOING TO THE FALL FORMAL?" She holds the phone so close to her face I see a blur of green and the white pearls of her teeth.

"Hannah's a friend from coding club," I say vaguely, not wanting to get into it again with Izzy about my app. "She needs a dress. And I'm not going, *she's* going."

Izzy pulls the phone back again, and now she's frowning. "Okay, I'll make a deal with you, Em. Your *friend* can borrow any dress she wants, as long as you borrow one and go to the dance, too."

I have no desire to go to the dance, and normally I wouldn't lie to Izzy. I'd just tell her the truth. But she's so far away, and I'm still kind of annoyed with her. "Okay," I tell her. "Fine." Just to get her off my back.

When we hang up, I feel a little pang of guilt. I'm not actually going to borrow a dress, or go to the dance. And I'm sure George will update John and he'll tell Izzy, and in a few

weeks from now, she'll FaceTime me with her disappointed face, which is way scarier than her green, gooey face-mask face. But I push that out of my mind for now and I text Hannah and ask her if she wants to come over and look through Izzy's closet tomorrow.

Dad shoots me a quizzical look when the doorbell rings the next afternoon, and I jump up quickly from eating the grilled cheese sandwiches I'd made for our lunch to answer it.

"You're expecting someone?" Dad asks, raising his eyebrows, finishing off his sandwich in one large bite.

"Yeah, some people from coding club," I say. Hannah is coming for the dress, Sam to work on his own profile in my Excel file.

"George?" Dad asks, sounding hopeful. George follows baseball and so does Dad, and every time they see each other, Dad likes to talk about some play or another with him, and George likes to show off all the stats he knows, and Dad gets all excited about that. Which, from a mathematical perspective, I guess I can kind of understand why George cares about that. But in my opinion, actually watching baseball is pretty much like watching grass grow.

I shake my head. "Not George." Dad looks vaguely disappointed, and I'm certainly not about to tell him that George is currently not even talking to me. So I leave him in the kitchen and go answer the door. Hannah and Sam are both standing out on the porch, having been dropped off at almost the exact same time.

Dad has walked out to the foyer, too, and looks with interest.

"This is Hannah," I tell Dad as I usher them inside. "And Sam."

I'm worried he'll ask them if they watch baseball. But he doesn't. "Nice to meet you both," Dad says. Then he adds, "I have to go into work for a few hours, Em." He kisses me on the forehead, then turns back to look at all three of us. "No wild parties, kids. Okay?" He laughs a little.

"Don't worry, Mr. Woodhouse," Hannah says. Her hair is crazy today, nearly covering her eyes, so maybe she doesn't get that Dad is just being Dad...joking. He winks at me, and walks toward his office to gather his things. I roll my eyes back in response.

"Come on, let's go upstairs," I say, and motion for them both to follow me. Dad's words are still resonating a little guiltily in my ears as I walk up the steps.

One time, when Izzy was a junior and Dad went away for a few days for a trial in Boston, she actually threw a wild party. It was supposed to be small, just a few friends. But before she knew it, it got out of hand, and there were twenty kids in our house. They were making so much noise, and someone had brought a water bottle filled with some kind of alcohol and they were passing it around. I'd sworn to Izzy beforehand I wouldn't tell Dad no matter what, so I'd sat on the floor in our upstairs bathroom, clutching my phone, worrying the police were about to come, we were all about to be arrested and all my hopes of Stanford would be ruined. I tried to block out the noise, to pretend I could be anywhere else but here.

Sometime after midnight, I'd heard a lamp crashing to the living room floor below me, and I'd been so tempted to text Dad, but instead I'd texted George.

Ten minutes later, he and his mom were at our house, ushering everyone out and home and then they helped me and Izzy and John clean up.

"You can't tell my dad," Izzy had implored John and George's mom, and she had frowned and said only if Izzy and John *promised* to never do anything that stupid again. They swore to her they wouldn't and, to this day, Dad still doesn't know about it.

We walk inside Izzy's room now, and I haven't been inside it since she left. It's dark and smells a little dusty. But I flip on the light, and everything is exactly as it was the morning she left me. I inhale deeply and catch just the slightest whiff of her strawberry shampoo. It makes me miss her, even though I wish it didn't.

"Take whatever you want from the closet," I tell Hannah, pointing to the walk-in on the left side of the room. "And bathroom's right there if you want to try anything on."

"Are you sure?" Hannah asks me, her eyes wide.

"I asked Izzy last night and she said it was fine." I leave out the part about how I promised to take a dress, too. Hannah hesitates for another second, but then walks into the closet and turns on the light.

I sit down on the floor, my back against Izzy's queen bed. Sam sits down next to me and I open my laptop to my Excel file database, his empty entry blinking in front of me. "Here you go." I hand my laptop to him. "Fill your information in."

I know my database is still rudimentary. That if we move forward with the project, we will need more categories, better information and more trial and error on the algorithm. And Sam is not the only new kid this year, of course. But for now, I can make a match for Sam based on this.

I look over his shoulder as he types in his interests, and see he's in choir, he plays volleyball and that he's bilingual, fluent in Spanish. I'm not sure why, but each one of those things surprise me about him in a different and weirdly disappointing way. Because I already know as I look over his shoulder those interests don't really match mine *(piano, math, coding)*, or only in the smallest way, if you're counting music as an interest in the vaguest sense. I still have physical features weighted fairly high, too. My hair is blond, my eyes blue. And Sam has deep green eyes and tar-black hair. Though we are about the same height…

"What's wrong?" Sam asks, handing the computer back to me, finished entering all his data.

"What?" I say. "Nothing."

"You're frowning," Sam says.

"Am I?"

At just that moment, Hannah steps out of the bathroom in a short green-silk slip dress. I remember Izzy wearing it once—to what dance, I can't remember now, but she'd gotten her photo taken with John there. He'd worn a matching green tie, and in the picture, Izzy clings to him, both of them smiling too wide, which I thought made them look a little like puppets. But Izzy loves that photo. She has it encapsulated inside a tiny square piece of plastic, a souvenir key chain from whatever dance they went to, and she'd hung her car keys on it all senior year.

Hannah looks totally different in this dress than Izzy had. For one thing, she's a little shorter than Izzy, so the dress hits right below her knees, not above. And for another, her hair is so red that it magnifies the green in a totally different way. She's put her hair back in a band, and now I can see that the dress is the same exact sea-glass color as her eyes. "Perfect," I say. "That dress is perfect for you."

"You think?" She spins around, glancing in the mirror, a little unsure.

I nod. I'm usually terrible at judging this kind of thing, but the way the color matches her eyes almost exactly makes it so obvious she's chosen the right dress, even to me.

"Hey, what about me, Emma?" Sam elbows me and grins. "Will you help me find something to wear?"

"My dad has a closet full of suits across the hall. I'm sure he wouldn't mind if you borrowed one." I say it completely straight-faced, though obviously I'm kidding. Sam is only an inch or so taller than my five-five, and Dad is six-two.

"I don't think they're my size." He laughs, like he didn't expect me to joke around with him, but he's happy that I did. I like the way his surprised laughter sounds a little different than his regular laughter, the way it bubbles up from his throat, clear and pure and almost musical.

"Fair point," I say, grinning. "And anyway, how about we match you to a date first? Then we'll worry about what you're wearing."

"Okay," he says. "Do it."

I hesitate for a second. "Actually, it's going to take a little while for the database to update." I hear the words come out of my mouth, a blatant lie, and I feel my face turning hot, wondering if he can see right through me or if he knows enough to call me on it. I shut the lid to my laptop. "I'll do it later and text you the results." The truth is, I don't want him looking over my shoulder when I run his match. Really, it'll only take a few minutes. But I already feel this weird disappointment settling in my chest, and I'm worrying I'm not going to like whomever he matches with. I want to be alone to process the results.

Sam doesn't question me, or seem to have any idea I'm not being truthful. He simply nods and says, "Okay, cool."

Hannah walks out of the bathroom again, holding on to Izzy's green dress on a hanger, and the three of us stare at each other for a minute, not saying anything. They both did what they came for, so… I can't think of another reason for them to stay. Though I wouldn't mind if they did. But maybe they're ready to leave? "Do you want me to drive you guys home?" I finally ask.

"Actually, could you drop me off at the mall instead? I need shoes," Hannah says. "Your sister's are all size eights and I wear a seven."

"I could go to the mall, too," Sam says. "I really will need something to wear." He turns to look at me. "Why don't you come with us?"

"Oh, no, I can't," I say quickly.

"Yeah, come," Hannah says. "You can help me pick out shoes. It'll be fun."

The mall is one of my least favorite places. There's not much I hate more than the tedium of shopping, in crowds of strangers. And helping Hannah pick out shoes doesn't exactly sound like it's in my wheelhouse. Even Izzy knew better than to try and force me to come with her to shop. Whenever I would go, I'd complain I was ready to leave much sooner than Izzy ever was, and she would tell me how annoying I was being, and how I would ruin the whole experience for her. I definitely don't want Hannah and Sam to get annoyed with me. "I promised my dad I'd get some things done around the house. I have a bunch of homework. And I should finish these matches..." None of these things are lies. I did tell Dad earlier I'd do the laundry and the dishes. I do have a lot of homework. I need to practice piano, and I would like to do the matches, alone. Still, I probably *could* go to the mall, if I really wanted to.

Sam's eyes are still on my face. He shrugs and smiles at me, as if to say, *No big deal, either way.* Hannah hangs Izzy's dress back up in her closet, and says she'll come back for it next weekend. I want to tell Sam he should come back next weekend, too, but then I can't think of a reason why he should, so I don't say anything at all.

I'm just pulling back into my driveway from dropping them off at the mall when Sam texts me.

Look who we saw walking into the movie theater together...

A second later a picture pops in, a fuzzy, grainy close-up of a couple... I can't tell who I'm looking at. I zoom in to make the picture bigger, and I think…is that Ms. Taylor? She's dressed way more casually than she does at school, where she always wears a floral dress and heels, and in this picture she's in jeans, flats and a black tee. But when I zoom closer in on her face I recognize her tortoiseshell glasses. It is her, and she's holding hands with a guy who's about her height with the same color hair and glasses and… Oh! It's Mr. Weston!

This is good, right? I text back.

Yeah, E! You totally wrote the code for love.

E. I focus on the letter for a second. I hate nicknames, but for some reason, I don't mind this one so much. Coming in a text from Sam it feels personal, special. No one else calls me that, and I like that now there is a piece of me that feels like it belongs only to him.

CHAPTER 8

Jason Richardson, Phillip's cross-country friend, matches to a sophomore, Jenny Hampton, who I don't know. But I don't really know Jason, either, except vaguely. He was in my health class freshman year, and the teacher paired us up for one stupid project where we had to spend the week writing an antidrug PSA together. Jason didn't have much to say on the topic, and was more than happy to put his head on the desk, sleep and let me do all the work, which was also fine by me, since I wanted the A+ on the project. When I refer back to the yearbook now, I see they're both brown-haired and athletic, that Jenny does girls' spring track, as well as soccer. I text Phillip about the results Monday morning before school, and ask him to let me know what happens with the match so I can keep track. He sends me back a thumbs-up emoji.

I run Sam's match, too, and he comes up as a ninety-seven percent match to Laura Jensen. She's in my AP Spanish class, she sits right in front of me and she talks *a lot.* I do just fine in Spanish. I always manage an A, but it's certainly not enjoyable for me to learn the way math is, and I don't go out of my way to talk too much in there.

I don't text Sam about his match right away, but instead I watch Laura in class on Monday morning. She's shorter than me, with long raven hair. Today she reaches back and twirls a strand around her finger all through class. And when she raises her hand, answers question after question *after question*, her voice is high-pitched, effusive. Izzy would refer to her as *bubbly*, and not in a bad way, either, like I would.

"Hey," I say to her as the bell rings, and we both stand up to walk out of class. "Do you have a boyfriend?"

She freezes for a second, then frowns at me. I suddenly realize this might be awkward, as we've never spoken directly to one another before, and I probably should've led with something else, though what, I'm not exactly sure.

"No," she says, hugging her books to her chest. "Why?"

And why did I ask her, really? I didn't ask Phillip; I didn't ask Jenny Hampton. I just told them their mathematical matches and let them figure out the rest. But maybe I wanted her to say *yes*, she already has a boyfriend. Maybe I want a reason to reconfigure my algorithm, for Sam. Because when I look at bubbly Laura, I can't picture them together. "I just..."

I finally stammer. "I'm working on a project for coding club, and—"

"I'm going to be late for class," she says unapologetically, cutting me off. And she turns down the hallway, walking away briskly toward the science wing.

My hands are shaking a little as I head toward calculus. I said all the wrong things, and now she probably hates me. Why did I even talk to her in the first place? I need to stick to gathering data, making the matches. I promise myself I'll tell Sam about his match at lunch, and let him do the rest on his own.

But then at lunch, he tells me a funny story about his chemistry teacher accidentally setting the end of her hair on fire in the lab, and he is so animated, re-creating Mrs. Hefferman's panic, that we are both laughing so hard we're crying, and the topic of Sam's match doesn't even come up.

I finally tell Sam about Laura at lunch on Friday, when he straight out asks me about his results. I'd been planning on telling him today, anyway, more evidence for our meeting later this afternoon that my app can work, that it has potential. I really need Sam to be excited, to back me up. But he asks me before I figure out a way to bring it up.

"Laura Jensen," I say flatly, thinking about the way she'd flipped her hair and run away down the hallway from me the other day.

"Laura?" he says. His voice is brimming with excitement, and I wonder if Sam is thinking of the right Laura. There are fourteen in the school. "Laura's in choir with me. She has a solo. She's really, really good." He smiles, like the fact that she's a *good* singer makes all the difference in the world. But yeah, he's thinking of the right Laura. I remember her singing in some concert Izzy was in last year, and Sam's right, she is a good singer. I'll give her that. Is Sam a good singer, too? Or does he just participate in choir to have something vaguely musical to put on his college applications? He's still talking. "I'm going to ask her to the dance at our rehearsal tomorrow afternoon."

"Great," I say, forcing a cheerfulness I don't actually feel. But Sam doesn't seem to notice.

Lunch is over and we both stand up, and before I know what he's doing, he leans in and gives me a quick hug. "Thanks, E," he says into my hair.

I like the way it feels to hug him, and he smells nice, kind of woodsy, like Christmas trees. And I know it's wrong, but a small part of me hopes that Laura will say no when he asks her to the dance tomorrow.

By the end of the day, I feel a little like I'm drowning as I walk to our coding club meeting, trying hard to keep my head above water. I'm still worrying about what's going to happen with Sam and Laura. And then Phillip texts me, with two more requests from his teammates for matches. And Jenny Hampton, who I have never met until now (but I recognize her immediately from her yearbook photo) grabs my arm in the hallway, gushing about how her friend Ellie wants a match for the dance, too, and can I do that? *Please, Emma*, Jenny says, holding on to my arm. *Pretty please?* I find myself nodding, bobbing my head just above the surface, completely overwhelmed.

I tell Jenny I will text her later, but first the club *needs* to go along with my idea over George and Jane's. If I'm going to match more people, we really need to perfect the algorithm to truly get it right. We need more research, more input from people who are more social than I am. And more data for the database from someone who knows how to skim socials, like Jane. And George. I need George to stop being mad at me and turn my idea into something animated and appealing, an app that people in the school could actually download and use to match themselves. So then the matching won't all be on me.

I walk into the meeting with all this on my mind. I'm the last one here, since I'd stayed after class for a few minutes in physics to ask Mr. Halpbern a question about the weekend homework, and had also gotten stopped in the hall by Jenny. And when I walk in now, everyone's eyes turn to me, so I get the uncomfortable feeling they've all already been talking about me.

"I updated everyone on your progress," Sam says. He smiles, and I relax, but only a little. At least someone in the room has my back. "Hannah and I both did," he adds. I look at Hannah and she nods and smiles, too. Okay, two people in the room have my back.

"I proposed that we take a vote," Ms. Taylor says, shooting me a small smile. She's wearing a red flowered dress and heels today, looking nothing like she had last weekend at the mall in the picture Sam sent. "But it's clear Sam and Hannah are on Team 1-Factor with you, Emma, and Jane and George are on Team Karma Can."

I glance at George and raise my eyebrows. *Karma Can?* He shrugs, but doesn't look away or give me his angry glare, and maybe he's not still mad at me? I haven't driven him to or from school in almost two weeks and, looking at him now, I realize how much I've missed his company.

"So—" Ms. Taylor is still talking "—that leaves Robert in the middle."

All of us turn to look at him. He was doodling in his notebook again, but his pencil stops moving, and he looks up, looks around, as if suddenly noticing what we've all been talking about around him. "Me?" he says, his voice cracking.

"I know it's not quite fair to put this all on you," Ms. Taylor responds. "You're new to the club and don't have much coding experience. So I would like to hear your opinion, yes, but then I'm going to make the final decision as the club's adviser."

Jane shoots George a smirk, like she thinks that means they've definitely won. But I bite my lip, not sure, thinking again about how Ms. Taylor looked in Sam's photo last weekend, holding hands with Mr. Weston. Falling in love beats recycling. At least, I would guess, since I've never been in love but I've recycled my whole life and it's pretty boring.

"Well…" Robert puts his pencil down, looks around at all of us. "Well, I still don't really get the karma points thing, and I don't know…I kind of might want a match, too." Jane's face falls. "But they're both good ideas," Robert stammers, and his cheeks turn pink. "Ms. Taylor, you should just decide."

Jane turns her gaze to Ms. Taylor; we all do. She doesn't

say anything for another minute before she turns back and nods at me. "I do think 1-Factor might be something special. Something unique that would stand out for the judges, and it would be easier to get more of the school involved in our project..."

Jane puts her head down on the desk, and I almost feel bad for her, except I think at least half the reason she hates my idea is simply because it's mine. No matter what she or Izzy or George thinks, I really do believe my school-wide matching app is a great idea. And I feel pretty validated that Ms. Taylor seems to think so, too.

"But we're a club," Ms. Taylor is saying now. "We have to all work together or we're not going to have a shot at winning anything, agreed?" Her gaze turns to Jane, then George.

No one says anything right away, and I hold my breath, thinking this is about to all fall apart. That Jane and George will quit and dissolve the club before going forward with my idea. But then George looks at Ms. Taylor and nods. "Agreed," he says.

"George!" I follow him out after the meeting, calling after him. He had been walking toward the parking lot with Jane. They both stop walking when I call out for him and turn to look at me. "Let me drive you home," I say.

"I can drive you," Jane says to him quickly, touching his arm in a way that I find weirdly offensive, like she's trying to take ownership of him. I want him to pull away, but he doesn't—at first. Then he shifts, and her hand falls away on its own. His eyes meet mine, and his expression softens. There he is. Just George, whom I've spent hours working on code with. Who indulges in talking to Dad about baseball. Who makes fun of me for my pizza choice.

"We're still co-presidents," I say. "And you can't stay mad at me forever." I need George for his animation, but I also need him to help teach and find roles for Sam, Hannah and Robert, and to convince Jane to work on the app. As much as I'm not a fan of Jane personally, she has skills I don't, and we do need her if we want to have a shot at winning.

George turns back to Jane. "Go ahead," he says to her. "I'll ride with Emma." She shrugs, as if she couldn't care less, and keeps on walking toward her car. George and I walk in step toward my car, and my body relaxes. "I mean, I probably could stay mad at you forever," George says to me, after Jane's across the parking lot. "You make it pretty easy."

"Well, so do you," I shoot back. "At least I didn't involve John and Izzy in any of this."

He stops walking and touches my shoulder lightly. "I am sorry about that. I was worried about you, Emma. But you're right, I shouldn't have said anything to John. I should've talked to you instead."

I nod, forgiving him, because he's George, and everything is easy with him, and I'm glad he's talking to me again, that we can be co-presidents again. "Karma Can was kinda cute," I say. "You did a nice job with the animation, the way you brought the can to life. But we have a better shot at winning with this. I just feel it."

"Agree to disagree," George says. "But I was outvoted. So here we are. And you know I want to win the state competition just as badly as you do, so I'll do whatever I can to make this app good."

We get into the car, and I turn out onto Highbury Pike, toward his house. There is this nice silence between us again. George flips NPR onto the radio and only the soft sound of talk radio fills the car. And for a little while, everything feels right with the world.

CHAPTER 9

Sam asks Laura to go to the dance with him, and she says yes, but though we all have the same lunch, she still sits at another table with her friends the following week, and Sam still sits at a table with me. I catch him watching her, from across the room, as I'm trying to talk to him about our project.

"Sam," I say, realizing he's not listening. I touch his arm to get his attention and he turns. His skin is warm, and I let my fingers linger a moment longer than I mean to. "Did you hear what I just said?" I'd asked him if he wanted to come over later to help me run the remaining matches.

"Oh, what, E? I'm sorry." I repeat my question, and he nods. "Yeah, yeah. I have choir right after school, but after that?"

"I have my piano lesson after school, anyway," I say. "So after that would be good."

"I didn't know you play piano." His eyes light up a little, like he's fascinated and surprised by the thought that I have some musical abilities. I remember what Ms. Taylor said, about a duet, and weirdly I envision this strange scenario where later when Sam comes over, and before we get to work on code, I play something on the piano, and Sam sings. And even though I only ever study classical, for a moment I picture it, and it makes me smile.

Sam's eyes have wandered back toward Laura. "You know, you could invite her to sit with us," I say, even though I don't actually want him to do that. It just seems like what I'm maybe supposed to say?

"Yeah," he says, sounding unsure. "Maybe I will." But he doesn't move, just watches her a little more. So I watch her, too. Her friend says something to her, and she throws her head back and laughs, her raven hair cascading down her back. I look away from her, back at Sam. He's still staring at her, but frowning now. I frown, too. Because it's impossible for me to tell from the way he's acting if my algorithm worked. If he even likes her at all.

I text Sam when I get home from piano later that day, and he texts back that he'll be over in twenty minutes. At my lesson, Mrs. Howard gave me a new Rachmaninoff piece to learn for the state competition in May, a piece she said she knew would *challenge* me. But now it feels more like a hurdle, and I pull it back out of my bag and sit down at the piano to look over it again while I'm waiting for him.

I love the piano, love the way the scale patterns and the time signatures make sense the same way calculus and coding do, but right now I feel overwhelmed by the difficulty of this particular piece. When I'd tried to play through it during my lesson I'd stumbled, pretty badly. Mrs. Howard said she wasn't at all worried, that I still have months to learn it. But I know I'm going to have to practice a lot to get it perfect, while also keeping up with all my AP classes, and working on our app. My heart pounds wildly in my chest as all that floods my brain now. I run my fingers over the keys, going through the scale patterns I know by heart, until their formulaic sequences relax me a little.

I have a keyboard up in my room, but downstairs, in the living room with Mom's worn blue couches, we also have Mom's old upright oak piano. One of my only memories of her still is her sitting here, playing piano, me watching the concave shape of her back as she hovered over the keys. As a toddler, I was content to sit on the living room floor listening to her play, enchanted by her music. And even now, all these years later, it's the one thing I do that makes me still feel connected to her. The one thing I know and understand about her that makes complete and total sense—Mom loved the piano, she was *good* at the piano. Just like me.

After I make my way through the scales, and I can breathe a little easier, I turn back to the Rachmaninoff. I go through it again, more slowly. I stumble still, but now on the second pass through, the notes make more sense, feel more formulaic than they had at first glance at Mrs. Howard's earlier. Maybe Mrs. Howard is right, that in a few months I'll get this down perfectly.

I hear the doorbell ring, and I lift my fingers from the keys, and go to answer it. Sam is standing on the porch. "I heard you playing," he says, walking inside. "You're really good, aren't you, E?"

My face warms with his compliment, but I answer him truthfully. "Yes, I came in first in the state competition last year."

"Why am I not surprised?" He smiles. "I took lessons for a few years in Phoenix, but my right hand and left hand don't like to work together. My vocal chords are luckily more co-operative."

I don't like to sing. I can do it. I have good pitch, but I find the whole thing unenjoyable and stress inducing. I suddenly want to hear Sam sing, but I don't know if it's the right time to ask him to. He's here to work on our project, so instead I invite him to come into the kitchen, grabbing my laptop on the way and bringing it to the table with me. I open up my Excel file to the database along with my flowchart software for the algorithm.

Sam looks at my screen, and his eyes widen. "You're going to have to explain this to me. It looks much more complicated than anything we ever worked with at my old school."

"It's not complicated at all," I say. "Actually, everything is very basic right now." He frowns, and I'm worried I said the wrong thing. The level we're at now really is beginner stuff: a spreadsheet and a flowchart. But I didn't mean any of that in a negative way toward him. "I mean…I can show you all this pretty quickly. You'll get it really fast…" I stumble over my words the way I just stumbled over the Rachmaninoff, wanting so badly to say the right thing to Sam. I want to see him smile at me again.

He does, and I exhale a little. "I really want to learn what all this is. Thank you for teaching me, E." His stomach rumbles, a low growl, and he laughs and puts his hand on it. "Sorry. Guess I'm hungry."

"We can order a pizza," I suggest. "Eat dinner and work at the same time?"

"Yeah? Pizza sounds great."

I grab my phone and open the Giuseppe's app to order. The last time I ordered pizza I must've been with George because it asks me if I want to reorder a half pepperoni, half mushroom and olives. "How do you feel about mushroom and olives?" I ask Sam tentatively, waiting for him to tell me how gross it is the way George always does. *Agree to disagree*, I hear George's voice in my head.

But instead Sam says, "Sure, sounds great. I love mushrooms and olives."

"Of course you do," I say, clicking to update my order. "Because you're smart like me."

He laughs and points back to my screen. "I don't know about that, E."

"I do," I tell him. "I'll explain this to you and you'll have everything figured out before the pizza even gets here."

By Friday afternoon, we've made matches for four more of Phillip's friends on the cross-country team, and one for Jenny

Hampton's friend Ellie. I update everyone at our meeting—we have ten couples matched for the dance now, including Hannah and Phillip and Sam and Laura.

"Okay," George says. "The dance is tomorrow night. Let's stop matching couples for now. Hannah, Sam and Robert, I want you to finish getting our application done for the state competition and get it submitted today with Ms. Taylor. And Jane, Emma and I will start working on improving our algorithm and database, and turning this into an app."

I'd brought all my work in on a thumb drive, and Jane is already scanning through my Excel file on her laptop. I watch her scroll, then jot something down, then scroll some more. The lab coat she's wearing today is embroidered in purple stitching around the cuffs of her sleeves, and I wonder if she did the stitching herself, if she knows how to sew?

"If we're going to make this user-driven," Jane says, and I blink my attention away from her lab coat, back to what she's saying, "we need a different way to populate the database other than us entering information from the yearbook."

She's right. "What are you thinking?" I ask her.

"Well..." She chews on the end of her pen. "I can set up a skim for socials. But I also think we should start with a survey, so everyone who wants to participate can enter their own information, too. You're relying on yearbook and social media profiles now to determine people's interests and their sexual orientation, but I think people need to be able to input their own preferences. It'll be more accurate."

"Good point, Jane," Ms. Taylor says from across the room.

I nod, agreeing with everything she's saying now, and I tell her if she works on designing the survey, I can start working on code in Swift.

George pulls out his own thumb drive, and shows us the animations he's been working on this week in Blender. He's taken the cute googly-eyed face he'd designed for Karma Can and put it onto a yellow heart that he's also given arms and legs. "I made it yellow to keep it gender neutral," George explains. "I'm thinking this can be our icon, and I can also animate it to guide people through the app. What do you think?" He's asking everyone, but his eyes fall on me, like my approval is what he really cares about.

"I think it's perfect," I tell him. He smiles at me, and his face relaxes.

"Oh, and—" Ms. Taylor interjects from where she's working with Hannah across the room. "We need a better name to go on the application." She turns to look at me now, too, like she thinks I might be upset, but I'm not.

"Of course," I say. "Something with the word *code* actually in it."

Ms. Taylor nods and explains for Sam, Hannah and Robert. Every year, people always try and use the word *code* in the title of their project in some way. Last year our title was Code Layup, having to do with some basketball term Brian and Daniel liked.

"How about The Code for Love?" Sam speaks up, and I remember how he texted me that phrase a few weeks ago, when he saw Ms. Taylor and Mr. Weston at the mall. How he said that I *wrote the code for love*. But then I think, *Love?* Is that what he feels for Laura? He didn't even mention her at all at my house the other night as the two of us had laughed and shared our pizza and I'd showed him how the flowchart worked.

"Simple. To the point. I like it," Ms. Taylor is saying now.

We all murmur in agreement. And Sam catches my eye. I smile at him, and he smiles back. He doesn't *love* Laura. He just came up with a good title.

"Okay," George says. "The Code for Love, it is."

Hannah stops over the next morning to pick up her dress. Her mom waits in the car in the driveway, because she's shuttling Hannah off to a hair appointment next. Hannah is practically buzzing with excitement about the dance—her whole body seems to vibrate with it as she climbs up the stairs with me.

"What do you think?" Hannah asks me, about her hair, as we walk into Izzy's room to grab the dress. "Up or down?" She stands in front of the floor-length mirror, sweeps her hair up with her hands, turns to the side, frowns, then drops it again, red curls bouncing against her shoulders.

"I'm not sure," I say. This is a question Izzy would've asked me last year. I would've just picked one, and then Izzy would've frowned and done the opposite. "Up?" I guess, wondering whether I've given the right or wrong answer.

Hannah grabs her hair again, piles it on top of her head with her hands and smiles a little in the mirror. "Yes, I think you're right," she says. *Am I?*

She drops her hair again, grabs me in a quick and unexpected hug and then takes the dress. "I'll see you later at the dance?" she says.

"Oh, no, I'm not going," I say quickly.

"What? Emma! You have to."

"Why?" I say. Then I add, "I hate dances." They are worse, in my mind, than shopping at the mall. Too many people, too loud. Everyone is sweaty and packed into the gym too close together. No thanks.

"But you set all those people up." Hannah is still talking. "And I need a friend there!"

"Well, Sam is going." I wonder if Laura will wear her raven hair up or down, and what color dress she'll wear. And if Sam will look at her the way he looks at me, when he smiles in that sweet way he does, like we share a secret.

Suddenly, Hannah's mom honks from the driveway, and the sound makes us both jump. Hannah frowns and glances at her phone. "I'm gonna be late for my hair appointment. But please come, Emma. Please?"

After she leaves I think about what she said. I do hate dances, but maybe someone should monitor all the matches I've made, to judge if my algorithm actually works. Our matches have agreed to go to a dance together, but will they actually get along? Will they like each other, never mind *love* each other? Mathematically, they should. *But will they?* Math is reliable and perfect. People aren't.

I text George and tell him what Hannah said, and I ask him if he's planning on going.

Yeah, he texts back. I'm going to pick Jane up at 6:30. Want me to pick you up, too?

Pick Jane up?

You're taking Jane to the dance?

Yep.

Oh, okay. Never mind…

Not like that…I'm driving her. Drive with us?

I don't know… If you're going I don't need to. You can monitor our matches without me. Text me later?

No way! This was your brilliant idea. I'm picking you up at 6:20. Be ready.

CHAPTER 10

The last time I went to the fall formal it was that time in tenth grade when Izzy set me up with Richard Hall. He'd held on to me too tightly as we'd slow-danced, and then surprised me with that disgusting kiss. I feel a knot in my stomach walking back toward the gym now, the floor in the hallway outside pulsating from the music. I remember that night again and it makes me feel a little nauseous, even though two years have passed, Richard graduated last year and tonight I'm walking in at an arm's-length distance, in between Jane and George.

I'd picked a dress from Izzy's closet and a pair of shoes to match. And I've done nothing with my hair, other than wash it and comb it. I chose the most modest dress I could find, black velvet, tea-length and with a cap sleeve. If I'm remembering correctly, Izzy wore it to our cousin June's wedding in Cincinnati, not to a formal dance, and had I run my choice by her on FaceTime, she probably wouldn't have approved. But I'd felt uncomfortable just running my hands across all the strapless and spaghetti strap options in her closet, much less actually *wearing* any of them out of the house. Anyway, Izzy's busy studying for midterms, and hasn't had time to FaceTime this week. She should just be happy I'm keeping my promise to her, that I'm here at the dance, even if this probably isn't quite what she had in mind.

"We should spread out," Jane says as we walk in. She's forgone the lab coat for once, and is wearing a long-sleeved lilac lace dress that looks weirdly like a doily, or like something she might've borrowed from one of the old ladies at the Villages, where I volunteer once a week. My dress is positively risqué in comparison. "Let's all try and find our matches and try to observe how things are going," Jane says.

George nods in agreement, and Jane walks inside the gym in front of us, heads right into the fray of dancing bodies, as if she belongs, seemingly not caring one bit that she doesn't. George and I stand there a little awkwardly by the door, watching everyone dancing out in front of us. The DJ is playing something fast, and the beat is pulsing way too loud. The gym still smells vaguely of sweat, and I don't care how dark it is, how much the committee decorated it last week, I still step in here and only see and smell PE class.

George nudges me with his elbow. "Look, there's Hannah and Phillip." They're dancing next to each other. Phillip bumps her hip with his and she throws back her head and laughs. She *is* wearing her hair up. All the red curls are piled on top of her head, making her face open and bright, her expression clear, radiant. Up was the right choice! "And Sam and Laura, over there." George points to the other side of the dance floor, and I can only catch a glimpse of Sam's face, the back of Laura's head (her raven hair is down, curled). "And one of the other cross-country guys over there…what's his name?"

I follow his finger and crane my neck to see. "Oh, that's Jason. And he's with Jenny."

"They all seem to be having fun," George says, and there's something strange in his voice that I can't place, like he's a little wistful. Or maybe he's still annoyed that I was right all along about this app being a good idea.

"Maybe I should've made you a match," I say, half teasing.

He chokes back a laugh. "Sure, right after you made yourself one." George has never had a girlfriend for as long as I've known him. He's like me—too focused on school and studying to have time to think about dating. And that's at least half the reason why we get along. We understand each other.

"Come on." George grabs on to my hand, pulling me farther into the gym, into the crowd. "Let's get a closer look."

Just as we make our way onto the middle of the dance floor, the song ends. For a second or two it's quieter. There are only the noises of couples laughing, chatting. The DJ announces it's time to switch things up, and a slow song comes on. All around me, couples move in closer, cling to one another, and there George and I are, staring at each other and trapped in the middle of all of it.

George holds out his hand to me. "Come on, let's dance."

I think he's joking for a minute, but I stare at him, his eyes hold on to mine and there isn't a hint of laughter in them. "We can make our way around the floor easier this way. Better for people watching," he adds.

I take his hand, he pulls me closer and we start to dance. But I don't feel awkward, the way I had dancing with Richard Hall here in this gym a few years ago, because this is George, and everything about him feels comfortable. He slowly inches us toward Hannah and Phillip, stopping when we're near enough to observe them, and then we stand in place and slow-dance.

I lean in closer to him; my cheek falls into the wool of his black suit jacket, and it smells good and familiar, like George: soap and just a hint of sandalwood aftershave. I inhale and close my eyes for a minute, and I forget I'm supposed to be watching Hannah and Phillip.

"Remember last year?" George says. "John and Iz went to this dance, and you and I worked on robot code instead?"

John and George and their parents had come over to our house to take pictures before the dance, and then after George and my dad had finished talking about the World Series, and we had both gotten bored of John and Izzy's endless poses and endless background changes, we'd gone upstairs to my room and pulled out my laptop to work on the robot code. Dad had come to check on us later, and we hadn't even realized it but a few hours had passed; it was already dark outside, and we'd missed dinner completely. *There's spaghetti in the kitchen if you kids are hungry*, Dad had said, switching on the light in my room, stepping inside. It was the rare night when he remembered about making dinner before I did.

"That was the night we decided we'd be co-presidents this year, remember?" I say. Before then, I'd wanted to, and planned to be, president of coding club alone, and I thought, like everything else with me and George, it would be a competition I would have to work really hard to win. But it was George who pointed out how well we worked together, how as co-presidents we could have everything—his people skills and animation, my coding skills and ideas. "I guess it's kind of crazy that we ended up here, tonight, huh?" I say now. If someone had told me last year at this time that coding club would lead me straight to the fall dance, *where George and I would be dancing*, I would've laughed and told them they were insane.

"It is crazy," George says softly into my hair, so I can barely hear him. But I think he says: "Kind of nice, too, isn't it?"

The song ends before I can say anything else, but George doesn't let go of me for a few seconds, and I don't let go of him, either. Until Hannah touches my arm. "Emma!" She squeals. "You came!" George and I both jump back, letting go of each other quickly.

Hannah grabs me in a hug, then stands back to examine me. "You look so pretty," she says, running her hand over the velvet of my dress. She does, too—the green of Izzy's dress is perfect for her eyes, especially with her hair up. But before I realize I'm supposed to tell her that, she has already moved on to George and is giving him a hug.

"How's it going?" George shouts to her now to be heard over the music. *Right.* I should've said that to her, too.

"I'm having so much fun! Phillip is so sweet and so cute."

I smile at her. Math came through for me, once again.

"I'm going to walk around," George says, tapping my arm lightly. "I'll find you in a little bit."

I nod and watch him walk away into the crowd, not realizing for a minute that Hannah is still talking. "I can't believe I'm lucky enough to date him, and that he actually likes me," she's saying now.

I hear her talking, but my eyes are still following George. And I'm thinking about the way my skin had felt warm, dancing so close to him. But then I lose him in the crowd, push the thought away and turn my attention back to Hannah and the reason I'm here. Our project. "Have you seen any of the other couples?" I ask her.

"I saw Sam and Laura, and they look like they're having fun. And then Phillip's friend Evan—he matched to a girl in my geometry class, Becca, and I saw her in the bathroom already and she said he was super nice."

The music is fast again, and Hannah starts dancing to it as she's talking to me. And I feel like I'm supposed to be dancing, too. I awkwardly swing my arms and sway my hips a little, and hope in the crowd of people, the semidarkness, no one sees or notices me. I look around, but it's so crowded and the faces are a blur as everyone is moving all around me. No one is paying attention to me.

Hannah grabs on to my hand and looks silly as she jumps up and down, but her energy is weirdly infectious and I mimic her moves for a few songs until we are both laughing and sweating. And for the smallest moment, I understand why Izzy always liked going to these things.

"Hey," Phillip says, pushing his way through the crowd and grabbing on to Hannah's arm. "There you are! I couldn't find you. Come back and dance with me."

"Go," I say to Hannah, remembering why she's here. Why we're both here. "Have fun."

"Do you want to come and dance with us?" she offers.

"No, I'm good. I'm going to walk around, find George. I'll catch up with you later."

Hannah clings to Phillip's arm, and the two of them disappear back into the crowd.

I scan the dance floor but don't see George, so I gravitate toward the edge of the gym, the long tables set up with bowls of punch and trays of cupcakes. I grab a cupcake and lick the vanilla frosting off, noticing Ms. Taylor and Mr. Weston are both here as chaperones, standing just a few feet away from me, holding hands.

"Emma!" Ms. Taylor says, and they both walk toward me. "How nice to see you here."

Maybe she believes I'm taking her advice, to be more social. "I came with Jane and George," I explain. "To monitor how our matches are going."

"Well, I'm glad you're here. And it's good to see you all getting along again," she says kindly. "It won't kill you to dance a little, too, have some fun." She turns and smiles at Mr. Weston, and it feels like a weirdly private moment between them, so I look away, and then I see George, quickly walking toward me.

"Cupcake?" I hold up my half-eaten one. George likes cake and hates icing, while I'm the opposite.

He shakes his head, and I drop the remainder of the cupcake in the trash. Then George grabs my hand. "I need to talk to you!" He's shouting to be heard above the music, and that makes him sound upset. Or maybe he is upset?

"You two have fun," Ms. Taylor says, and she and Mr. Weston wander off, still holding hands.

"Did you see that?" I say to George. "Our very first match is actually working out." But he ignores me and pulls me toward the exit of the gym, into the hallway where it's quieter.

"We have a problem," he says, speaking at a normal level now, but he's frowning and still sounds upset.

"What?" I say. "Is one of the couples not getting along?"

He shakes his head. "Much worse. Dammit, Emma," he snaps at me, seemingly out of nowhere.

His words sting. I feel a little like he slapped me, and I pull away from him.

George sighs and looks down at his feet, so I do, too. He's wearing black leather shoes so shiny and brand-new looking that I wonder if he bought them just for this occasion. Normally he wears jeans and gray Converse, and actually, I don't know if I've ever seen him dressed up before. "I knew this was a terrible idea," he's saying now.

"What?" I look back up, and meet his eyes, trying to decipher the expression on his face. Hurt or disappointment or anger?

"The app," he says.

"It was not a terrible idea," I say through gritted teeth. "Didn't you just see how happy Ms. Taylor and Mr. Weston looked in there?"

He shakes his head and doesn't say anything for a minute. The expression on his face is anger, *yes*. He's mad at me, but I have no idea why. "I overheard Phillip and some of the cross-country guys talking outside the bathroom," he finally says.

"So…what? They don't like their matches?" I don't believe it, even as I say it out loud. Hannah and Phillip are having a great time, and she told me Evan and Becca were, too. Jenny and Jason also looked pretty happy in there.

"No…they like their matches, all right. But not the way you think."

"George, I don't know what you're saying or why you're so angry. Just spit it out." I'm frustrated, and I'm still sweating from dancing, and it's too hot out here. I blow on my bangs to get them off my sweaty forehead. This is exactly why I hate dances.

"The guys on the cross-country team all apparently have a little game they play, a competition, to try and see who can get an underclassman to hook up with him first," George says. I can't process what he means or how this relates to us. I shake my head. "That's why they all wanted matches. They're using us, Emma. They're using our app to help them with their disgusting game. And now we have all these freshman and sophomore girls believing we've matched them to a person they're supposed to fall in love with. And we have all these senior and junior cross-country guys betting on who has sex with one of them first."

"What?" I hear what George is saying, of course, but his words don't make sense. The cross-country boys match with these girls, mathematically. Of course they should want to date them. And some people who date in high school do have sex, so maybe that's all George heard. "Maybe you misunderstood?"

"Oh, I didn't misunderstand." His words are so sharp they hurt, and it's hard to breathe.

I take a step back and sink down on the bench in front of the large glass trophy case behind me, filled with championship trophies from years of sporting events I've never attended. George stays standing, and we stare at each other.

"Misunderstand what?" Jane has walked out of the gym, along with Sam. I peek behind him for Laura, but it's only him and Jane.

"I found her for you," Sam says to George. "What's going on?" He notices me sitting down, and shoots me a worried look.

George repeats for them what he just told me. "Crap," Jane says. "We have to warn the girls. And I just saw Hannah and Phillip getting ready to leave—we have to go get her."

"But my algorithm matched them…" I'm still trying to breathe, to process everything in my head. Math is better than people. Math doesn't lie or leave you or hurt you. "And Hannah is having so much fun," I say weakly. But Hannah really is having so much fun, and Phillip genuinely seems to like her. This doesn't make any sense at all. Is it possible George is making this into a bigger thing than it should be because he still isn't happy with the club using my app for our project? "Are you trying to sabotage my app?" I say now.

"Jesus, Emma, do you really think I'd do that?" George's face reddens. He's definitely angry now. He turns away from me, shutting me out of the conversation he's having in a huddle with Sam and Jane.

I hear Sam saying he's texting Hannah. And then he and Jane and George run off toward the parking lot to look for her. Should I follow them, or should I stay here on the relative safety of this bench? Before I can decide what to do, I lose sight of them. George's words echo in my head. *Jesus, Emma.* They thrum in my chest, and they hurt. I know deep down that George would never sabotage our project. George is too good, and George wants to win. Why did I even say that out loud? George isn't the one I should be mad at. *Phillip.* Stupid Phillip is ruining everything.

My phone dings with a text from Sam: they found Hannah, and George is driving her home. George wants to know if I can find another ride. I text Sam back that I can.

I hold my phone in my hand a minute longer, trying to think of something else to text back to Sam. Something I can say that would make this right. But I don't know what that is.

So instead I text Dad and ask if he can come pick me up.

CHAPTER 11

I wake up the next morning, and the events from the dance last night come crashing back to me all over again, so vividly, as if I'm still sitting right there in front of the trophy case. I'd turned off my phone and stuck it in my night table drawer after I got home last night. I'd closed my eyes and willed it all away, wished for sleep to overtake me. I groan and put my pillow over my head, not wanting to deal with it now, either, wishing for more sleep. But I'll never fall back to sleep. Not when I feel this giant nervous pit in my stomach, knowing that somehow Izzy and George were right to be worried about me all along. I'm in way over my head.

I squeeze my eyes shut, and toss and turn for a few more minutes before I finally give up and pull my phone out of my night table drawer, power it on.

The only text is one from Dad, saying he went into work for a few hours and didn't want to wake me before he left. That I looked like I needed some sleep after last night and he hoped everything was okay. Can we talk over dinner? I'll pick something up on the way home. Text me later and let me know what you want.

When he'd picked me up from the dance last night, I'd gotten in his car and refused to say a word the entire ride home. Dad asked if I'd had fun, and then, when I didn't answer, he asked if something was wrong. I'd just shrugged and looked out the window, not wanting to discuss any of it with him, worried if I did, I'd scream—or worse, cry. Finally, he pulled into the garage. I told him I was really tired, and I'd gone straight upstairs and gotten into bed. It had taken me hours to fall asleep, as every time I closed my eyes I kept seeing Hannah's bright, excited face as she was dancing, and George's red, angry one looming over me.

I glance at the time now, and it's after eleven. I never stay in bed this late, not even on Sundays, and I do have a calculus test and a Spanish quiz tomorrow. I need to practice piano today, too. I force myself to get out of bed and get some work done.

I go into the kitchen, brew some coffee for a mocha. Then I sip it at the kitchen table, and pick up my phone, glancing at it again. I think about texting Hannah, but I'm not sure what to say to her. Should I apologize? She was having a great time at the dance when I saw her, and I only gave her what she asked for: a match. Still, I can't help feeling this is all my fault and that she might hate me right now. Maybe instead I should text Phillip and yell at him for ruining everything?

He'd seemed genuinely upset when we'd lost states last year. How could he do this to us now?

I'm still considering what to do when the doorbell rings. I walk toward it slowly, wondering whether or not to actually answer it. It would be just like George to storm over here if he was still angry. But also, part of me hopes it *is* him, because then he can help me figure out what I'm supposed to do next.

I look through the peephole, and it's not George. It's Sam. He's standing there on my porch, looking down at his sneakers, a paper bag in his hands. I have never felt happier to see anyone, and I open the door quickly before I realize that I'm still in the clothes I slept in, and that my hair is a total mess. I quickly pull it back into a ponytail with the hair tie on my wrist.

"Did I wake you?" Sam asks, taking in my outfit—my old stretched-out gray sweatpants and my Stanford sweatshirt.

"No, no. I got up a little while ago."

He holds up the paper bag. "I brought donuts."

I open the door wider. "Come on in. You want a mocha?" Then I clarify that it's just half coffee, half milk, with a packet of Swiss Miss mixed in.

"Sure, sounds great." He follows me into the kitchen where I make him his own cup, hand it to him and then invite him to come sit with me on the couch. I curl up on one end, tucking my feet underneath me, sipping on my mocha. Sam sits next to me, puts his cup down on Dad's Phillies coaster on the coffee table and leans his elbows on his knees, turning his head to look at me. He offers me a half smile before opening the paper bag. "Glazed or chocolate?" he asks me.

I consider it for a moment, because really you can't go wrong with either one. "Glazed," I finally decide. He hands me a donut, and I take a bite, chewing around the edges, letting the sweetness of the glaze melt in my mouth, soothe me a little.

"I am a firm believer that donuts fix all things," Sam says.

I laugh a little, but the donut catches in my throat and then I almost feel like I might start to cry. "I made a mess out of everything, didn't I?" I don't know what it is that lets me feel comfortable enough to speak honestly with Sam in a way I couldn't with Dad last night. Maybe it's just that he's been on my side with this app the whole time. Or maybe it's that he's here right now, that he brought me donuts. Or maybe it's the sweet half smile on his face, the kind way he's looking at me now like he truly wants to help, wants to make everything better. "Does Hannah hate me?" I ask as I finish off my donut and lick the glaze off my fingers. He holds out the bag to offer me another one but I shake my head. The first is already settling as a nervous lump in my stomach, and I feel a little sick, imagining Hannah hating me.

"Hannah was upset last night when we drove her home," Sam says. "But I don't think she hates you, E." Poor Hannah. She was so happy earlier in the day, in the evening, laughing and dancing. "You'll make her another match and she can forget all about this." Sam is still talking.

"Oh, no way. I'm done," I say quickly. George was right, Izzy was right. Phillip was right when he laughed at me. I'm not equipped to match people, not even using math. "We can all go recycle now and get our karma points."

Sam laughs and shakes his head. "First of all, we already submitted The Code for Love in our competition application, and Friday was the deadline. We can't change it now. I double-checked with George on that this morning." I sigh, realizing he's right. The deadline has passed—we can't change our application. We either go forward or we drop out. "And second of all," Sam continues, "this still has tons of potential. We just need to reconfigure it to account for the Phillips of the school somehow. You really shouldn't feel bad, E. You had no way to know what those guys were thinking."

But I can't help but wonder, if I were more like Izzy, would I have known? My whole life I've had a hard time understanding other people; why did I think this was going to be any different? Because this wasn't really being social, this was supposed to be *all about math*. Numbers don't lie. Except guys like Phillip do. I sigh again, and bury my face in my hands. "It doesn't matter...this is still my fault. I can always count on math, but this time it failed me. And everyone is mad at me now."

"Hey." He reaches across the couch cushion and pats my knee gently. "I'm not mad at you." His hand lingers on my knee for a few seconds, so I can feel the warmth of his fingers through the thin fabric of my sweatpants, and I move in a little closer to him. If math has failed me in this particular situation, failed Hannah, then was it wrong about Sam and Laura, too?

I look up again and his face is closer to mine. I get this weird feeling that it might be enjoyable to kiss him, that the pressure of his lips against mine might feel thrilling, not disgusting, and I move my face in even closer to him, so our lips are almost touching but not quite. But we're close enough that I can feel the warmth of his breath against my face. If I moved just the smallest bit closer, my lips and his lips would touch.

"E," he says softly, extracting his hand from my leg, moving back. "I had a good time with Laura last night. I like her. Math didn't fail you at all. Phillip and his friends are just jerks."

"Right," I say, my face suddenly flaming hot. I never get embarrassed, but now I feel so truly and desperately embarrassed. It washes over me, hot and sticky, unexpected and unfamiliar, and I want to run upstairs, slam my bedroom door shut, turn my fan on high and hide on my bed underneath it.

But if Sam and Laura actually had a good time last night, if they genuinely like each other, then that means my algorithm isn't a complete disaster. That our project isn't completely ruined. And I know that's a good thing. But it's still hard to breathe, and my face still burns too hot.

"I should probably go," Sam says, standing. "I'll leave you the donuts, though, okay, E?"

"Yeah," I say. I stand up to walk him to the door, and he reaches over, gives me a quick hug. His arms feel gentle and kind, and my embarrassment lessens, because even though I did the wrong thing, read the situation all wrong, he's not upset. "And thanks," I say. "For the donuts, and for..." I can't articulate the rest in words for a minute. Finally, I say, "Making me feel better."

He nods, like he gets it. "Anytime, E. Anytime."

Izzy's FaceTime chime an hour later is so predictable I'm annoyed with myself for not having thought to preempt it with a text to her, telling her not to listen to George, and that I'm fine. *Everything is fine!* But the truth is, I'm still not fine, and I pick up, relieved to see her there, even if it's just on my screen, and really, she's 2,764 miles away. Still, I can't believe George involved her again, after just apologizing to me last week for doing it the last time.

"Whatever George said, don't listen," I say before she can say anything.

"George?" She frowns. "What happened with George?"

For some reason, I think of that moment last night, the two of us dancing, my cheek pressed into the wool of his jacket. But then I quickly remember the way, only twenty minutes later, his angry words had felt like a slap. The dance meant nothing, the same way Sam's kind hand on my knee meant nothing.

"Never mind," I say. "What's going on, Iz? I thought you had midterms."

"I do, but Dad texted me and asked me to check in on you."

I sigh. Not George at all. *Dad.* I should've thought to mollify him with…something last night. Some excuse or explanation. Since Sam had showed up right after I woke up, I haven't remembered to text Dad back this morning yet, either. I feel bad that I worried him enough that he texted Izzy to check on me.

"Well, I'm fine, Iz. Really."

"That's not what Dad said. He said you went to the dance, and something happened and you seemed upset and then you wouldn't talk to him about it."

I bite my tongue because I know if I tell Izzy the truth

about what happened, she'll tell me that she *told me so* about my app. And Sam is right. Now that we've submitted it for the state competition, we're going to have to figure something out. I'm not dropping out of the competition, not failing as co-president my senior year.

"But you *went* to the dance," Izzy finally says. "That's good. I'm proud of you, Em."

"Yeah," I say. "Well…" I let my voice trail off, not wanting to elaborate more. I'm thinking about what Sam said, about how our app isn't bad, or a total disaster; it just needs more work. Hannah needs a new match, and we need to account for jerks like Phillip. "Hey, Iz," I say. "If you had to pick the number one thing that makes you and John work, that makes you love him, what would it be?"

"Did you actually dance with a boy last night?" Izzy's eyes widen, then go fuzzy on my screen.

"No," I say too quickly. I did dance with George, but that doesn't really count. I'm not going to tell her about that. "That's not why I'm asking. I'm just trying to figure out what's the most important thing to make two people fall in love."

Izzy frowns again. But then she answers my question. "He makes me laugh," she says without hesitation.

"He makes you laugh?"

It's like the thing Dad said about Mom's eyes. And I have no idea how to quantify that. Izzy's answer is no help at all.

CHAPTER 12

George texts everyone and calls an emergency coding club meeting for Monday after school. As soon as I get his text, I'm a little annoyed with myself that I didn't think to send one first. But that's part of what makes our co-presidency work, isn't it? George is just naturally better with people than I am.

I text George back separately and ask if he still needs a ride to school in the morning.

Yep, he texts back.

I stare at that one word, trying to read into it. Does this mean he's not mad at me, or does it just mean that Jane can't pick him up for some reason?

I consider texting him again to ask him, but then I don't. And when I show up Monday morning, he gets in the car and says hi, almost like nothing ever happened at all. So I decide not to tell him yet that I've been thinking about what Izzy said about John making her laugh, and that I've been taking another look at my algorithm, considering that maybe I have the categories weighted all wrong. We drive to school in silence, and I can't tell whether it's that nice silence we usually have or whether George is really mad at me.

"You study for calc?" George finally asks as we get out of the car and walk toward the school together. He doesn't sound mad at all. He sounds quiet and sweet and kind…like George.

I nod. *Of course I studied.* If he thinks this app is going to distract me from my real goal this year, becoming valedictorian, beating him, then he doesn't know me at all.

"It's not your fault, what happened at the dance, you know," George says quietly. "If anything, it's my fault."

"No. I never should've said you were trying to sabotage the app. I know you wouldn't really do that." I stop walking and turn to look at him.

His face is downcast; he's staring at his shoes—back in his beat-up old gray Converse today, which look much more *George* than the shiny black shoes and wool suit from Saturday night. His clothes look so much more George, but I haven't ever seen him looking this dismayed before.

"This is not your fault," I say gently. "You didn't even want to go along with my app to begin with. And you are not responsible for Phillip using us." As I say all this out loud, I start to feel angry again. That's what Phillip did—used us. *Used me.*

George shakes his head. "I heard Phillip say some things last year. I should've known. I should've said something at our meeting. It was just…one of those things, where I didn't really think about it until after I overheard them on Saturday, you know? And then I felt so stupid for not realizing it all along."

"You shouldn't feel stupid. I know Phillip, too, and it never would've occurred to me, ever," I say.

George looks up, cracks a small smile. He picks up my hand and squeezes it. "That's because you're such a good person, Emma, with such a kind heart." I suddenly feel warm from his unexpected compliment, from his hand holding on to mine. "It would never even cross your mind to consider what Phillip and those guys might be doing. That's why this is all on me."

I squeeze his hand back. Maybe it doesn't matter whose fault it is? "Our project is still very beta," I tell him. "There's mistakes, but we're going to test and figure them out. We'll fix it. Together, okay? We're co-presidents, right?"

George doesn't let go of my hand for another few seconds. And then once he does, he smiles at me, a real genuine smile, and he nods. For once, somehow, I've managed to say the right thing. And I walk into school feeling just a little bit lighter.

"I've designed a new survey," Jane says after school at our emergency meeting. She opens up her laptop and sets it out on the table in front of all of us. "And after what happened with the cross-country team…well, I think I can fix things going forward."

We're all gathered in our normal Friday afternoon meeting space, except for Robert, who has marching band practice Mondays after school, and couldn't make it.

I glance at Hannah as Jane is talking. Her hair is down today, and covering most of her face. She has her head down on the desk as she's listening to Jane, and she either won't or doesn't want to look up to meet my eyes—all that's visible is a sea of messy red curls. I look back toward Jane, and Ms. Taylor hovers over her screen, a worried look on her face, so I guess either Jane or George told her what happened at the dance.

"The survey is twofold." Jane is still talking. "One, we get the user to enter his or her own likes and dislikes and sexual orientation to go into our database for matching. And two, it allows users to note any persons in the school who've exhibited *past bad dating behavior.* If a person gets more than one bad mark, we filter him or her out of the database for matching completely."

No one says anything for a moment, and Jane's words settle. Until Ms. Taylor says, "I don't know, Jane. There's a lot to unpack here. Bad dating behavior could constitute a lot of things. And we wouldn't want anyone to be unfairly called out."

Jane frowns, like she can't believe Ms. Taylor would question her. I think about what George said this morning, how he knew that Phillip was a jerk and how he wishes he would've said something beforehand. If George knows, then other people know, and why shouldn't that kind of information disqualify someone from getting one of our matches? It absolutely should. As much as Jane normally annoys me, this is a brilliant idea, and it will fix the problem we ran into this weekend.

"I don't think anyone would be called out unfairly," I say.

Both Jane and Ms. Taylor turn to look at me, shocked expressions on their faces, like neither one of them can believe I'm defending Jane. "We're never going to publish or announce the names of the people who are marked with bad behavior in the survey. We'll simply exclude them from the database, so they'll never come up as anyone's match. And if one of them tries to make a match, they'll get a response that no matches are found for them. No one will ever have to know why but us."

"I don't know…" Ms. Taylor still looks skeptical.

"Also," Jane chimes in, "we'll only do this if more than one person says someone has exhibited past bad dating behavior. So it would have to be something chronic. I think that's more than fair."

"I agree," George chimes in. I meet his eyes across the room and offer him a smile.

"So do I," Sam says quickly.

"Me, too," Hannah says, lifting her head from the desk, looking at me for the first time. Her hair still covers her eyes so I can't really see what she's thinking, or how she's feeling. But I remember the way she threw her head back and laughed Saturday night as she was dancing with Phillip and I feel a little sick to my stomach.

Ms. Taylor nods—she's only our adviser, after all, and here we are, all agreeing with each other for once.

"Okay," Jane says. "I'm going to set up a SurveyMonkey. Anyone in the school who wants to participate can take the survey, and then once enough people in the school take it, we can repopulate our database and try again."

★★★

George is staying after the meeting to take down dance decorations and plans to take the late bus home—he'd signed up to volunteer to work toward his NHS service hours. I'd rather stab my eyes out than touch dance decorations—I always get my quarterly hours volunteering to play piano at the Villages, a local retirement home. So I'm walking out to the parking lot alone after the meeting when I hear Jane, calling after me.

I stop and turn. She's running toward me, her silly lab coat flapping out behind her in the October wind. The air has finally turned and it's chilly today, crisp, suddenly somewhere halfway between fall and winter, and I shiver a little, wishing I'd worn something heavier than a hoodie this morning.

"Thanks for backing me up in there," she says, out of breath, when she finally catches up to me.

"Yeah," I say. "I mean, it's a really good idea. I'm glad you thought of it."

"I know we've had our differences in the past, Emma. But I do really want to win the state competition this year. It'll look great on my college applications, and next year I want to be president. So even though your app wasn't my first choice, and even though Saturday was kind of a disaster—"

"Kind of?" I interrupt her, surprising us both, and we both laugh a little bit, which makes everything feel just a little easier between us for the first time.

"Well, even in spite of all that, I want this to work, to be the best it possibly can be. So, no hard feelings?"

She holds her hand out awkwardly, and I'm not sure if she

wants to high-five me, or shake my hand, or wave. But she grabs my hand to shake, and it's the first time I've ever really stood that close to her. Her lab coat sleeve shifts up a little bit, and then I notice it: the edge of a jagged pink line. A scar?

I'm about to ask her what happened, but then she seems to notice it, too. She quickly pulls her hand away, pulls her lab coat sleeves down and turns and runs off to her own car before I can say another word.

CHAPTER 13

At lunch the next day, Sam and I are eating and talking about music. He's telling me about Laura's solo in their upcoming choir concert. And I'm telling him about the piano piece Mrs. Howard has me working on for the New Jersey state competition in May that I also plan to perform today for the elderly residents of the Villages when I volunteer after school: Rachmaninoff's *Prelude #6*.

"My left hand is my weakness," I tell him. "And this piece really highlights that."

"I'm sure you'll get it, though, E. I don't picture you ever failing at anything." He says this between bites of carrot and hummus. His mom must've been working all weekend again.

It sounds like a compliment, but he's not wrong, either. I

work and I work and I work until I can do whatever I set out to. At least when it comes to schoolwork and piano. And still, I'm not really sure how I'm supposed to respond to Sam, or anyone, who says something like that to me, so all I say back is, "Yeah." Which makes Sam smile at me in that infectious way he has, so suddenly I'm smiling back.

"Besides," he adds, "I heard you play a little through the door that one day and you sounded awesome to me."

We're so into our conversation that we don't notice anyone has walked up to our table at first, until she sits down next to Sam. "Hey," she says, and we both stop talking and look at her.

She's tall with dark curly hair and deep brown eyes—and she's vaguely familiar, a senior like me, I think, but I don't remember ever having any classes together and I don't remember her from middle school, either. I've just seen her around the halls.

"You're Emma Woodhouse, right?" she says, staring at me. I nod, but not before wondering if I should lie in this situation and say that I'm not. "I'm Mara Maloney. I'm the co-captain of the girls' cross-country team."

At the words *cross-country*, I suddenly know this is going to be about Phillip, and I push my tray away, done with my lunch, feeling a little nauseous.

"We heard about what happened with the guys' team at the dance and your coding club project."

Yep. For once, I've read a social situation right, though I wish I hadn't. "Look, I honestly had no idea about their bet," I say.

"Yeah, yeah, I know that." Mara smiles, revealing a row of pearl-white teeth. "We were all talking at practice this morning, and we feel really bad about what happened. We don't want your project to be messed up because of them."

"It's not," Sam interjects. "We're…reconfiguring things."

"Well," Mara says. "I want to help you, if I can. We all do. The whole girls' team—we all agreed this morning. You can match us up or whatever." She pulls out her phone, and puts it on the table, pushes it toward me. "Put your app on my phone and we'll all use it."

"We're not exactly there yet," I say, gently pushing her phone back toward her. "We're working on a survey now and then we have to repopulate the database and reconfigure our algorithm."

Mara's eyes glaze over, and she squints, looking confused. I'm losing her, and she actually wants to help. I need to say something else.

"What I mean…is…" I stammer. "Is that we'd love your help, we just don't have an app up and running to put on your phone quite yet."

Mara nods, understanding now.

"Hey, why don't you exchange numbers," Sam suggests. "And Emma can text you as soon as the app is ready. The club would love your help."

Mara smiles brightly. I get her number and promise her she and the other girls on cross-country can be our first test subjects when we're back up and running again.

"See," Sam says, smiling, after she walks away, "I told you this was all going to work out."

★★★

I drop George off after school, and then I head over to Highbury Retirement Villages. On most Tuesdays, I volunteer to go in and play piano for the residents after school. I've been doing it since the beginning of junior year when I first needed something to fulfill the volunteer requirement for NHS. But now it's become something I actually kind of enjoy doing, and I think I'd still come even if I didn't need the volunteer hours. I have a little following, about fifteen residents, mostly the same ones who like music, who come to hear me play, and it gives me a chance to work out my pieces in front of a very nonjudgmental audience. They clap for everything.

Today I've brought the Rachmaninoff, even though I can't play it at full tempo yet like I was telling Sam at lunch. I'm months out from the competition, but I need the practice performing it in front of a crowd, even a slightly hard of hearing one.

"Emma!" Mrs. Bates calls out for me when I walk in, waving wildly from across the room where she's sitting today. Her other arm is linked with her husband's. Mr. Bates has dementia, and if it weren't for that, I don't think Mrs. Bates would be living in an assisted facility at all. She's eighty-six, but in great shape, mentally and physically. She runs a yoga class here, and she'd probably be off traveling through Europe if Mr. Bates were still just as fit. She comes to hear me every time I play, and sometimes afterward she grabs me and tells me stories about when she was my age. She apparently also used to play the piano. I get the feeling she likes having someone young to talk to for once.

I wave back to her before taking my seat at the piano and getting right to it. I play through the Rachmaninoff at half speed, then play through a few of their favorites: *Clair de Lune* and *Moonlight Sonata*. The notes and the rhythms of these songs I know by heart are numbers and patterns, and they always soothe me, so I relax when I play. Today, my mind drifts and I find myself thinking about Sam. The way he'd looked at me at lunch when he said he didn't picture me ever doing anything less than perfect. He's at choir now, and he's probably looking at Laura, singing her perfect solo. That makes me feel weirdly annoyed and I hit the last few notes of *Moonlight Sonata* louder and harder than I should. But all the residents burst into applause when I'm finished.

I stand up and gather up my music. Mrs. Bates leaves her husband's side for a minute to come talk to me, as she usually does. She's small and trim, with bright red hair that's teased up on her head, and she's dressed in leggings and a big red sweater that look much too young for her. "Tell me, Emma, what's shaking in high school this week?" She moves her hands as she talks, and the row of bangle bracelets on her wrist jingle.

"Not much, Mrs. Bates. Just studying, working hard. The usual."

"Stanford accept you yet?" she asks.

I shake my head. "I haven't even applied yet. So…who knows." I shrug. The early action deadline is next week, but Ms. Taylor thinks I'll have a better shot if I apply regular admission in January. She says I'm taking, and doing well in, so many AP classes this fall my application will be stronger with my first semester senior year grades. Plus, we'll know by then whether we're a finalist in all-state for coding club, and as long as we are, that could also help.

"Oh, they will," she says. "It's just a matter of time."

I smile at her. She's so kind, even though, really, she doesn't know that much about me. But she's part of the reason why I like coming here each week. If Mom were still alive, or if I ever talked to my grandma in Miami more than once or twice a year, I imagine she might sound something like Mrs. Bates.

Suddenly there's shouting from the corner of the room. An aide is trying to help Mr. Bates up and he's yelling at her to get her hands off him. Mrs. Bates casts me a quick apologetic smile, a wave goodbye and walks toward her husband, her bracelets jingling the whole way. "Honey," she says gently. "That's Roberta."

"I don't know any Roberta," he says back. Mrs. Bates puts her hand on his arm, and his demeanor calms down. "We're late to pick up the children, aren't we?" he says suddenly.

"Honey, the children live in the city now, remember? They have children of their own."

He shakes his head, confused. He doesn't seem to remember at all.

"It's all right," Mrs. Bates says, standing up on her toes to kiss her husband softly on his cheek.

His expression softens, and he hugs her.

"I've got you now," I hear her saying to him as I walk out. "Don't worry, Jack. I've always got you."

CHAPTER 14

Jane has her survey up and ready on SurveyMonkey by the end of the week, and we start spreading the word at school, sending out the link to anyone who wants to take it. Sam talks to the choir, and Robert to the marching band. Hannah tells the swim team, and George tells everyone in our classes. I start with texting Mara, who promises to share it with the cross-country and volleyball teams. By the end of October, we have nearly three hundred responses to the survey. That's seventy-five percent of the student body.

We repopulate our database with survey responses, combined with a skim Jane set up for socials and our original yearbook data. George has his heart animated, with moving arms and legs now, and we get Hannah and Robert to work on designing the screens for our app. Sam is working on the algorithm with me, and that feels like the last and also most important piece we need to get right before we put it all together in Xcode.

Sam and I haven't made much progress by the end of our meeting on the last Friday in October. The regional competition is just a month away, and I ask him if he wants to come over tomorrow, so we can work. Hannah overhears, and offers to come, too. "I still need to return your sister's dress," she says. "And anyway, I want to learn more actual coding from you."

It feels like she's not mad at me anymore, or maybe she never was? Maybe, like George, she understood that I couldn't possibly have been able to fathom Phillip's motives. But I'm just happy that she's talking to me. I tell her she's welcome to come. "And if you're done with finding a match yourself, I wouldn't blame you," I add. "The girls' cross-country team offered to be our next test subjects, so you're totally off the hook."

"Why would I be done?" Hannah says, frowning, like I've confused her.

"I just thought..."

She laughs and shakes her head, and her red curls fan out against her back. "No," she says, "I want us to get this right, and then I want another match. And maybe you'll make yourself a match this time, too?" she adds.

"No," I say. "I don't have time for a boyfriend." Hannah raises her eyebrows, surprised, but doesn't say anything, and I quickly turn the subject back to her. "But don't worry, I'm going to perfect our algorithm and then I'll find you a perfect match."

★ ★ ★

George's mom is off work today and is picking him up, so he stays behind to work through an animation issue with Ms. Taylor while he waits for his mom to arrive. I walk out to the parking lot after the meeting by myself, and almost bump right into Phillip and Jason, leaving practice.

"Em," Phillip says, shortening my name, a curl in his voice, so it almost sounds like he's taunting me. I bite my lip, but I don't correct him again. He steps right in front of me, so I can't just ignore him and keep walking.

I sigh and cross my arms in front of my chest. "What do you want, Phillip?"

"What'd you tell Hannah about me? She won't text me back."

"And Jenny's ghosting me, too," Jason adds.

"I don't even know Jenny. And I didn't tell Hannah anything." All of this is technically true. It was George and Sam and Jane who'd told Hannah what was going on while I'd sat in front of the trophy case feeling paralyzed and helpless. But I don't feel that way anymore. Now that I've had a few weeks to let what happened simmer, I'm angry. "It wasn't enough that you quit coding club, was it, Phillip? You had to try and destroy our project this year, too?"

"You practically begged me to take Hannah to the dance, and I did what you wanted, didn't I?"

I shake my head. "I did not ask you to make some kind of demeaning bet with your friends and try and use her."

Phillip's face burns red, nearly matching his hair. "Who told you that?" he fumes.

I've said the wrong thing. I know I have. But I feel my own face turning red and hot with anger. Phillip made me think I could trust him and then he almost ruined everything. "It doesn't matter who told me," I say. "What matters is that now we know the truth and we're blocking you from any more dating matches."

My voice shakes a little, and I think Phillip and Jason are going to demand an explanation or keep me from walking the rest of the way to my car, but instead Phillip starts to laugh. He laughs so hard that his whole body shakes. "You really… think…you'll…" He gasps out words in between laughter, and then shakes his head, unable to finish his sentence. Jason chuckles a little.

They're both laughing at me now, and I think about what Izzy said, about how I shouldn't be matching anyone. But Izzy is wrong. I understand this situation perfectly. And then I think about how Mara came to talk to me at lunch, how the girls' team heard what happened at the dance, and how maybe the whole school will start using our app to find dates and then I really will prevent Phillip from dating anyone at our school.

"Laugh all you want," I finally say, pushing past them to make my way toward my car. "But Jane figured out a way to exclude you from our database. You'll never get a date now."

The next afternoon, Sam, Hannah and I are sitting at my kitchen table, laptops open, all attempting to do research on what scientific factors are the biggest indicators of lasting love so we can definitively reconfigure our algorithm. I'm staring at an unhelpful journal article on my screen about pheromones and attraction. But I'm still thinking about my run-in with Phillip in the parking lot yesterday and wondering if I should mention it to Hannah now. She's reading something on her own screen, her mouth open a little, looking engaged and determined. It's much better than the way she'd looked last week, sad and depleted, and maybe I shouldn't mention Phillip to her ever again?

"I think we need another survey," Sam says suddenly, and I push Phillip out of my mind and turn my full attention to him.

"What kind of survey?" Hannah asks, shutting her laptop, propping her chin up with her hands.

"We need to survey people who've been in love for a long time."

I think about the response I got from Dad, about Mom's eyes. And from Izzy about how John makes her laugh. "People in love say stupid, unquantifiable things," I say.

Sam smiles at me and shakes his head. "No, we won't give them that option, E. We'll offer them all the categories we have in our database and in our algorithm—interests, activities, values, background, appearance, etc. Then we'll have them rank each one by most to least important in their lasting love."

I consider what he's saying, excited about the prospect of actually getting this right. "In other words, we'll use math to figure this out." Of course. That's the most obvious, the most accurate, way to calibrate our algorithm. Why didn't I think of that?

"Okay…but where are we going to find people who've been in love for a long time?" Hannah says. "My parents are divorced. And yours are, too, right, Sam?"

He frowns—like he hasn't thought of this part. "True," he says.

"I mean, do people even stay in love for a long time anymore, or is that like a myth?" Hannah asks in all seriousness.

I think about Mr. and Mrs. Bates at the retirement village last week, the way Mrs. Bates so calmly called him *honey*, and attended to him, even in his confusion. The Villages has a thousand cottages, and there are many older, married couples there. "Actually, I think I know exactly where we can find them," I say.

We design a very simple, on-paper survey—ten questions that can be taken with a pen or pencil. I go into Dad's home office and make three hundred copies, and then I drive the three of us over to the Villages.

I've never been here on a Saturday before, and the parking lot is packed. I remember what Mrs. Bates said, about their children being in the city with their own children now, and I wonder if they ever come and visit on the weekends, or if Mr. and Mrs. Bates are stranded here, all alone. I think again, guiltily about what will happen to Dad if I really do move to California next year. Of course, he's much younger than Mr. and Mrs. Bates, but he'll be all alone in Highbury, too.

"It's cool that you volunteer here," Hannah says as we all walk inside the front lobby of the Villages. She casts me a sideways glance so even though she says the word *cool*, I hear the word *surprising*.

I shrug. "I need volunteer hours for NHS." But even if I didn't, I'd probably still want to keep coming here on Tuesdays because I honestly do enjoy playing for the residents and talking to Mrs. Bates.

We sign in at the desk, and the woman behind it tells us most of the residents are eating lunch in the dining room. We walk by the room where I usually play piano, and it's empty now, but we quickly find Mrs. Bates in the dining room, just next to it. She's eating with Mr. Bates, and a table full of other women I don't recognize. No one's visiting children are anywhere to be found, which makes me feel a little sad.

"Emma, you came to visit us *and* you brought friends?" Mrs. Bates stands up when she notices me, her voice a full octave higher with excitement, and she quickly orders one of the staff to pull over chairs for us. I introduce her to Sam and Hannah, and she shoots them both warm smiles.

"Are the kids here, honey?" Mr. Bates asks her, looking toward us eagerly, like he wants very badly to recognize us.

"No, honey, not the kids. It's Emma, the gal who plays that beautiful piano for us on Tuesdays." His face is blank, not even a glimmer of recognition. Not that I'd expect him to remember me or my piano playing when he can't even remember about his own kids. "Finish your lunch." She leans over and kisses him gently on the temple. Then she turns back to us. "I'm so happy you came to visit us. This is just delightful!" She claps her hands together again and her bracelets jingle.

"We actually came because we need your help with a school

project," I tell her. Then I simplify the details, not wanting to get into coding or technology with a table full of octogenarians who may or may not even know what an app is. I tell her only that we brought three hundred copies of a survey that we need people who've been in love for a long time to take. And that we want to tabulate the results for a project we're all working on together.

"Oooh." She claps her hands together. "I love a good project. Why don't you leave those with me, and I'll make sure they're all filled out by the next time you come back to play piano for us. Now." She turns toward Sam. "Tell me, honey, are you *the boyfriend*?"

By *the boyfriend*, I'm pretty sure she means *my boyfriend*, and I feel my face turning red and hot at her assumption. Sam catches my eyes, and shoots me that smile he has, that feels like it's just for me. His green eyes sparkle a little in the fluorescent light and he looks more amused than embarrassed by her question. But this is the second time I've felt embarrassed in front of Sam lately, and I hate the red-hot feeling.

I clear my throat. "Sam's just a friend," I clarify emphatically for Mrs. Bates.

"Okay," she says, smiling. She winks at me, like she doesn't believe me, or she thinks we share some secret.

And it makes me wonder…when we get the surveys back from her, when we reconfigure our algorithm, what if things are different? Maybe Sam and Laura won't match any longer. And if they don't—is there any way Sam might match me?

I remember again what Izzy said to me, right before she left, about how maybe I needed a boyfriend this year. And how ridiculous that was and is. Socially awkward, academically minded girls like me don't have boyfriends. Do they? But Izzy also said to be more social. Is that what I'm doing here this afternoon in a weird way?

I think about that as I walk out of the Villages in between Sam and Hannah. Hannah makes a joke about how I've led them to the one remaining place on earth where people actually stay in love forever. All three of us are laughing as we get to my car. And I realize everything feels so much different now than it did just a few months ago, the morning Izzy left me.

CHAPTER 15

The following Tuesday at school, I'm feeling pretty good about everything. I'll pick up my surveys later when I go play at the Villages, and then I can finally start to reconfigure my algorithm. We'll start coding the app this week, and by next week, we'll have a test app running on TestFlight that people can actually download and then use to match themselves. The regional tournament is almost four weeks away, the week after Thanksgiving, and we should be more than ready with a solid prototype by then.

Then last period, during AP Physics, the school secretary comes over the intercom and interrupts Mr. Halpbern: "Can you send Emma Woodhouse straight to Mr. Dodge's office?"

Mr. Halpbern looks at me, his mouth a circle, his eyes

expressing the shock that I'm feeling. I have never once in my entire life been called out of a class to go to the principal's office. In fact, I'm pretty sure if Mr. Dodge even knows who I am, it's only because I ended junior year ranked first in my class.

"You'd better go," Mr. Halpbern says, sounding as concerned as I feel. I gather my things and stand, and George shoots me a worried look as I make my way out toward the hallway.

When I get to the front office, I walk in and spot the white of Jane's lab coat across the room. She's already sitting in a chair outside Mr. Dodge's office. "Hey," I say to her. "Do you know what's going on?" Since we were both called down, I have a strange feeling that this has something to do with our coding club project. But then why wasn't George called down? Why me and Jane?

She shrugs, and I sit down next to her. We can see through the glass that Mr. Dodge is on the phone, but we can't make out what he's saying. He hangs up, and Jane tugs on the sleeves of her lab coat with her fingers, nervously clutching the material in her fists.

Mr. Dodge opens the door. "Girls," he says pointedly, staring at us. He ushers us into his office, offering us the two chairs across from his desk. I'm already frowning as we sit down, feeling annoyed that he called us *girls*, which feels somehow both dismissive and demeaning. I'm not sure how a person is supposed to react in this situation. But I'm mad that I'm missing the end of AP Physics, and also confused about what's going on.

"Why are we here?" I ask bluntly.

"Well." Mr. Dodge folds his hands in front of him on his desk, twiddling his thumbs. "I've gotten a few complaints from the boys' cross-country team. Apparently you two created some kind of..." He looks down and checks his notes. "App that *allows women to demean them*?"

Laughter gurgles in my throat and I can't stop it from coming out. Both Jane and Mr. Dodge look at me and frown, so I know right away my first reaction, to laugh, was the wrong one. I think about the way Phillip laughed at me on Friday, in the parking lot, and then I realize whatever is going on here is all his doing. Or maybe it's my fault, for saying the wrong things to him. "That's ridiculous," I say, now completely serious. "If anyone's demeaning anyone, it's the other way around."

"So you didn't create an app?" he asks.

Jane and I look at each other, and I'm really not sure what to say next. Jane surprises me by speaking, her voice sounding louder, more forceful, than normal. "We're working on a project for coding club, an app, yes." Then she explains about what happened with Phillip and the boys on the cross-country team at the dance, and about how she designed a survey to try and prevent that going forward.

Mr. Dodge is frowning the whole time. "Look," he says. "You're both good girls." There he is, calling us *girls* again. "But the boys say they didn't do anything wrong. And they feel bullied by this app, so I'm going to have to ask you to shut it down."

Shut it down? No way! Not when we're finally getting it right.

Before I can say anything, Jane speaks again: *"Bullied?"* She sounds incredulous. "So you're fine with the fact that the cross-country team is betting on which underclassman they can have sex with first? But you're not okay with us asking people to flag bad behavior?" She's breathing hard; her hands are shaking.

"If you had some proof about this…*bet*, then of course I would investigate that," Mr. Dodge says. He stares at both of us, as if he's waiting for us to hand over some sort of proof we might be hiding in our pockets.

"George overheard them talking," I finally say, and Mr. Dodge frowns. "They said it all out loud."

There's a knock on the door, and we turn. Ms. Taylor peeks her head in. Mr. Dodge motions for her to come all the way in and close the door. "Sorry," she says. "I got caught up with a student." She addresses Mr. Dodge. "But I read your email, Bill. And honestly, I'm shocked you're calling these two fine students out of class."

He reiterates to her what he told us. That the cross-country boys feel *bullied*, and he wants us to stop working on the app. I feel like I should say something else, anything, but I'm not sure what. All I know is we can't stop working on the app. And also, now I really truly hate Phillip, and I can't believe I ever thought he'd want to help coding club win.

"Absolutely not," Ms. Taylor says. I'm surprised by her forceful tone—usually she's so calm and soft-spoken—but also relieved she's jumped in to defend us. It wasn't too long ago that she'd been skeptical about the survey questions, too. "Bill, first of all. No one is being bullied. Everything is being done anonymously and confidentially. And second of all, if you bring anyone down here for bad behavior in this case, it should be those boys. I can't believe you're singling out Jane and Emma right now." Her face is red, and she's making an expression I've never seen before: Is she livid?

Mr. Dodge looks away from her, down at his thumbs on his desk, and frowns. When he looks back up, I expect him to say something really ridiculous, like *Boys will be boys.* As if none of us can be expected to hold Phillip and his friends accountable for anything. But instead he looks back up at Ms. Taylor again and his face softens a little. "Now, Anna, you know that's not my intent. I know Jane and Emma are good students. I'm just investigating a complaint I got, that's all. We have a zero tolerance policy for bullying at this school, so if someone makes a complaint..."

"Oh, Bill, please." Ms. Taylor shoots him a steely look.

"We've already submitted our project for the state competition," I interject, suddenly finding the words I want to say. "We can't change it now or we'll have to withdraw. I'm counting on this for my Stanford application. We're all counting on it for college applications. And I promise you, our app is completely inclusive. We're trying to *prevent* people from being treated badly or being bullied."

"Yes." Ms. Taylor smiles at me, like she's proud of me. Like maybe she thinks I'm actually finding a way to stand out, or stand up for myself, or to be something else other than *a math brain*. "Emma's absolutely right."

The bell rings for the end of the day, and Mr. Dodge looks at Ms. Taylor, then at me and Jane, and holds his hands up in the air. "You girls can go," he says. "But I don't want any more done on this *app* until we figure this out."

Jane and I stand up and Ms. Taylor sits down and takes my seat. She winks at me, as if to say, *Don't worry, I've got you covered.* Or maybe she's saying, *Ignore what he just said. Go. Get to work.*

Jane and I walk out together, toward the parking lot. My hands are still shaking. So are Jane's. "Do you think he's going to kill our project?" Jane asks, sounding worried.

I shake my head. "I think Ms. Taylor will work everything out." But my voice falters a little because even as I say it, I'm not totally sure. "Hopefully," I add.

"Mr. Dodge was probably totally the Phillip Elton of his high school." She rolls her eyes. *"Girls, we have a zero tolerance policy for bullying,"* she mimics his voice. "What a jerk."

I laugh a little. "Yeah. Well, you were pretty awesome in there."

"So were you," she says back, quickly.

"I don't know, if he called us *girls* one more time, I was about to scream," I say.

She nods in agreement. "Right? And why did he call me and you in instead of you and George, anyway? You two are the co-presidents."

"Because it would've been way harder to mansplain bullying to George," I say, and Jane snickers a little. "No, I think it's actually all my fault. Phillip confronted me on Friday and

I might have said something about how you were designing a survey to keep anyone from dating him." I shrug.

She shakes her head. "This is not your fault, Emma. Or mine. Or George's," she adds. "And I actually think it's pretty great that you confronted him."

"Really? You do?" I'm still unsure. Maybe it would've been better if I'd said nothing at all. Then Phillip wouldn't have complained to Mr. Dodge and we wouldn't be in danger of having our whole project ruined, again.

She nods. "Why should Phillip and his friends just be allowed to do whatever they want with no consequences? Anyway, this is me..." We've reached her car, and she goes to open the door, but then she stops and turns back toward me. "Actually, Emma, are you doing anything now? I know Mr. Dodge told us not to work on the app, but that only makes me want to work on it more." I smile because I feel the same way. "Maybe we could go to the diner and order some fries and get a little work done?" she suggests.

Izzy used to hang out at the diner after school all the time with her friends, but it was something I always schemed to get out of, not having the mental energy at the end of a school day to listen to all that idle chatter and gossip. I actually wouldn't mind going with Jane now to get some work done, but it's Tuesday, and I have to get to the Villages. "I can't. I have to go volunteer at the retirement villages right now."

"Oh," Jane says, frowning again, her face going back to that expression that's familiar to me. "Well, never mind, then."

"Why don't you come with me?" I say quickly, before I really think through whether it's something I should say or not. I tell her about the surveys Sam, Hannah and I dropped off on Saturday, and how I plan to collect them now after I play. "Then maybe we can go to the diner and get to work on tabulating the surveys after?"

Mrs. Bates just loves that I brought Jane, and makes her sit beside her and Mr. Bates during my performance. When I'm finished playing, I walk over to them, and Mrs. Bates whips out the full stack of filled-out surveys from underneath her chair. She hands them over to me proudly.

"Thank you," I tell her. "This will really help us, Mrs. Bates."

"Oh, your friend Jane told me all about your little project. I hope you two will fix yourselves up, too. What about that handsome boy who was here the other day? What was his name?" She snaps her fingers and Jane shoots me a funny look.

"Sam," I say as I take the stack of surveys from her, hoping we can get out of here without any more embarrassing questions. "But Sam already has a..." I'm about to say girlfriend, but then I correct myself because I'm still not sure how he and Laura feel about one another. "Match."

Jane offers her a tight-lipped smile. "I don't want a boyfriend, Mrs. Bates. I'm too busy with homework and coding club."

Mrs. Bates smiles at her, and shakes her head like she doesn't believe her. It's suddenly like I can picture Izzy at eighty-six years old, and here she is, right in front of me, bangle bracelets and all. "It was nice to meet you, Jane." Mrs. Bates pats her on the shoulder. "Come back and see us another time, okay? We can always use more young people around here."

At the diner Jane and I both order cheese fries, and I put the stack of answered surveys on the table in between us. Jane pulls her laptop from her bag so we can begin to tabulate and note the responses.

"You're really, really good at piano," Jane says as she powers on her laptop. "I had no idea you even played."

"Thanks." I shrug. Why would she know? I don't really ever talk about it at school, and I haven't ever talked much to Jane, period. "Playing at the Villages is an easy way to get my service hours for NHS." I pause for a second before admitting something I haven't ever admitted out loud, not even to Izzy. "And also…I've grown pretty fond of Mrs. Bates. My mom died when I was really young, and my only living grandma lives in Miami so we don't see or talk to her much."

Jane nods. "I can see why. She seems really nice. Though… she told me three times I *could be such a pretty girl* if I took my lab coat off."

That sounds like Mrs. Bates. She doesn't always filter what comes out of her mouth, which is part of the reason I like her. I appreciate her honesty. But it does make me uncomfortable at times, too.

"Why do you wear the lab coat all the time?" I ask. Jane frowns, and this tenuous truce, or whatever it is we have come to now, this afternoon, might already be over. "Never mind," I say quickly. "Forget I asked."

She doesn't say anything for a minute, and I half expect

her to throw her laptop in her bag and run out of the diner, leaving me with the stack of surveys, two orders of cheese fries and the check. But then she slowly pushes up her right sleeve, rolls her arm over and shows me what I got only the smallest glimpse of a few weeks ago. Her entire forearm is marked with jagged pink and purple scars, going all the way up to the crease of her elbow.

"What happened?" I ask softly.

"The summer before sixth grade, I was in a car accident and it messed up my arm pretty bad. I started middle school with these really ugly fresh scars all over my arm and people never even bothered to learn my real name. Everyone called me Freddy Krueger instead. I cried almost every night for three years. I begged my mom to homeschool me." She traces the scars on her forearm with her pointer finger now, and I can't imagine the Jane I've known in coding club the past few years—serious, brilliant, confident Jane—crying every night, or wanting to be homeschooled, or worse, being teased so relentlessly at school.

I find myself staring at her arm, but not because I think her scars make her ugly or nightmarish, but because I wish I'd known about them before. I would've liked Jane more, understanding that, underneath, she was a little a raw, and that she felt like she didn't fit in at our school. Just like me.

She pulls her sleeve back down, and I quickly look away, ashamed for staring. I wonder if without the lab coat Jane feels naked, exposed at school, the way I've felt this year without Izzy.

"I guess I made a choice, you know?" She's still talking.

"I could continue to be Freddy Kreuger in high school, or I could be the nerdy lab-coat girl. I want to be this girl in the lab coat instead."

I nod. "I used to think it was some kind of a fashion statement I didn't understand. But now I think I get it." I pause for a moment. "I don't understand people," I admit. "Not just you, I mean…any people." I think about all the people who were so mean to her in middle school. Why would anyone act that way? "Numbers make sense to me. People not at all." I shrug, but even as I say it, I'm not sure it's completely true. I think I do actually understand Jane now.

"Yeah." She offers me a half smile. "I agree with you. People are the worst. Numbers are easy."

I've respected Jane's talent and intelligence in coding club for the past few years, but now, for the first time, I actually wonder if I might truly like her, if it's possible we might even become friends.

I catch George up on what happened with Mr. Dodge on the way to school the next morning, and he frowns, looking anxious. He had texted me after school yesterday to ask if everything was okay, and I told him it was and I would explain what had happened in the morning, thinking it would be too hard to try and explain over text. And besides, I was engrossed in entering all the survey responses last night—I stayed up late inputting them all and then started to reconfigure my algorithm flowchart. I got hyperfocused on that, like weirdly if I got everything right there'd be no way Mr. Dodge could still shut us down.

"He should've called me in," George says now, after I tell him everything. I'm not sure whether to be offended that George believes I can't handle anything on my own, or if I should feel grateful that George wishes he could've helped.

"Jane and I handled it," I say. "And Ms. Taylor was there when we left."

"So how did you leave things?" George asks, sounding worried.

I shrug because I'm not exactly sure. I pull into the school parking lot, and George suggests we stop at Ms. Taylor's office before class.

When we get there, we can see through the glass: she's sitting behind her desk, and Mr. Weston is sitting on the edge of her desk, saying something to her. She throws her head back, and laughs, and George glances at me. "They really do like each other, don't they?" He sounds weirdly surprised, like he hasn't realized how we built our whole app off this theory until right this very minute.

I shoot him a look, and knock on Ms. Taylor's door. "Come in," she shouts, and Mr. Weston jumps off the edge of her desk, takes a step back and stands up straight.

"Emma, George," he says to us. Then he turns back to Ms. Taylor. "I'll see you at lunch, Anna?"

She nods and smiles at him as he walks out. Then she turns her attention to us. "I'm glad you both stopped in. I was going to call you down during first period."

George takes one of the seats across from her desk, and I take the other. "Well," I say, suddenly feeling really anxious, the way George has been sounding since I picked him up. "What happened after Jane and I left?"

She smiles at me. "Let's just say I worked everything out, and you don't need to worry. We'll proceed with the project as planned."

"Mr. Dodge just…got over it?" I ask, skeptical.

"Phillip rescinded his complaint this morning and assured Mr. Dodge there was no bullying going on."

"He rescinded it? Just like that?" George raises his eyebrows.

"Oh… Phillip may have had a little nudge from his guidance counselor, who threatened a phone call to his parents. Mr. Dodge can be caught up with *proof*, but, George, your word is enough for me," Ms. Taylor says. "Phillip and I had a nice chat about being respectful." My eyes widen, as I'm super impressed by Ms. Taylor right now, but she shrugs like it's no big deal, and she's only doing her job as our counselor. "Anyway, I promised Mr. Dodge he wouldn't get any more complaints about our app, so we have to make sure we're really being inclusive and thoughtful about everyone's feelings going forward."

"Of course," George says.

"Good." Ms. Taylor smiles at both of us. "Why don't you get to class, then, and I'll see you at our meeting later this week."

CHAPTER 16

Based on the results from our survey at the Villages, it's clear that common interests are the most important factor for staying in love, and I finish redoing our algorithm so that it weights extracurricular activities and likes and dislikes the highest. Jane has the database up and running on the server; it includes her survey results, socials skim and yearbook data. And on Friday, we're all sitting at our meeting, discussing how we'll get everything into app form and ready to present at the regional competition right after Thanksgiving in Princeton, three weeks from now.

Our plan, moving forward, is to let the app be user-driven—people who want to will be able to download it and make their own matches. But for now, while we design and code the app and get it functioning, I'll be adding people into the algorithm on my laptop and texting out their results.

"Okay," Ms. Taylor says, clapping her hands together to get our attention. "In addition to working on designing the app screens and coding the app, we need some of you to tabulate the data and the accuracy of the matches we're making. I'll start," she says. She looks right at me and smiles. "This is not normally something I'd tell my students, but in this case…I guess I should tell you all that Mr. Weston and I have been dating for two months now. So even in its prior form, I don't know that your algorithm was completely off."

I think about the way he made her laugh in her office the other morning, and then I clap, which is clearly the wrong response, because everyone turns to stare at me, and there's an awkward silence. Jane is wearing her lab coat with the purple embroidery on the sleeves today, and it's cold in here—she has it buttoned up, making her look weirdly like that Muppet. Is it Beeker or Bunsen? I can never remember which is which. But then I think about what Jane told me the other day about why she wears the lab coat, and I shoot her an apologetic smile. She smiles back before turning and saying to Ms. Taylor, "I think George and Emma and I should work on getting the app up to speed, and the new members should work on tracking the data."

"But, Jane," Ms. Taylor says. "We have to teach them to code, too, or where will you be next year when George and Emma are off at college?" George looks at me, and I wonder if he's thinking the same thing I am, that college feels so far away still, and I haven't finished my applications yet, and how can they all already be thinking about a time when we're gone? It feels so far away, and so frighteningly close, too.

"We can do both," Sam volunteers, and Hannah agrees.

We all look to Robert, and he's so quiet and barely speaks up at these meetings, but then he surprises us all when he says, "I'll track data. And…also, I still really want a match, too."

I wait to start on the matches until later that night, once I'm home, by myself. At the meeting we started designing app screens and figuring out where the animations will go. But now, all alone in my bed with my laptop, I can enter names in my app simulator and get people's matches.

I work on the girls' cross-country team first. Maybe unsurprisingly, given our new higher weight on common interests, Mara matches with Liz, the other senior co-captain of the team. Helen Brimley, who sits across from me in calc, matches to Dave Redstone, who is also in our calc class, and when I look, I see they're both also in their church choirs. The other six girls are underclassman who I don't know, but I put their matches in, feeling confident this is working now. I type all the matches into a spreadsheet where we can keep track of their progress, and then send the information in a text to Mara.

Omg, she quickly texts back. I match Liz?

I'm not sure if she's confused or upset or surprised, so I clarify and text back, Yes, 98%.

This is so cool! she texts back. So, she's definitely not upset.

I do Robert's match next, and he matches Ben Parker, a sophomore. They are both in chess club and in marching band together, and in a tidbit picked up from Jane's social media skim, they are both huge *Star Wars* fans. I don't know Ben, but I look him up in the yearbook, and he has a sort of nice lopsided smile, and dark curly hair.

I decide I'll do Hannah next, and save Sam for last. I don't want a match of my own, or a boyfriend as Izzy suggested before she left me in August, what feels like so long ago now. My senior year is supposed to be all about numbers, and coding, and getting into Stanford. I don't have time for anything else.

But what if Sam and I do match? I couldn't ignore the algorithm in that case, could I?

I think about that morning when Sam sat on my old blue couch, close enough to me that I could almost feel his lips on mine. Sam is kind and smart, and if I *had* to date someone, say, to set an example with our app, maybe I'd want it to be him? But I push the thought away, and type Hannah in first to see her match.

George Knightley flashes up on my screen.

Wait...George?

I delete it and try again. Maybe I hit the wrong key? But nope, it comes back the same way the second time. *Hannah Smith* and *George Knightley.* I look in the database—they have coding club in common, of course. Hannah swims on the school team, and George swims on a club team in the summer. George's favorite book is *The Hobbit*, and...so is Hannah's. And they both love baseball and anime.

I pick up my phone and text George. You want to hear something funny? I ran Hannah's match and you match her.

What?

You and Hannah are a 96.3% match.

Red-haired Hannah...in coding club?

Yeah...what other Hannah would I mean?

...

The three dots come up, then disappear. Then come and disappear again.

Do you want me to take you out of the database and rerun her match? I finally type. I'm thinking he will. George doesn't want a girlfriend. He doesn't have time to date. And anyway, George is so...*George*. How could he possibly date Hannah?

No, he types back quickly.

No?

What kind of example would that set for the club? If I match her, then I match her. Your math isn't wrong, right?

It is basically the same argument I just made in my own head for how I would feel if I happen to match Sam. So I can't argue with him. Though I also have this weird feeling rising in my chest. *Annoyance*, I think. Or...*dread*? I like Hannah. And George is my friend. But together they will be something altogether different. Something I might not like at all. And that bothers me.

But like George says, the math isn't wrong, so I sigh and move on.

I run Sam's match. And again, he matches Laura. *Stupid choir.* When I check the database, there's also the fact that they are both bilingual…and I didn't realize before, but she also plays volleyball, just like he does.

For some reason, I'm unreasonably angry, and I slam my laptop lid shut, done with matches for the night. I go downstairs, and even though it is late, after nine, I'm the only one home. Dad is working late, again. The kitchen is dark. But I don't turn on the lights.

I find a pint of mint chocolate chip in the freezer and I don't even get a bowl. I sit at the kitchen table in the dark and eat it right out of the carton with a spoon.

CHAPTER 17

"I think something's still off with my algorithm," I say to George in the car the next week on the way to school. After a few days of thinking on it, that's the only possible explanation for how George and Hannah somehow match. And how Sam *still* matches Laura. She's started sitting with us at lunch now, and she's nice enough, but every day this week I've been thinking how she and Sam just don't seem like they should be dating. Something feels off.

"I don't think so," George says as I park and we both get out of the car to walk toward school. "You know Liz, cross-country co-captain?" I shake my head. I know of her, know she matched Mara, but I don't *know* her. "She found me at lunch yesterday and she is so happy that she matches Mara.

She's wanted to ask Mara out for two years, but was worried Mara didn't feel the same way. Except apparently Mara does feel the same way, has for a while, and she was too scared to say anything to Liz, too." I guess that's what Mara was saying when she texted me Omg!

"All right, well, that's one. I'm not saying the algorithm is completely wrong. Maybe it just needs to be tweaked."

"Robert and Ben are going to a movie on Friday," George says. And now it's just annoying that he knows all this stuff I don't. I sigh as we walk into the school. I guess it should have occurred to me to follow up with everyone this week, but my mind was still on perfecting the math, the algorithm itself. Of course it occurred to George, though. "And Hannah and I are going out to dinner on Friday night," he says.

"You are?" I stop walking, turn to look at George. He shrugs, and he has this weird defiant look on his face, like maybe he wants me to tell him *not* to go. But why would I do that? What reason could I possibly give? "I mean, of course you are."

"There isn't anything wrong with the algorithm," George says again. "And besides, we only have two weeks until the regional tournament. Full steam ahead."

I get to lunch a few minutes late, staying behind in English to ask a question, and by the time I get to our table, Sam and Laura are both already there, laughing and holding hands. I stand back and stare at them for a second, thinking that maybe George really is right. There's nothing wrong with my algorithm.

"Hey, E," Sam calls out to me, waving me over. I walk to the table and sit down. He flashes me a smile, but doesn't let go of Laura's hand. "Do me a favor. Laura and I are having a debate—settle something for us."

"What's that?" I ask, plunking my tray down on the table. But I take a minute to observe them before I start to eat, noticing how close they're sitting together, how they're both smiling, like they really do like each other.

"Which one's a better song: 'Bohemian Rhapsody' or *Rhapsody in Blue*?" Sam asks.

"Easy," I say, taking a bite of my sandwich. *"Rhapsody in Blue."*

"No," Laura says. "I disagree! Freddie Mercury's voice beats everything."

As a pianist, I'd take Gershwin over Freddie Mercury any day. Plus, Gershwin has patterns that make sense. "Bohemian Rhapsody," not so much.

"See," Sam says, laughing. "I told you E would agree with me." He reaches up to high-five me. I reluctantly high-five him back.

Laura rolls her eyes and bumps his shoulder gently with her own. "Of course she agrees with you. You two are both such nerds."

"Compliment accepted," Sam says with a grin, bumping Laura's shoulder back.

I eat my cheese hoagie, watch the two of them laughing with each other, and I think again about what George said this morning. Maybe my algorithm *is* perfect. Maybe Sam and Laura actually are good together.

"What should I wear on my date with George?" Hannah asks after school. She's come home with me so we can work more on our app before our meeting tomorrow. Jane's on her way over to work with us, too. Hannah's question catches me off guard, as I'd been in the middle of trying to explain Xcode to her, showing her how to make George's new photo frames come to life in the app, when she blurted out her question about her outfit, seemingly out of nowhere.

"I don't know," I say, my tone sharper than I intend. "Do you want to learn to do this or not?"

"I do," she says, frowning. "Sorry."

"No," I sigh. "I'm sorry. I didn't mean to snap at you. We just need to get it done, that's all." Thanksgiving is next week, and Sam is going to Phoenix, and Hannah will be at her dad's in the city, and the following Tuesday, when we're back in school, we have to go to Princeton to present our app to the regional judges. "And honestly," I say now, "George is...*George*. I don't think he'll even notice what you wear."

"So you think jeans and my cute green sweater and flats?" She's still talking about her outfit, and it's such a question for Izzy, *not me*, that I'm tempted to FaceTime Izzy, hand Hannah my phone and go upstairs to my room to work alone so we can actually get stuff done.

But then the doorbell rings. *Jane.* I don't answer Hannah's question about her outfit choice, and instead jump up to get the door.

"Sorry I'm late," Jane says, walking in. She throws her school bag on the bench by the door next to mine and Hannah's and pulls her laptop from her bag. "On the way out of school I kept getting stopped by people asking for matches. Mara and Liz apparently have *a lot* of friends, and they've been telling everyone about our app."

She pulls a list of names out of the pocket of her lab coat, hands it over to me. I unfold it and look—there are about twenty names and phone numbers on here. I'm glad that people are interested in our app, but I'm worried about making the code as workable as possible before regionals. It won't matter how many matches we have if our code isn't running smoothly. "We really need to clean up code today, get the app presentable before the holiday."

"I know," Jane says. "But the more matches we make and track, the stronger our presentation can be for the judges."

I consider what she's saying. She's right. "Okay, why don't we have Hannah run these new matches. And you and I can work on getting the code right."

We walk into the kitchen, and Hannah is back looking at her laptop. She's forgotten about her outfit, or has decided I'm useless with these things and has moved on. She looks up, smiles, says hi to Jane. And Jane tells her that we need to have her switch over to running new matches now so the two of us can clean up the code. "Oh, okay, cool," she says, sounding breathless, excited that we are entrusting her with her own job.

The three of us sit around my kitchen table, laptops open, all working quietly, until Jane yawns really loudly and stretches her arms above her head. Hannah and I look up at her. "Sorry," she says, laughing. "Do you have any caffeine, Emma?"

"I can make you my special mocha," I say, explaining about my combination of coffee, Swiss Miss and whole milk.

She smiles. "Coffee and hot chocolate—what's not to love?"

"Ooh, can I have one, too?" Hannah asks.

I stand up to go make a pot of coffee, and they both close the lids on their laptops for a few minutes, too. As I'm preparing the drinks, I hear Hannah ask Jane about her outfit, and Jane tells her she *looks cute in everything.* Why didn't I think to just say that when she asked me?

Hannah laughs in response, and the sound of her laughter from across the room makes me suddenly feel lighter myself. It's nice not to be working in my house alone, and I realize I'm actually enjoying the fact that both of them are here, with me.

The next night, after coding club, I'm sitting in my bed with my laptop, still cleaning up the code, feeling weirdly glum about being home all alone and by myself tonight. As I work, my mind drifts to think about what everyone else is doing with their Friday night. Robert and Ben went to a movie; Sam and Laura are *hanging out* at her house, as they'd mentioned at lunch. Hannah and George are out to dinner. It's silly but I'm wondering what Hannah did end up wearing to dinner, and whether George noticed—and how their date will go. I should want it to go well; it'll only be further proof that my algorithm works. But I can't shake the feeling that I'm kind of hoping it doesn't. The thought of George and Hannah as a real bona fide *couple* makes me feel a little ache in my stomach. In coding club, George and I are the co-presidents. We're supposed to be a team. But if he's dating Hannah, then where does that leave me and what does it mean for the club?

A notification pops up on my screen that Jane just updated the back end code on GitHub. So I guess she's working, too.

I pick up my phone and text her. I'm home by myself, working on code, too. I actually think we're the only two in coding club not on dates right now.

She texts me the *eye roll* emoji.

I'm not sure whether she's eye-rolling at the fact that she still doesn't really love the matching app, and here we are, spending our Friday night working on it. Or that everyone else in coding club jumped all in with it. Or that she thinks dating, in general, is lame.

I'm still considering that as FaceTime chimes. I'm expecting it to be Izzy, but then I see it's Jane. I pick up, and the first thing I notice is that she's not wearing her lab coat—she has a gray Princeton T-shirt on, and her long black hair is piled up on her head in a messy bun. But it was silly to think she would always wear her lab coat, even at home. It's kind of like her armor at school, I guess. And I feel sort of honored that she FaceTimed me without it. That she trusts me enough to show me who she really is, even if it's filtered through my phone screen.

"Hey," she says. "I figured it was easier to talk than to text."

"Yeah," I agree. "What are you working on?"

"Oh…just trying to speed up the match creation without breaking it altogether." She sighs.

I nod. "I'm working on the intro screen to add George's new heart button to enter the survey."

"Cool," Jane says. Then she grimaces. "Okay, are we both ridiculous? FaceTiming to discuss how we're *coding love* on a Friday night, while everyone else is out there dating right now?"

I think about what Izzy would say: *lame!* But Izzy isn't here, and Izzy and I have never agreed on what's lame and what's not. "No," I say. "We're not ridiculous. We're smart. Who wants to be out dating, anyway?"

"Exactly," she says, making a face. "What a waste of time and energy. And who has time with all honors and AP classes?"

I nod, agreeing. "Let Sam and Hannah and Robert and George go test out our matches," I add. "You and I can stay home and do the real work." I don't say this part to her out loud, but it feels a little weird to put George in the other camp. Because up until now, he has always been the math brain, with me. But now he's on a date, with Hannah. At least I have Jane.

"Yeah," Jane agrees with me, and then I prop up my phone on my pillow, and continue working on code, and she does the same, so we work and chat a little bit about our classes and what teachers we like and don't like.

After a few minutes, I hear some commotion in the background on her end, someone yelling something, but I can't make out what. She stops talking midsentence and turns her head.

"Do you have to go?" I ask.

"No." She sighs. "Hang on, I have to shut my door." She disappears from the screen for a minute, and then the yelling in the background is suddenly muffled, far away. "Sorry, my parents are fighting again." She's back on my screen. And I think it's weird the way her expression is still blank, neutral. If Dad were downstairs yelling, at anyone, I'd probably burst into tears. But Jane seems oddly resigned to it.

"Do they fight…a lot?" I ask, and even as I ask it, I realize maybe I shouldn't. Maybe it's not my business. But Jane nods in response, like she's okay with me asking. "But they're not divorced?" I ask, puzzled. Hannah's parents are divorced and so are Sam's, and a bunch of Izzy's friends' parents were.

Jane shrugs. "They say they'll never get divorced. They *love* each other." She rolls her eyes. "So basically, love makes people stupid."

"Well, that probably shouldn't be the tagline for our project," I say, completely straight-faced.

Jane bursts out laughing. "Right? We should go with 'Love is the worst' instead."

And then I'm laughing, too, and I feel something warm bubbling up in my chest, something different. And maybe it is this unfamiliar feeling that there is someone else in Highbury who thinks like me, who actually understands me.

CHAPTER 18

On Monday after school, George and I are walking out to the parking lot to head home, and I'm still wondering how his date with Hannah went on Friday night. This morning I was running late, and we were both rushing to get into school on time so we didn't really have a chance to talk. I've spent most of the day thinking about how to bring it up on the ride home. I also want to tell him how Jane and I were joking about taglines for our app over FaceTime on Friday night, because it's the kind of irony he would appreciate. Except maybe now that he's dating Hannah, he wouldn't even find it funny.

But I don't have a chance to bring it up. Just as we get outside school, my phone rings, and I look down and see it's Dad at work. Dad never calls me from his work number, and in general, if he wants to tell me something, he texts me.

I pick up quickly. "Hello?"

"Is this Emma?" It's not Dad's voice at all, but a woman's, and suddenly I can't breathe and I stop walking. George doesn't notice and keeps going toward the car without me. "Emma?" she says again.

"Yes."

"Honey, this is Kristy." Kristy has been Dad's legal assistant since before I was born, but I haven't talked to her in probably a year or two at this point, and I certainly wasn't expecting to hear her voice, which is why I didn't recognize it at first.

"What's wrong?" I ask, because I can't imagine a scenario in which Kristy calls me and nothing is wrong. I'm shaking, and now George notices I've stopped walking and has turned and come back for me.

You okay? he mouths. I shake my head.

"Honey, I don't want to alarm you, but your dad passed out at the office and had to be taken to the hospital this afternoon."

"Passed out?" I repeat the words but don't understand them. The parking lot is a sudden swirl of colors and lights, and I sit down on the curb so I don't pass out myself.

"He's at Princeton-Highbury General."

"Princeton-Highbury General?" I repeat again, like suddenly I've lost all ability to speak words of my own and can only repeat back what she's saying without really understanding or processing what it means.

George hears what I've said, sits down next to me, and now he's frowning, too.

"Where are you, honey? Do you need me to come pick you up and take you to the hospital?" Kristy asks.

"No," I say. "I'm at school. I have my car."

Kristy might have wanted to say more, but before she can, I say, "Bye," and hang up the phone.

"What happened?" George asks.

"My dad…he's…Princeton-Highbury General…" I'm trying to find the words to repeat to George what Kristy told me, but I don't know them anymore or I can't remember them, and I really can't remember how to speak much at all. All I can think is, *Please, please, please let Dad be okay.*

George holds out his hand. "Give me your keys."

"What?"

"Your keys, Emma. We need to get to the hospital and you can't drive like this."

I do what George is asking, hand him my keys. My hands are shaking, and George takes my arm, lifts me gently off the curb and holds on to me. He steadies me the whole way through the parking lot to my car and helps me get in.

It is weird to be in the passenger seat, to see George in the driver seat of my car, and this is something I might comment on if I weren't also hyperventilating. George adjusts the seat and the mirror and pulls out. "Just breathe, Emma," he says. "I'm sure everything is going to be fine."

"You don't know that," I say, my voice breaking.

He stops at a red light, turns and puts his hand on my arm.

"You're right, I don't know that," he says. "But try not to panic yet, okay?"

The light turns green, and George speeds down Highbury Pike, faster than I normally would drive. I put my head against the seat, close my eyes and pray that George is right.

George drops me off at the front of the ER, and I run in as he goes to park. It's packed inside, but I make my way up to the front desk, and have to wait in line. Finally, I'm at the front, and I ask for Dad.

George runs in, and I wave him over to where I'm standing.

"Woodhouse?" the nurse says, scanning a list in front of her. "I don't see him."

"What do you mean you don't see him?" I'm talking too loud, almost yelling. "Kristy said he was taken here."

"I'm sorry," she says, holding up her hands. And I know I have to explain more, or ask more questions, but I can't find the words, and when I try, I start crying instead. If they can't find him, does that mean he's dead? I can barely breathe I'm crying so hard.

George steps forward and explains what he thinks happened, and where Dad would've been coming from. "Check again," George says to her. "Please."

"Woodhouse?" Another nurse steps forward, and hands the first nurse a chart. "He was just admitted. Third floor. Room 301." She points toward the elevator, and I run in that direction, hearing George thank them behind me.

It takes forever for the elevator to come and then to rise up to the third floor, and it's hard to focus on anything because my eyes are still teary, and I didn't think to ask why Dad was admitted or what condition he's in. I picture him in a coma, tubes and wires coming from his large body. My breath is ragged in my chest and I can barely stand. George grabs on to my hand and it feels more like it's to hold me up, to keep me from falling, than to try and comfort me. I don't let go of him. I can't.

Finally, the elevator makes it to the third floor; room 301 is just across from it, and George and I run toward it. I stop at the doorway when I see Dad. He's sitting up in bed, reading something on his iPad. No tubes and wires at all, except for an IV.

"Dad. You're alive!" I run into his room and give him a huge hug.

"Emma, honey, of course I'm alive. I was just trying to figure out how to connect this thing up to the Wi-Fi to text you. My phone is back at the office but I had my iPad with me in my briefcase. How did you know I was here?"

I hold on to him so tightly, and he's warm and smells the way he always does, like his Old Spice aftershave, and I'm so relieved I can't let him go for a few minutes. "Kristy called me," I say. "But all she said was that you collapsed and then the nurse couldn't find you and I thought you were dead."

"Oh, Em." Dad holds on to me tightly and kisses the top of my head. Dad suddenly notices George standing nearby, too, and he waves to him. Then he tells us both we should sit down on the small daybed next to his hospital bed. I reluctantly let him go and sit with George.

"What happened?" I ask him. "George and I were just leaving school when Kristy called. He drove me here."

"Thanks, George," Dad says, and shoots George a smile. Then Dad turns back to look at me. "Now, it's not a big deal and I don't want you to freak out, Emma. But there's just a minor problem with the old ticker." He thumps his palm lightly against his chest, then grimaces a little.

A problem…with his heart? And he passed out?

"Did you have a heart attack?" I shriek at him. He opens his mouth, then closes it, like he's considering how to sugarcoat things for me. "Dad! Tell me what's going on," I yell at him.

"A very, very small heart attack," he finally admits. "There's a little blockage, and the doctor's going to do a minor procedure, put in a stent tomorrow morning. Then they say I can go home tomorrow afternoon, good as new."

"Dad! You could've died."

"But I didn't," he says. "I'm right here, Em."

"You have to take better care of yourself."

He chuckles a little. "I told the doctor you were going to say that."

"This isn't funny!" I yell at him again, but I'm so relieved that he's here, that he's breathing and talking to me. I try and focus on the words he just said. *Small. Minor.*

He holds out his arms again, and I stand up and give him another hug. He strokes my hair back with his hands. "I know," he says. "But I'm fine. I'm not going anywhere. I promise you, Em."

I want to spend the night at the hospital with Dad, but he insists that I go home, sleep in my own bed and get my homework done, though I don't know how I'll be able to concentrate on anything. I refuse to leave until I hear what Dad already told me directly from the doctor—that he will be fine, and that the procedure he'll have in the morning is fairly routine and minor.

My hands are still shaking nearly two hours later as we ride the elevator back down, and George insists he'll drive me home. I tell him I'll be okay if he goes to his house first. I am capable of driving the whole mile back to my own house, but he says he's coming over and he'll text his mom to pick him up on the way home from work. I don't argue with him, because the truth is, I feel grateful for his company. I don't think I want to be alone.

It's dark outside, and already after seven by the time we get to my house. I know I need to FaceTime Izzy and tell her what's going on, but I need to calm down a little more first. I don't want to freak her out, too. Not when she's 2,764 miles away from home, and Dad.

"You hungry?" George asks as we walk inside my kitchen and I flip on the lights.

"Not really," I say. My body and my mind are still numb and shaky, and it's hard to feel anything else, hard to remember anything else. "Are you?"

"A little. And you should probably eat something. I'll order us a pizza."

"Sure, whatever you want."

George orders it on his phone, and he doesn't even comment on my mushroom and olives. When he's finished he grabs me a glass of water and puts it on the table. "Have some water," he says. "Take a deep breath. I know this is scary and unexpected. But everything's okay."

I smile at him, take the water and force myself to take a few sips. "Hey, thanks for taking me to the hospital today, and just…being here now." For a few hours I forgot about everything else—school, and coding club, and our app. And George and Hannah's date on Friday. And all there was, was my worry about Dad. And George, who was being so kind, trying to help me.

"Of course," George says. "You would've done the same for me."

I nod, hoping I would've known that was the right thing to do, if the situation were reversed. "It's weird," I tell him. "I was so young when my mom died, but I still have this memory of waiting in the hospital waiting room with Dad and Izzy, finding out she wasn't okay. And even the idea of stepping in a hospital has freaked me out ever since. Honestly, if you weren't there, I feel like they would've needed to admit me, too."

George smiles, puts his hand on top of mine reassuringly. "I'm just glad he's going to be okay."

"Me, too," I say.

We sit there and stare at each other for a few minutes, and George doesn't move his hand, and I don't move mine, either. And then George says my name, *Emma*, and it sounds different than it usually does in his voice, soft and ethereal.

"What?" I say softly, still staring at him, neither one of us moving our eyes or our hands, and I have this weird feeling like there's something else I'm supposed to say here and now, something I should know how to say. Or do. But I don't move. I just sit there, holding on to George.

The doorbell rings, and we both jump up, moving our hands back quickly. "Pizza," I finally speak, and George frowns. I wish I'd said something else instead. But I stand and walk to the door. My hand is still warm from where George was holding on to it, and I put it in my pocket.

I open the door, and it's not pizza at all, but George's mom. I frown when I see her because this means George is going home now and I'm not ready for him to leave yet.

"Emma, honey. George texted me what happened. Do you need anything?" she asks me, a worried look on her face.

George must hear her voice because he walks in from the kitchen and grabs his school bag from the bench by the front door.

"Do you want to come sleep at our house tonight, Emma, so you don't have to stay here alone?" Mrs. Knightley is still talking, fretting over how she might be able to help me.

The thought of sleeping in a strange house, in a strange bed, sounds way worse than sleeping in my own house alone. "No thanks," I tell her. "I'm just going to eat the pizza George ordered when it gets here, do some homework and go to bed."

"Are you sure?" she asks. I tell her that I'm sure, that I'll be fine now that I know Dad is going to be fine. "Okay," she says reluctantly. "But George is just a text away. You let us know if you change your mind or if you need anything. Anything at all."

"I will," I promise.

George shoots me a half smile, and goes to walk out with his mom. But then he stops for a second, turns back and gives me a hug. He embraces me tightly, and I lean into him. My head falls into his chest, and I remember that feeling of dancing with him, when everything felt comfortable and safe and easy. I hold on to him longer than I should, breathing in the warmth of his sweatshirt and his sandalwood. When I'm holding on to George, I do believe that everything's going to be fine, that I'm fine.

But then he lets go first, steps back. "Text me if you need anything, okay?"

"I'll be *fine*, really," I say again, extra emphasis on the word *fine* to try and convince him it's really, really true. Because when he's not hugging me anymore I feel weirdly…not fine.

"Okay." He nods, convinced. "I'll see you in the morning," he adds softly.

"Yeah," I echo back. "See you in the morning."

The pizza comes about five minutes after George leaves. When I open the box I see he ordered an entire pie with mushrooms and olives, which makes me smile. If the pizza got here before his mom, I bet he would've even eaten a slice, though he thinks it's gross, just to make me laugh and try and cheer me up.

Great pizza choice, I text him. Mushrooms and olives forever!

You had a rough day, he texts back. I hope it makes you happy.

How could it not? Mushroom and olive pizza would make anyone happy.

Agree to disagree, Emma.

I smile at the words in his text, picturing the way his face would look if he were still here saying it to me out loud. But I'm still not hungry, so I put the pizza in the fridge for later. At least laughing a little over the pizza makes me finally feel calm and normal enough to FaceTime Izzy.

"Em, oh my gosh." She picks up, sounding, and looking, frazzled. Her hair is piled on top of her head in a messy bun, and she's wearing her ratty old pink DC sweatshirt that she got when Dad took us there to see the Smithsonian one spring break in late elementary school. "Dad just texted me and told me what happened." I guess he finally got the Wi-Fi to work. Now I feel bad I waited so long to FaceTime her. "I was working on a paper all day, and I haven't eaten anything, and now I'm trying to look up flights..." Her voice breaks, and she wipes at her cheeks with the back of her hand.

I was freaking out about Dad, and I was only twenty minutes away from him when I found out what happened. *And* I had George to drive me to him. I can't imagine how upset Izzy must be all the way across the country.

"Iz," I say, wanting to calm her down. "It's okay. He's okay. You don't need to come home." I explain to her what the doctor told me, about how putting in the stent is a minor procedure that will open up Dad's artery, and how he'll have to rest for a few weeks and work on his exercise and diet, but that he'll make a full recovery. This was *a warning*, and he got lucky. We all got lucky.

"But what am I doing here three thousand miles away?" she shrieks.

"2,764 miles," I say softly, correcting her.

She frowns and keeps talking. "I should be with Dad. And what about you? Are you all right?"

I think of all the times last summer I begged her to stay, how I thought I didn't know how to exist without her. But so far this year, I've managed pretty okay. I do wish Izzy were here, but not because I need her to take care of me. Just because it would be really nice to hug her right now. "Iz," I tell her. "I can take care of myself just fine. And Dad will be home from the hospital tomorrow, and I'll take care of him, too. You don't have to worry. Really."

There's a weird silence on Izzy's end, and she stares at me for a minute with her mouth open, not saying anything. She plays with her hair, nervously redoing her bun. Finally, she says, "But you'll call me if anything changes… The second anything changes."

I nod. "I'll make sure Dad FaceTimes you tomorrow when he gets home from the hospital, okay? Go finish your paper. Don't fail out of college. That would really not be good for Dad's heart."

"I'm not going to fail out of college!" she shrieks again.

I smile and shrug. And I reach my finger up to my phone screen, letting it linger on Izzy's sad pretty face for just a moment before we hang up.

CHAPTER 19

The plan all along has been that Izzy and John would stay in California for Thanksgiving, since they'll be home for Christmas break just two and half weeks later. But after Dad's health scare, Izzy calls him and says she wants him to buy her a last-minute ticket to fly home for Thanksgiving. Dad assures her he really is fine. She'll see him in a few weeks over Christmas break, and he tells her it's too expensive, and too much travel, for her to fly home twice in such a short period of time. "That's just the way things go when you go to school so far away," Dad tells her. He doesn't sound upset about it, more matter-of-fact, and I can't help thinking about how if I get into Stanford he might be saying the same exact thing to me next year. How can Izzy and I possibly *both* be that far from him?

Dad's health aside, I'm still sad about a Thanksgiving without Izzy, and without our pie bakeoff. Every year, for as long as I can remember, Izzy and I have each secretly found and baked a different pie recipe for Thanksgiving. We don't tell Dad whose is whose, and then we make him eat a slice of both and declare the winner. I've won the past three years. Last year, I made a macadamia nut white chocolate chip, while Izzy stayed more basic with a cream cheese pumpkin pie. Chocolate and nuts *always* beats pumpkin in Dad's book—it was almost like she wasn't even trying.

Dad asks me a few days before Thanksgiving what pie I plan to bake this year. He's off from work until after New Year's to recover, and he's been working on eating healthier, so he's actually been home after school and cooking plant-based dinners for us every night, too. It's been kind of nice not to come home to an empty house, and to have an actual home-cooked vegetarian meal.

"What's the point?" I say when he asks me about the pie. "Izzy's not even here. And you shouldn't be eating pie," I remind him.

"The point is, your pies are delicious. Dr. Hiller said I'm allowed to indulge *once in a while*. And I told Mrs. Knightley you were bringing one."

"Mrs. Knightley?"

Dad frowns. "I forgot to tell you, didn't I? Mrs. Knightley called to check up on me this week, and she invited us to have Thanksgiving dinner with them this year. I think they're missing John just as much as we're missing Iz."

I nod, thinking about how George and Mrs. Knightley

were so nice to me when Dad was in the hospital. And how George hugged me before he left that night and I hadn't wanted him to leave. How I felt something weird and empty when he'd let go of me. I've driven him to school a few mornings since then, and have been extra careful to walk into school far enough apart that we don't accidentally touch. "Wouldn't you rather eat here, just the two of us, though?" I ask Dad now.

He shakes his head. "I think it'll be nice to spend the day with friends instead of all alone, don't you?" And it occurs to me that maybe it's good for Dad to have a place, other than here. He'll need it when I'm gone next year, too.

Dad is still looking at me, waiting for a response. "Yeah, sure," I finally say. "I'll bake a pie to bring to the Knightleys."

We have the whole Thanksgiving week off school, so when we show up at the Knightleys at three p.m. on Thursday, I haven't seen George since last Friday, at our coding club meeting. He and Jane and I have all been working on our own this week, updating code in GitHub, and I know he's been working on tweaking the animation, because I get a notification every time he makes an update.

Hannah texted me on Saturday, before she left to go to her dad's for the holiday, that she and George went on a second date, for coffee. She said it was *great*, with a heart emoji. I texted back a thumbs-up, but I didn't ask her for more details. I'd sat there staring at the heart emoji for a while, trying to analyze why she put that there. She loves me for setting her up with George, or she already *loves* George, after only two dates? Or maybe she just overuses heart emojis? Because she has texted them to me a lot so far this year.

I'm still debating this when we ring the bell at the Knightleys', and I'm wondering if I should ask George how he enjoyed the dates with Hannah. Purely to collect data for the upcoming competition, of course.

But then George answers the door, his eyes go to my pie and he holds out his hands to take it. "This smells amazing," he says. I went with the same macadamia white chocolate chip pie as last year. As Dad pointed out in the car on the way over, zero points for creativity, but one hundred points for taste. *No one is judging this year*, I'd reminded him, which only made me miss Izzy more.

"Thanks," I say now, and George steps aside and ushers us in. I notice he's wearing jeans and a UCLA sweatshirt and socks. His hair is sticking up a little more than usual, like he just woke up from a nap. Dad has gotten dressed up for dinner in a nice shirt, tie and dress slacks, and he'd told me to put on a dress, so I already feel awkward and out of place.

"You look like you're feeling better, Mr. Woodhouse," George says to Dad.

"Yes, I am. Thanks." Dad smiles at him. "Oh, you know what I wanted to tell you, George? I've been doing a little eBay browsing while I'm off work and I put in a bid on a 1980 signed Mike Schmidt baseball."

"No way!" George reacts, and I tune them out the way I always do when they talk baseball, walking inside behind them.

Mr. Knightley is on the couch, watching football, and invites Dad to join him. Dad prefers baseball to football, but nonetheless, he abandons me, sits down with Mr. Knightley and takes off his tie. I follow George back to the kitchen, where Mrs. Knightley is wearing jeans and a sweater and an apron and checking the oven.

"Mom," George says. "Emma brought a pie."

"Macadamia nut white chocolate chip," I offer.

She turns and gives me a wide smile. "This looks wonderful, Emma!" She surprises me by pulling me into a hug, holding on tightly, in a way that makes me think she's wishing I were Izzy, or forgetting for a second that I'm not. I've talked with her lots of times, most notably last week, when she picked George up from my house, and that night of Izzy's crazy party when she and George came to rescue me. But she has never once hugged me before.

"Do you need any help with the dinner?" I ask her, extracting myself from the hug.

She steps back and shakes her head. "I've got everything under control here. I've even got some veggies roasting in the oven for you, Emma. Why don't you kids go hang out and I'll call you when dinner is ready?"

Every holiday meal for as long as I can remember, Izzy and I were always in the kitchen, always in charge of preparing things. So it's a weird feeling to be shooed away from the food. But this is not my kitchen, not my meal, and I don't really want to hang around to have an awkward conversation with Mrs. Knightley, anyway. I appreciate that she remembered to include vegetables for me and I thank her.

"Come on," George says. "I'll show you what I've been working on with my animation today."

I follow him upstairs. At the top of the steps is a huge loft area, complete with a Ping-Pong table and some arcade games. George grabs his laptop off the desk, flops down on a red bean bag and drags another one over for me. I sit, and wish I hadn't listened to Dad and worn a dress. I pull it down, and tuck it around my knees.

"I animated a second heart," he says. "It matches the first one. Look." Two identical yellow hearts walk across the simulator on his screen, and meet in the middle to hold hands. "I think we should add this to the last screen, when the match pops up. And maybe on the first screen, they could hold up a sign that says The Code for Love."

"It looks really good, George," I say, and it does.

George puts his laptop down, and we kind of stare at each other. I think about what I wanted to ask him, about his dates with Hannah. And how as a mathematician, coder of this app, I should want to track the data, all the data. Even George and Hannah. Especially George and Hannah. But I don't say anything for a minute.

"You look nice," George says, speaking first.

"Oh… Okay." I'm kind of flabbergasted, not sure what I'm supposed to say in response. I told Hannah that George doesn't notice that sort of thing. I guess I was wrong? "Well, Dad thought this would be a more formal dinner than we're used to. But apparently he was confused," I explain.

George smiles. He nods toward the Ping-Pong table. "You know how to play?"

"Do I know how?" I laugh, incredulous. We have a table in our basement, and Izzy and I have a running tournament every single summer. It's practically the only sport I'm good at. If you can consider Ping-Pong a sport, which, for the record, I do.

I push up the sleeves of my dress, stand and go grab one of the paddles.

"I'll make you a friendly wager," George says, picking up the other paddle, pushing up the sleeves of his sweatshirt. "If I win, you'll run your own match through our database."

"What? No way," I say.

"Afraid I'll beat you?" His eyes are shimmering behind his glasses against the overhead lights, brimming with laughter.

I shake my head. There is no way George will beat me. I've beaten Izzy three summers running. "So what do I get when I win?" I say.

He thinks about it for a minute. Then he says, "I'll do the oral presentation at regionals next week."

It's always the worst part of the tournament, having to make the oral presentation to the panel of judges, in ten minutes or less. In the past, the club presidents have always done it, and I've been dreading having to do it this year. George and I had planned to equally divide the talking and go in there together. "The whole thing? By yourself?" I say. He nods. "Okay, deal. I serve first."

I hardly even give him a second to react before I toss the ball and do a hard slam serve onto his side, catching him a little off guard.

As with everything we do together, George is a formidable opponent, but I win the match by a point in game five. "Best of three," George says quickly as I put my paddle down on the table.

I laugh and shake my head. I'm sweating now, and I try to push my dress sleeves up even farther. Why did I wear wool? George takes off his sweatshirt—he's wearing a white tee underneath, and it's more fitted than what he normally wears, showing off his muscular arms and broad shoulders from swimming. I quickly look away, because it feels like a weird thing to notice.

"Nope," I say. "A deal's a deal, and I won, fair and square." I walk across the table to him, and hold out my hand so we can shake on the match. He takes my hand, but doesn't shake it exactly. He holds on to it, gently touches my knuckles with his thumb. I meet his eyes, and he opens his mouth to say something. Then changes his mind and doesn't say anything. We stand there like that for a minute, both breathing hard, not talking, holding hands.

"I'll still do the speech with you," I finally say. "We're co-presidents, aren't we?"

"Co-presidents," he says softly, his hand still on mine. I should let go, but I don't. "But aren't you even the least bit curious to see who you'd match?" he says.

I think about Sam, who texted me a picture from a hike he was on with his dad this morning in Phoenix. Wish you were here, E! But Laura is his match. In coding club last week we discussed the fact that one person's highest match might not be the other person's highest match, and how we might go about solving that dilemma. But even if Sam were my highest match, I'm not his. He's dating Laura. And the two of them have kind of started to grow on me as a couple.

I look back at George, standing right in front of me, breathing hard, holding on to my hand. He's Hannah's highest match, but what would happen if we ran his name through the app?

"Not even the slightest bit curious?" George prods again.

"Nope," I say, forcefully enough, so I wonder if maybe it's possible I'm lying, a little bit, even to myself. "Not in the least."

"George! Emma! Dinner," Mrs. Knightley calls us from downstairs. George quickly drops my hand, and as I follow him down the steps, my fingers are still warm and tingling. I ball my hand into a fist, trying to fight back the weird feeling of wanting just another moment, alone, standing there like that with him.

CHAPTER 20

Jane and Sam and I are sitting near each other on the bus ride to Princeton the following Tuesday afternoon, and Sam is showing the two of us photos on his phone from his Thanksgiving trip back to Phoenix. He slides through mountains and sunsets and tall-armed cacti and then a huge Thanksgiving turkey on a platter, which I have to look away from, as I think about that poor beautiful bird who was murdered. But Jane is really interested, asking questions about the desert biome and climate in Phoenix. I tune them both out and look through my notecards again, rehearsing my presentation one more time in my head.

"Hey, Emma." George says my name and touches me on the shoulder. I remember the way his hand had lingered on mine on Thanksgiving and I close my eyes for a second.

He and Hannah were sitting a few rows back when I'd gotten on the bus, but he must've moved up to the seat behind me while I was listening to Sam and looking at my notecards and I didn't notice. He leans over the seat now. "You ready?" He moves his hand, and I reach up to rub the warmth away from my shoulder.

"As ready as I'll ever be, I guess?" I say.

George shoots me an empathetic smile. "It's just regionals. All we have to do is score in the top five to go on. We'll be fine."

I nod. I know all that. There's only one other high school in our region that even has a serious coding club like we do. And in all our years participating, we've never scored lower than third in the region, and that year, when George and I were freshmen, the president really bombed our oral presentation, and our project, coding solar energy, was kind of lame and poorly coded. Still, I've never been responsible for part of the oral presentation before, and I don't want to be the one to mess it up.

"George!" Hannah's red head bops up from four rows back. "I want to show you something funny!"

George gives me an apologetic shrug, and moves back to his seat with Hannah. "They're good together," Jane says.

I guess she and Sam are done discussing the desert, because now he has his head against his seat, eyes closed, headphones on. I didn't realize Jane had been paying attention to George, and I turn back around to face her. "Really? You think so?"

Liz and Mara just seem to fit together when I see them walking down the hallways holding hands—they *look* like a couple, but when I look at George and Hannah, I still see them as George…and Hannah. And it bothers me that they've paired off in coding club, that they're together right now, when I wish George were up here, acting like a co-president, going over our presentation with me.

"It's nice to see George look so happy," Jane is saying now.

Does he look happy? Happier than usual? I try and turn around again, but all I can see from here are the tops of their heads—bright red and sandy blond. The sounds of Hannah's laugh float across the bus, and I wonder what funny thing she's showing George and whether or not he actually thinks it's funny, too. I wait for it, but I don't hear him laugh, and it feels like this tiny bit of proof that Jane is wrong about him, that George isn't happier with Hannah at all.

The oral presentation is first on our schedule at 9:50 a.m., and George and I go into a classroom to present to the judges, while the rest of the team stays behind in the cafeteria to show off the trifold we made to represent the app's features. Later this morning, we'll have a team demonstration of the actual app to a different panel of judges.

George and I make it through the oral presentation without any mishaps, both of us reciting the speeches we'd rehearsed. My portion of the speech is in technical terms, about how we coded the app, and George's is about the results and how the app has helped people in our high school. As we leave the room together, we both sigh with relief at the same time. George laughs at our simultaneous sighing, and so do I. *There it is*, I think. *George's laughter.* Coding club is what makes him happy. Winning will make him even happier.

"What do you think the judges thought?" George asks me as we walk back to the cafeteria to find the rest of our team. "It was hard to read their faces," he says. "But I thought that one old guy looked unimpressed."

I know exactly which guy George means, as there were only three judges in the room: one was a woman, and the third was a younger man. The older man had looked kind of skeptical, and for some reason he made me think of Mrs. Bates and her husband, and I threw an improvised line into my portion of the presentation that mentioned how our survey respondents were over sixty-five. "I don't know. He was so stone-faced. It was hard to tell what he was thinking."

We walk into the cafeteria and Sam waves us over, excitedly. "Jane did great!" he gushes, and Jane smiles a little, and shrugs, her cheeks reddening from the compliment. "I think she really impressed the judges when she explained how she optimized the back end."

"Well..." Jane stammers, her cheeks still bright pink. "Sam and Hannah and Robert all did well, too. How did it go with the oral presentation judges?"

"Okay," I say. "I think?"

George nods in agreement and adds, "Not bad."

"Good effort all around," Ms. Taylor says, walking over from behind Jane. "Now let's get ready for the demonstration." She checks her watch. "We have twenty minutes."

The demonstration goes well, with every member of the club chiming in to explain what he or she worked on in the code, and then we take the bus back to Highbury with little fanfare. There are no award ceremonies at the regional competition. Ms. Taylor will get the results emailed soon.

She emails me and George that she has our scores by lunch the next day, and George and I call a quick meeting after school so we can see the score sheets and figure out how to proceed. My heart pounds wildly in my chest as we walk into the room after school and she waves the score sheets in the air. "Second place," Ms. Taylor says, smiling.

Second. I feel my face fall; my stomach drops a little.

"Not bad," George says, his voice calm, even, and I glance at him. He's not smiling or frowning, just looking normal, like George. He catches my eye and shrugs a little and it makes me think that, inside, we're both feeling the same way.

It's fine. We still advance to the state competition in February. But I can't help but feel disappointed. Last year we came in first in the region, and I always thought during my senior year—my co-presidency—that we would be first, too. This also means we have a lot of work to do in the next few months if we want to have any chance at winning states and advancing to nationals.

"It looks like what you got marked down for is the fact that it's a user-driven app, but you didn't actually have any user data to present yet," Ms. Taylor is saying, looking through the score sheets, then passing them around for us all to see. "So—" she's still talking "—we have three weeks until Christmas break. Let's get our app on as many students' phones between now and then as we can. Then, after break, we can begin to track that data."

★★★

We leave after a short meeting, and Jane is offering to drive Sam home as we all walk out and I'm watching the two of them, so I almost walk right into Ben. He's standing in the hallway, just outside the door, waiting for Robert. It's the first time I've seen him in person, but he looks almost exactly like he did in his yearbook photo.

"Hey," he says to Robert, touching him lightly on the arm. "How'd you guys do?"

"Second place," Robert says. "Not bad, right?" He looks to me for confirmation.

"Well...we did...fine." I can't keep the edge of disappointment from my tone.

"We did great," George interjects, managing to sound more positive than I do, though I would guess deep down he's disappointed, too. "But, we still have a lot of work to do before states."

Ben smiles at Robert, revealing slightly crooked front teeth that weren't visible in his yearbook photo, but it makes his smile kind of more endearing in person. "I thought you might need a ride home," Ben says to Robert.

Robert nods, and waves goodbye to us, and the two of them walk off together toward the parking lot.

"Okay," Jane says, turning to me. "You know I was skeptical of this whole app at first. I mean, I'm a cynic who doesn't really believe in love. I have to admit, though, it's kinda cool now to see that we're making people happy."

And I know I should be thrilled that Jane is pretty much apologizing, but instead I'm distracted by Hannah, who is laughing as George whispers something in her ear, and I hate the feeling that they are sharing some private joke, without me. So all I feel instead is this weird twisting feeling in my stomach.

"Love is still the worst," I say quietly to Jane.

"Oh, yeah," she quickly agrees. "The worst."

CHAPTER 21

The week before school is out on Christmas break, Izzy flies home from California on the red-eye. She walks through the front door of our house while I'm eating breakfast before school, as if she'd never even left.

"Em!" she squeals, and runs into the kitchen to grab me in a hug. I hug her back, hold on to her tightly. She feels like a stranger and a memory all at once. She pulls out of the hug first. "Look at you!" She tugs on the end of my ponytail, frowns, puts her hands on the sleeves of my sweatshirt. "This is what you're wearing to school today?"

"I've survived the last 122 days without your fashion advice," I say pointedly. "Yes, this is exactly what I'm wearing to school."

"Oh my goodness, Iz." Dad walks in, lugging her giant suitcase behind him. He wipes sweat from his brow. "You're only home for three weeks. And you still have half a closet full of clothes upstairs. How much could you possibly need?"

Izzy goes and kisses him on the cheek. "I told you I could carry that in, Dad. Aren't you supposed to be taking it easy?"

"I'm supposed to be getting in shape," Dad says, doing a half-hearted bicep curl. Then he hugs Izzy to him, kisses the top of her head and closes his eyes a little, so I know how happy he is to have her home and how much he's missed her. I've missed her, too, but if I don't leave now I'll be late to pick up George. "I have to leave for school," I say, to both Izzy or Dad or neither.

Izzy pulls out of her hug with Dad, grabs on to my arm. "I got no sleep on the plane. I need to take a nap. But, Em, after school we'll hang out, okay?"

I'm staying after for coding club. We've planned to meet every day this week to get as much done as possible before the break. But I tell Izzy I'll be home for dinner and we'll talk more then.

"The prodigal son has returned," George says to me, rolling his eyes when he gets into my car. *Right*. John is home, too. Of course they took the same flight. George's sarcasm surprises me, though.

"I thought you and John get along?" I say.

He nods. "We do. It's just…in my parents' eyes, John is the sun, and I'm just some shadow cast behind him."

"That's ridiculous," I say. "You're way better than he is."

George chuckles, and I realize how that came out. "I mean, I like John…enough. But he's not you."

"And that's a good thing?" George says, tilting his head to the side, looking vaguely amused.

"Yes. For one thing, John couldn't code his way out of a cardboard box. For that matter, neither could Izzy."

"But they could probably both make it look really beautiful and then not even care that they were inside a cardboard box because they'd just pretend it was a mansion," George says.

Now it's my turn to laugh, because George is so spot-on. "The first thing Izzy said to me was, *This is what you're wearing to school today?*" I mimic her, making my tone squealier.

George laughs again, reaches his hand out and touches the sleeve of my sweatshirt. "It's your navy blue. You always wear this one on Wednesdays."

I pull into my parking spot and turn off my car. His hand lingers on my sweatshirt, and I turn and look at him. "How do you even know that?" He's right, though. I am partial to my navy blue hoodie on Wednesdays. It's my *halfway through the week is the hardest day to face I might as well wear my most comfortable sweatshirt* look.

"You've driven me to school almost every day this year." He shrugs, pulls his hand away and gets out of the car, like it's no big deal. But if he were to ask me what he was wearing on any particular day, or if there is a rhyme or reason to it, the truth is, I would have absolutely no idea.

At lunch, there's a line of people wrapped around our little table, waiting for us to help them load our app onto their phones. Mara spearheaded the campaign during our lunch; Liz and also George and Jane did it during their lunch, and this has been going on all week. So far, we've gotten our app on about seventy-five other students' phones. Jane will be able to track who requests matches, what the results are, and after break, we plan to follow up.

Sam and Laura are talking about their Christmas plans, not being super helpful. So everyone waiting is talking to me, asking *me* questions. It's weird how I don't know or recognize most of them, how you can go to a school for four years, walk its halls and almost be valedictorian of your class, and still not know so many people who *surround* you day in and day out. And also, even weirder? Now they all seem to know me.

"Hi, Emma!" There's a blonde girl standing in front of me now, holding out her phone. I don't know her name, and I'm not sure I've ever even seen her before.

Sam is supposed to be taking down emails while I help people download TestFlight, but he and Laura are deep in conversation. I glean bits and pieces of what they're saying—Laura is going to be here over the break, and Sam is going to be skiing with his mom and aunt's family. She'll be lonely without him.

"Write down your name and email here." I take the notebook from in front of Sam, who barely even notices, and pass it over to the blonde girl. I glance at her name as she writes: *Riley.* She passes the notebook back to me. "Okay, now you need to go to the App Store to download TestFlight. You'll get an email invite later and you just need to follow the instructions to get the app on TestFlight from there."

"This is so cool," she squeals, sounding a lot like Izzy did this morning. "Thank you, Emma!"

She walks away, and then there's a boy behind her, whom I do recognize. He's in NHS with us. "Hey, Garrett," I say, surprised to see him. He offers me a half wave. "You're going to try our matching app?"

He shrugs. "Why not?" I arch my eyebrows, not able to hide my surprise at his interest. "It'll help you and George out, right?" I nod. "And besides, I like the anonymity. I can see who I'm supposed to be dating without putting myself into any embarrassing social situations. You know what I mean?"

I nod. I actually do understand what he means, and I make a mental note that we can add this point to our presentation for states.

I finish helping Garrett and a line of ten others stretches behind him. My stomach rumbles and I glance at my watch. Only ten minutes left of lunch, and I haven't even gotten to take a bite of my sandwich. "Sam." I nudge him with my elbow, and he finally stops talking to Laura and turns to look at me. "I need help."

He turns, notices the line of people. "Oh, sorry, E." He shoots me an apologetic Sam smile, and I instantly forgive him.

"It's okay," I say. "Just help me with the rest of these."

"I'll help, too," Laura interjects, putting her half-eaten sandwich down. "What can I do?"

I'm not sure how she can help, since she's not even in coding club. But before I can figure out what to say, Sam turns and smiles at her. "That would be great," he says. "Here, you take down emails. I'll help people get TestFlight, and Emma can eat her lunch."

Before I can say a word, Sam has taken over the next person in line, and Laura is carefully writing down her email. I take a bite of my sandwich and watch them. In between people in line, Sam leans over and whispers something to her, and she shakes her head a little and laughs.

"Emma." She pushes the notebook toward me. "Can you read my writing okay for this email?" Her script is perfectly neat, and I nod. She smiles at me, and gets down the email of the next person in line.

I wonder if maybe I've misjudged Laura all along—if she really is a kind person and a good match for Sam. And if that's all true, then maybe my algorithm really is working perfectly. And if we get user-driven data to back it up—maybe we can win at states. That thought makes me smile as I finish off the rest of my sandwich.

I have this weird feeling after coding club later as I'm driving George home, when I remember that Izzy is at my house again. I'm excited that she's finally home, and I want to spend time with her. But also now I'm used to being home alone, doing what I want when I want to. I think of all the times last year I felt uncomfortable tagging along with Izzy and her friends, and I don't want to be back in that place again. I hope Izzy won't expect me to now that she's back.

"Earth to Emma," George says, tapping my shoulder.

"What?" I say, and I realize he must've been talking but I haven't heard a word.

"I was saying my lunch was so busy today. Jane and I had probably twenty-five people waiting to talk to us. I have to send those emails out tonight."

I nod, thinking about how Laura had to help so I could eat. "Yeah, mine, too."

"People are really excited about this." George's voice almost sounds excited, too, and I'm tempted to say, *I told you so.* Except we only came in second in the region, so really, I haven't proven anything yet, have I? I imagine saying this to him when we do win states, though, and the thought makes me smile.

"Hey," I say as I turn into his driveway, remembering his comment about John this morning. "If you want to get out of the house, we could go to the diner tonight and send out those emails together. We could study for the calc midterm, too."

He frowns. "I would, but I promised Hannah I'd take her to see the Christmas light show at the mall tonight."

"Oh..." I feel weirdly disappointed. "Well, of course. Never mind, then."

"Maybe we can study together later this week?" he says.

"Yeah," I say softly as he gets out of the car. "Maybe."

Izzy is waiting for me in the kitchen when I walk in. I imagine she slept all day. She's recently taken a shower—her hair is still damp, and I can smell her strawberry shampoo strongly when I walk in. That and...cookies? She pulls a tray of tree-shaped cookies out of the oven.

"Wanna help me decorate them?" she says, putting the tray on the counter. I'd bought the ingredients for our yearly sugar cookies last weekend, anticipating we'd make them together, after my midterms, and now I swallow back disappointment that she made them without me and didn't even think to wait for me.

She doesn't wait for me to answer her now, either. She passes over a tube of icing and some green sprinkles. "We have to let them cool first," I remind her. "Or the icing will run."

She shrugs and flips her hair over her shoulder. Details are not her strong suit. And now she looks a little hurt, like I've rejected her. I reach for her hand. "We can decorate them after dinner, okay?" I say.

She sighs. "I guess it'll have to be tomorrow, then. John and I are going to dinner and then to see the Christmas lights at the mall. That reminds me, can I take the car?"

I think about George, also going with Hannah to see the lights, and I frown.

"You could totally come with us," Izzy adds, misreading my expression. She tilts her head, making her pleading eyes at me. I used to feel guilty saying no when she made that face, but now that I haven't seen it in months, it's not affecting me as much. I hate the mall, and I don't much love Christmas lights, either.

I shake my head. "No, you go ahead without me. I have to study for midterms, anyway."

Izzy frowns but she doesn't press me like she used to. Instead, she just says, "Are you sure, Em?" I nod and then she shrugs and lets it go.

I probably should study for midterms, but we've been reviewing during all my classes for the last week. So truthfully,

I'm already pretty prepared. Instead, I take out my notebook with the emails from lunch today, and I FaceTime Jane. We've been on FaceTime together all week, tracking whom we are sending the app to and how many downloads we get.

"I heard you got twenty-five people today," I say when she answers. Her face fills the screen. Home Jane—Jane without a lab coat, with her long black hair up in a messy bun—always looks entirely different to me than school Jane, who is quiet, precise, protected. I like home Jane, because she seems more honest, more unfiltered, more like me.

"Yeah, twenty-four actually," she says now, scanning her notebook with her eyes. "How'd you do?"

I scan down the list quickly counting. "Nineteen."

She turns her eyes away from me, to her laptop. "From the twenty we added yesterday, thirteen have downloaded the app and twelve have gone in and made matches. I just sent that info off to Sam. He and Robert are going to follow up with those people tomorrow. And George and Hannah and I will continue to add names at lunch, too."

When she mentions George and Hannah, I think about their date to see the lights at the mall tonight, and tell Jane about it.

"They are definitely a good match," she says.

"Yeah," I agree half-heartedly. "I guess so."

"Actually, Sam told me he and Laura are going to see the lights tonight, too," she says. "I guess that's like the thing to do when you're dating someone around Christmastime in Highbury." She raises her eyebrows, and maybe she thinks it's as ridiculous as I do. I fail to see the romance in electricity—

instead, I think about the science, all the wasted kilowatts and energy. "You know," she says. "Maybe we can use this?" I guess I've read her eyebrow raise completely wrong.

"Use this how?"

"We could go over there tonight, too, see how our matches are working out firsthand. Observational data. It'll be more accurate than what Sam and Robert get interviewing people at lunch tomorrow."

As much as I'm not dying to go see the Christmas lights, it's not a terrible idea. But Izzy took the car to go with John, and they already left without me. Dad went to have dinner with an old college friend who's in town. I tell Jane I can't go because I have no way to get there, and I feel relief that I still have an excuse, a way out of it. Because the thought of the crowds and the lights, and watching George and Hannah holding hands—or kissing—sounds awful to me.

"It's no problem at all," she says. "I'll pick you up in an hour." And then she disconnects from FaceTime before I have a chance to say anything else.

CHAPTER 22

Izzy spots me the moment Jane and I walk up to the lights display entrance, like she has some kind of weird radar that allows her to hone in on me, wherever I go.

I haven't been to see the lights here since we were kids, and Dad used to take us, and all I remember is that there are displays surrounding the entire outside of the mall parking lot—cartoon characters, and Christmas trees, and reindeer, all made out of Christmas lights. There's some school choir caroling tonight, too, singing "Silent Night" a little off-key as we approach. It's a pretty mild night for December, but it's overly bright and too loud out here, and it smells so strongly of pine and cinnamon I sneeze.

"Em!" Izzy shouts, and waves for me to join her and John,

who are standing in front of the tall, lit-up tree, perhaps unsurprisingly with George and Hannah. George turns at the sound of my name, and shoots me a confused glance.

"Oh, hey! Emma's here," Hannah calls out, causing Izzy to whip around with surprise, like she can't believe someone else would actually notice my presence, aside from her. I sigh and walk toward them, Jane following close behind me.

"I thought you had to study?" Izzy lets go of John, grabs me in a half hug.

"I'll study later," I say, noncommittal. Izzy frowns, knowing this is not like me. Or not like the Emma she used to know last year, anyway.

"Who's this?" she asks, taking in Jane's lab coat and arching her eyebrows a little.

"This is my friend Jane, from coding club," I say. "We're going to walk around. We'll catch up with you later."

I grab Jane's arm and walk to the other side of the crowd, practically dragging her, as much to get away from Izzy's questions as from George's weird stare. I suppose we could've asked Hannah and George to help us gather data, but they're here on a date. I noticed they were holding hands, both smiling. They're the exact kind of data we're hoping to collect. And maybe Jane is right. Maybe they really are good together. Only more proof my algorithm is working, so I'm not sure why that thought bothers me so much.

"You're lucky to have a sister," Jane is saying now as we walk. "I hate being an only child."

"Yeah, I know. I am lucky." I suddenly feel a little bad I wasn't nicer back there with Izzy. "But Iz and I are so different, and I guess I just kind of got used to being by myself more when she was away at college this fall."

"I get that," Jane says. "I remember her last year at school. She was on the dance team and the lead in *Hello, Dolly!*, wasn't she?"

"Yep," I say. "She's super talented and awesome, and has always had a ton of friends."

"Ugh," Jane says. "Gross." She laughs, and I know she's kidding. Kind of. "Seriously, though, I don't get people who feel like they belong in high school. You're lucky," she says again, sounding a little more bitter this time. "Six months and you're done. You'll be off in Palo Alto next year."

"Maybe," I say. The closer it gets to the application due date, the more I think about the math, the small percentage of people who apply to Stanford who actually get in. And the more I doubt that I might be one of those people. I'm also applying for a scholarship Ms. Taylor recently found for me at Carnegie Mellon, which she thinks I have a better shot at. And I'm applying to Rutgers and Penn State as backup schools. "I'll be in Palo Alto, *if* I get accepted," I say to Jane now.

"You will," she says, sounding so sure.

But I think about Dad being here in Highbury all alone, and what if something else happens with his heart and Izzy and I are both in California? I swallow back the metallic taste of panic. Maybe it wouldn't be so bad if I only got accepted to Rutgers. Then at least I'd still be close by to Dad.

"And even if you don't go to Palo Alto—" I realize Jane is still talking "—then you'll go somewhere. Not high school. I'll be stuck here for another year."

"You can be president of coding club," I say brightly, like it's something to look forward to. But really, I'm not sure it's been as great as I'd thought, to be in charge. I kind of enjoyed myself more last year when coding club was all about coding, only about coding, without the extra pressure to succeed, or the feeling like it's all on my shoulders because the project is and was my brainchild.

"Look," she says, switching subjects, pointing toward the hot chocolate stand. "There's Robert and Ben."

Ben grabs two hot chocolates from the booth, and hands one to Robert, and then they hold hands and start walking back toward the display. They stop in front of the closest one, take it in, turn to talk to each other and sip their hot chocolates.

"Is that Snoopy on top of his doghouse behind them?" Jane asks, her eyes drawn to the display. She tilts her head and squints.

"Yeah…I think so?"

She walks over to get a closer look, and I follow her. Ben says something to Robert, and he laughs, his face looking much more animated in the bright twinkle of the Christmas lights than I've ever seen it in coding club.

Robert turns and notices me and Jane. "Oh, hey, guys," he says, and Ben lifts up a hand to wave. I wave back.

"Emma and I came to track data." Jane cuts right to the point. "You two sure look happy. *Check.*" She makes a checkmark in the air with her finger, and Robert's face turns red. Ben laughs, and says Jane is right, they are happy. "Have you seen any other couples we've matched?" she asks them.

Robert nods. "Yeah, a bunch. We just saw those two girls from cross-country."

"Mara and Liz?" I ask.

He nods. "Yeah, I think so. And that guy in my geometry class…Ian. But I don't know the girl he was with. I just know you helped him at lunch last week," he says to Jane.

"Ian and Brianna," Ben offers, and he points them out to us. They're standing over by the next display, which appears to be birds—three doves, maybe—in a lit-up tree. Ian is really tall, and so is Brianna—though not quite as tall as him. Still, I'd bet she's almost six foot. She leans her head on his shoulder.

"Bri and I play in youth orchestra together," Ben says. "She's really nice. And Ian's a good guy."

Jane and I thank them, and wander over to that display. We stand there, observing them for a moment. Their arms are linked; her head is still on his shoulder as they wander over to the next display: reindeer. It appears they are having fun, that they like each other. That their match is successful. *Check*, as Jane said. But it's also a hard thing to quantify just from looking at two people from a little ways back: happiness, love. How can you really tell what two people are thinking and how they're feeling, just by looking at them from a distance?

"E, is that you?" I turn at the sound of Sam's voice. So does Jane. "Janie, you're here, too?" His voice is thick with surprise. And…*Janie?* I've never heard anyone call her that before, and it sounds much too unserious to suit her. But Sam breaks into a smile and so does Jane. Or *Janie*. He gives us each a hug.

"Where's Laura?" I say, looking behind him.

"Oh, she just left. She has to study. But I wanted to stay and see all the displays. Highbury does Christmas *way* better than Phoenix. Our mall did fake snow and carols. No lights like this." Because Sam seems super impressed by the lights, I swallow back my instinct to tell him how stupid I think the whole thing is. Jane tells him how we came here to observe our matches, observational data and all that. "Oh!" Sam says. "I just saw Lance, from choir, with his match. I think her name's Helen?" I nod. Her name *is* Helen. I paired them up a few weeks ago in our very first test batch. Lance had asked Sam about a match and Sam had sent him to me. Helen is in my AP Physics class. She's quiet, with curly black hair and tortoiseshell glasses. Lance is painfully shy, to the point he refuses to talk in class. But for some reason, he's totally different when he opens his mouth to sing. I've heard him sing at assemblies before and his voice is deep and velvety.

"How'd they look?" Jane asks.

"Good? Here, they were back this way near the big tree." We follow Sam around the displays, back toward the front where we saw Izzy and George and Hannah when we first got here. And on the way there, we spot a few more matches that we point out to each other. They're all here together. Some are holding hands, some aren't, but they still seem to be enjoying one another's company. When we finally do spot Lance and Helen, they're standing under mistletoe, kissing, which seems like a very good sign to me.

"What do you think we should be looking for exactly?" I ask Jane, interested in her opinion, as we stop and watch Helen and Lance move out from under the mistletoe, hold on to one another's arms and move on to another display. "How are we quantifying any of this, really?"

She frowns, like maybe she's not sure. Then Sam says, "If our matches are here, spending time together and appear to be having fun, then we can call that a success, yes? We're just telling people who they're compatible with, mathematically. Everything else is up to them."

"Yes," Jane agrees.

But is it really just that simple? George and Hannah have caught my eye again. They're sitting on a bench together now, sharing a cup of hot chocolate. George blows on it, before handing it over to Hannah for a sip. She takes it, and whispers something in his ear, and then he smiles. Until he notices me watching them, and he hands the cup back to Hannah, says something to her and walks over to us, alone. *Is that happiness? Or not?*

"I thought we were taking the night off coding club, but I guess I was mistaken," George says with an easy smile, so I don't think he's annoyed, more curious what we're doing and why he doesn't know about it.

"We need data on our matches," Jane says with a shrug. "This seemed like an easy way to get it."

"I knew you had plans," I add. "And I didn't want to interrupt them."

"We can help you," George says quickly.

"No need. You're here on a date," I say. "So technically, you're already doing your part to help, aren't you?" My voice is supersweet, saccharine, and the words sound all wrong as they come out, even to me.

George turns and looks at me, opens his mouth to say something, then shakes his head a little. "Hannah and I will start on the other side. You three can continue on this side. We'll cover more ground this way."

"Good idea," Jane interjects. "Let's all take notes on the matches we see here, and then email them to me later. I'll start a data file for our results."

I watch George for another minute as he walks back toward Hannah, holds out his hand and she takes it to stand up from the bench.

"Emma," Jane says, tugging on my sleeve. "Come on, there's Garrett and Alyssa over there." I nod and start to follow her, and when I glance back over my shoulder one more time, George and Hannah have already disappeared into the crowd.

CHAPTER 23

Dad invites the Knightleys over for Christmas dinner, to reciprocate for their hospitality at Thanksgiving. But Mr. and Mrs. Knightley have already made plans to go to Cancun for the week, just the four of them. Izzy is bummed that she wasn't invited, that she and John won't be together at Christmas.

"But you get to be with us," Dad says, like that's going to console her. "And Christmas is a time for family," Dad adds.

She forces a smile. "You know I love you guys. But…it's not the same." Once the Knightleys leave for Cancun, she gets a little pouty and stays in the same pajama pants for three days in a row.

"Aren't you going to take a shower?" I ask her on Christmas morning, after we open our presents, mostly gift cards that Dad wrapped up in big boxes to be funny. But even I notice that Izzy's hair looks pretty greasy and she doesn't smell great, either.

"I'll do it before dinner." She sighs, and I can't get over how much she seems not herself with John away. It's strange and also slightly disturbing.

"It's only one week," I remind her. "Four days left, Iz." But John doesn't have cell service or access to Wi-Fi in Mexico and they can't even text or FaceTime, and Izzy has already used the word *unbearable* multiple times today.

I would never tell Izzy, but I'm actually kind of glad that John is gone, and that the Knightleys can't come over here, either—that Dad and I get Izzy all to ourselves for once. Because Christmas feels like it used to be when we were younger. Izzy does shower after I mention it to her, and puts on clean sweats. Then we play Ping-Pong in the basement, eat all the cookies I baked yesterday and we bake more together. Izzy does a reread of her favorite books every year over Christmas break, and in the afternoon she reads *Pride and Prejudice* on the couch while I practice my Rachmaninoff on the piano, and Dad reads through the *New York Times* on the love seat.

We decide to do our Thanksgiving pie contest for Christmas dinner—I try something totally new, a red velvet cheesecake, and Izzy goes all out with a candy cane pudding pie. Dad picks hers as the winner, but I'm happy to see he limits himself to only having a tiny sliver of each to try and stay on his diet. And even I have to admit, Izzy's pie is pretty amazing.

"Victory at long last!" She pumps her fist after Christmas

dinner when Dad declares her the official winner of the first annual Christmas pie contest. Her face is more relaxed, and her hair is clean, and she seems vaguely like her normal self.

I laugh. "I'll get you next year, Iz." I suddenly remember again that next year at this time I'll be home from college, too, that poor Dad will have just spent the whole fall all alone. That thought makes me infinitely sad, so I push it away for now.

After dinner, Dad goes into the family room to start a fire, but Izzy and I stay at the table for a while, eating the pies with our forks straight from the tins, until we're both so full we can barely move.

We stumble to the living room, and Dad stokes his fire, and Izzy cues up *It's a Wonderful Life*, her favorite Christmas movie, and one that always bores me with its impracticality, so I know I'm about to take a nap, which I'm perfectly okay with.

Izzy lays on one end of the couch; I lay on the other, our feet touching in the middle. Dad throws a big plaid blanket over us, and smiles. "Is there anything better than this?" he says. "Both my girls at home on Christmas, watching a movie with me."

And for a little while, everything and everyone else feels very far away.

The Knightleys fly home on New Year's Eve day, and Izzy and John already made plans to go out tonight, even before he left for Cancun. This is Dad's last week home before going back to work, and he's been cooking and freezing healthy food all week. Today he's working on a huge pot of his famous chili, only now he's doing it all vegetarian, which works way better for me, anyway, since I'd never eat the other version of the recipe he made with beef.

"Em," he says. "Izzy's going out. But you should invite some friends over to have dinner with us tonight. I made way too much. Even for freezing. We'll be eating chili for a month."

Dad probably assumes anyone I'd invite won't have New Year's plans, like all Izzy's friends do. But he's assuming right. Jane and Hannah both have already been texting me this week that they're bored. I text them to invite them for chili, and they both text back they'll be right over.

Jane arrives twenty minutes later in a pair of plaid lounge pants and a sweatshirt, her hair piled up messy on her head. It's the first time I've seen her in person without her lab coat, and that makes me happy. School Jane is apparently on break, too. "Can I sleep over?" Jane asks when she walks in. "My mom doesn't want me driving home super late. *Too many drunk people on New Year's Eve*, she says. Either that or I promised her I'd be home right after dinner."

I nod and let her in. Dad definitely won't care if Jane sleeps over. Izzy has had plenty of friends sleep over. But I've made it to nearly the end of high school without ever having a friend sleep over. I always thought sleepovers sounded terrible. All those hours of having to talk to someone? But Jane is easy to talk to, and I don't want her to have to leave in an hour right after dinner. And I don't really want to spend New Year's Eve by myself, either. I've gotten kind of used to having Izzy around again this week, having someone else to cook and watch movies with again. And I've grown to actually like Jane these past few months. I'm glad she'll be here to keep me company while Iz is out.

Hannah shows up a few minutes later, and I'm about to ask her if she wants to sleep over, too. But when she takes off her coat, I see she's wearing a pretty long-sleeved green dress and heels. Oh, and is she wearing lipstick, too? "I thought we'd just have chili and maybe watch a movie," I say instead, frowning, looking again over her outfit. "And if you want to sleep over, Jane is going to."

"Oh, I would but…after you texted, George texted me and invited me to go to a party with him and his brother tonight. He said they were already coming here to get your sister so they could pick me up in a little bit, too. You don't mind, do you?"

"We don't mind," Jane says quickly, flashing Hannah a smile.

I bite my lip, and frown a little. Because I kind of do mind, though I can't exactly articulate why. Who cares if Hannah only wants to stay a little bit and then go out? But since when does George go to parties with John and Izzy's friends?

Dad walks out into the hallway and says hello to Jane and Hannah before I can say anything. "I hope you girls are hungry," he says, and he ushers them both into the kitchen, where he sets out bowls of chili and corn bread.

It's like Izzy hears the bowls hitting the table from all the way upstairs, because thirty seconds later, she's in the kitchen, too, looking ridiculous, wearing her red checkered bathrobe, her hair up in big pink curlers. She is going all out for this reunion with John, like he's going to forget how she normally looks after one whole week.

"Oh," she says, catching sight of Jane and Hannah, her mouth actually falling into an O of surprise. "I didn't know you had *friends* over, Em. Sorry for how I look," she apologizes to them.

Jane shrugs, like she doesn't care or even notice, and she digs into her chili. "This is delicious, Mr. Woodhouse," she says, and Dad beams.

Hannah stares at Izzy, wide-eyed, and reaches for her own mess of red curls to smooth them down, somewhat self-consciously. I wonder if she's nervous going out with a group so much older than her for New Year's Eve? I couldn't have even fathomed how to handle that as a freshman, and I think maybe I should say something vaguely comforting. But then, of course, Izzy does it first. "Hey, I hear you're coming with us." Izzy smiles reassuringly at Hannah in between spoonfuls of chili.

"Yeah…I mean…I hope that's okay. George invited me."

Izzy shoots her another smile. "Sure, you'll have a great time. Jessi throws the best New Year's Eve parties."

I struggle to remember which one of Izzy's friends is *Jessi*. And I can't. I wish I'd paid more attention last year because for some reason I want to picture exactly where George and Hannah are going to be tonight, what they're going to be doing. And why Hannah looks so dressed up and so nervously excited at the same time.

Izzy rushes through her chili and goes upstairs to get dressed, and we're almost finished when the doorbell rings again. "I'll get it," I say. Izzy is still upstairs, and Dad is eating his chili and asking Jane and Hannah to tell him more about our app and how we're preparing for the competition. Jane is talking about how she worked with the servers, and Hannah is telling him how she implemented the UI, so no one else even moves but me.

I open the door, and there's George, standing on my porch, all dressed up in the same suit he wore to the fall formal. He steps inside the foyer and his cheeks are ruddy from a week of Mexican sun, his nose peeling a little.

"Hey," I say, reaching out to gently hit him on the arm. "How was your trip?"

"I guess it was good…if you like the beach."

"The beach is the worst," I say in all seriousness.

"Right?" George says. "Sand is the most annoying substance in the world, and then it gets everywhere. In between your toes…seriously, so gross."

We both smile a little, like we're thinking we're the only two people in the world who feel this way about the beach, and we can't understand how everyone else doesn't agree with us. "How was your break?" he asks.

"Nice actually. Iz and I have just been hanging out. Baking and playing lots of Ping-Pong. It's been kind of amazing to turn my brain off for the week."

"Ping-Pong," he says. "I still want a rematch." He suddenly reaches his thumb up to my chin. "Here, you have a little something…" A wayward spot of chili I haven't noticed until right now. He wipes it away gently with his thumb, and then doesn't move his hand away right away. We stand there just staring at each other for a few seconds, George's hand on my face.

"George!" Hannah squeals from behind me, and he quickly drops his hand. I take a big step back. Hannah runs up and gives him a hug, reaches a hand up to touch his nose. "You forgot your sunscreen," she admonishes him.

"I didn't!" he's saying. "The sun was just too strong, and it didn't work..."

He's still talking about his sunscreen, but I turn, and suddenly notice Izzy standing at the bottom of the steps. I didn't hear her come down, and I reach my hand up to my chin, wondering how long she's been standing there.

George notices her, too. "John's in the car, with the heat on. It's chilly outside."

"We should go," Izzy says, grabbing her coat. She shoots me a weird look, and I have a feeling she wants to say something, but she doesn't.

"Have fun, and be safe!" Dad calls from the kitchen, and then the three of them are gone.

Dad goes into his office after dinner, saying he needs to prepare to get back to work later this week, and Jane and I sit on the couch and scroll through Netflix looking for a movie. We end up deciding on an old generic romantic comedy. Jane says, "Research," as she selects it, but I can't tell if she's kidding or not. Tom Hanks and Meg Ryan bore me, and it's obvious from the beginning they're going to get together, but there's no logical reason for it, either. It's like the screenwriters just made it up and think everyone will buy in to the fact that they'll fall in love because they tell us it's so. I'm already yawning halfway through.

"Do you ever wonder what it would be like to fall in love with a guy who adores you as much as Tom Hanks adores Meg Ryan?" Jane says out of nowhere in the middle of the movie. "To just feel something like that…something more intense than you've ever felt before. So intense that it would make you dumb and crazy. And happy. Just really, really happy. Meg Ryan looks so happy, doesn't she?"

I'm so surprised she's asking me, in light of what I know about her parents and how we both agree that love is pretty stupid. And how what we're watching right now is a movie, not real life. But she's still staring at me, waiting for a response. Finally, I shake my head. "Not really. No."

"Really? You never even think about it? Not even a little bit?"

I shrug, and think about George trying to beat me at Ping-Pong so I'd make a match for myself in our app, and how there was no way I was going to let that happen. "I know we joke around," I say. "And…I'm not saying I'd never want to fall in love. Someday I might want to get married or have kids."

"Oh, I'm never getting married and having kids," Jane interrupts me to add. "But…maybe it wouldn't be the worst thing to feel something for another person? Hannah looked so happy when she was leaving with George, didn't she? I don't know if I've ever really just felt *happy* like that." She pauses. "What if you and I are missing out on something?"

"We're not," I say quickly. "I'd much rather be hanging

out here in my pajamas than out at some party right now, wouldn't you?"

"Yeah," Jane says, but there's a note of hesitation in her voice, so for a second I'm not sure what she's really thinking.

I notice it's nearly midnight now, so I flip the movie off so we can watch the ball drop in Times Square. Right as it hits the ground, Jane's phone lights up with a text. She picks it up, looks at it and smiles.

"Who's that?" I ask, not realizing it might not be my business until after I already ask.

"Oh…just Sam, saying Happy New Year," she says.

I glance at my own phone, but no one's texted me. "He's back from skiing?" I ask.

"Just got back today," she says, and I get the feeling they've been texting over break. He hasn't texted me, but then I've mostly been with Izzy and haven't texted him, either.

She picks up her phone to text him back. "Tell him I say Happy New Year, too," I tell her. Then I scroll through Netflix some more. "Oooh," I say. "How about a horror movie instead of this sappy romance?"

Jane laughs, puts her phone away and asks if we have any popcorn.

CHAPTER 24

The morning I head back for the final semester of my high school career, Izzy surprises me by waking up early and cooking me French toast for breakfast before I even make it downstairs.

"Wow," I say, walking into the kitchen. "It smells great in here."

"Can I drop you off at school so I can have the car today?" she says. Now that Dad is going back to work, she'll be stuck here all day without a car if she doesn't take mine. *Ah, an ulterior motive.* She makes great French toast, though, so I don't even care.

"As long as you pick me up, too," I say. "And I have to go to the Villages after school to volunteer, so you'll need to go with me since I won't have time to drive you home first." She makes a face, but then nods to agree to all that. "Oh, and we need to pick up George on the way to school this morning. I've been driving him this year."

She slides a piece of French toast on my plate and sits next to me at the table, watching me eat it. "George likes you, you know, Em," she says quickly, matter-of-factly.

"Yeah, George and I have become pretty good friends this year," I say in between bites.

"No. I mean, he *likes you*. Wants to date you."

"What?" I stop eating, turn to her and laugh. "That's ridiculous, Iz. He's dating Hannah."

She shakes her head. "Only because you guys have this silly app for your competition. You can't write a code for love, Em. I was one hundred percent kidding when I told you to do that the day I left for LA."

"Actually, you *can* write a code for love. And we did." I shove the last of the French toast into my mouth, and stand up to put my plate in the sink and gather my things for school.

Izzy follows after me. "Okay... So then tell me why George *matches* Hannah or whatever in your app. But he's actually in love with you?"

In love with me? Something flutters a little in my chest, and I have to stop and catch my breath. I think about all the words Jane used to describe love the other night—*dumb* and *crazy*, and *happy. Really, really happy.*

"That's ridiculous," I say to Izzy. "George and I are friends. Co-presidents of the coding club. That's all. What would even make you think he's *in love* with me?"

"The way he looks at you," she says. "It's so obvious, Em."

I roll my eyes. *The way he looks at me?* What does that even mean? That's not something quantifiable, something I can reasonably wrap my head around. Izzy has no idea what she's talking about. We *did* write the code for love—our matches are all working out great. Izzy doesn't know everything there is to know about love, no matter how amazing her relationship with John is. "I have to finish getting ready," I say. "Or I'm gonna be late."

"I have bad news," Sam says at lunch, plopping down next to me. He's walked in a few minutes late, and I've already started eating the leftover vegetarian chili I brought from home. Maybe it's the break, or maybe it's that everyone who wants to use our app already is, but lunch has been quiet today. I have, so far, been sitting at our table all alone, and haven't said a word to anyone. I'm happy to see Sam, though—it's been twelve days since I've seen him last—but I also notice that, strangely, he's alone.

"What's that?" I say. "Where's Laura?"

"Oh, she's home sick. But that's not my news. Ian and Brianna broke up over the break. And so did Bethany and Tyler."

I stare at him and nod, then eat a little more chili. "That's not good, right?"

"Well..." I consider for a moment what this means for our app, for us, for the upcoming state competition. But I don't think it's as bad as Sam thinks it is. "We're in high school. It's not like we're telling people who they should marry or anything. Just who they match best within our school. So,

I guess it's bound to happen. Some couples aren't going to work out, right?"

"Yeah?" Sam smiles, looking reassured, and he sits down next to me and opens his lunch box. He pulls out an orange, a small thermos of soup and a sandwich on a full hoagie roll.

"Wow, nice lunch today," I say.

He laughs. "My mom was off the past few days, and she totally stocked the fridge."

I motion to my thermos of chili, instead of my usual tray of cafeteria-bought lunch. "My dad has been off, too, and was cooking for the first time in, like, ten years. And Izzy and I made six dozen cookies. Want one?" I push the small Tupperware of cookies toward him, and he takes out two halves of a broken star, holds them up and puts them back together before taking a bite.

"You and Jane have a fun New Year's Eve?" he asks as he devours the cookie.

I push the Tupperware toward him and he takes another. "We did," I say. "Did you and Laura go out?" Though even as I ask the question it occurs to me that maybe it would be weird if they had, given that he was texting Jane when the ball dropped.

He shakes his head. "Nah, just stayed home and watched the ball drop with my mom. I haven't seen Laura since before we went skiing actually." He says it pretty matter-of-factly, like his distance from Laura is neither here nor there. It's certainly not devastating him, like how Izzy was acting like someone died when John was in Cancun for a week.

And I'm not sure what to make of that. But he doesn't

seem to notice my consternation and he asks if he can have another cookie. "Go ahead." I push the container farther toward him. "Help yourself."

Izzy is waiting in the parking lot for me right after school as promised, and then she drives me over to the Villages and pulls up in front to drop me off. "What time do you want me to come back?" she says.

"You don't want to come in and hear me play?" I assumed she would, and I really wanted to introduce her to Mrs. Bates.

She makes a face. "No. This place gives me the creeps."

I sigh and get out of the car. If Izzy gave it a chance, she would actually really like Mrs. Bates, but I don't have time to argue with her. "Come back in an hour," I say, before I walk inside.

I haven't been to the Villages to play in a while. Between Dad's heart attack, Thanksgiving, regionals and Christmas break, it's been about a month since I've been here. I haven't practiced piano as much as I should've, either, but the New Jersey Music Teachers Association competition isn't until May, and if there's any place I can safely sound rusty, it's here.

I walk inside and go straight to the piano. Only about five residents are here today, including Mrs. Bates, who smiles and waves at me. I wave back, and can't help but notice that Mr. Bates isn't with her, which is unusual. It's the first time I've ever seen her without him. She looks a little smaller than I remember her, her cheeks sunken and more wrinkled.

I play through all the residents' favorites, and then try my way through the piece Mrs. Howard gave me right before

Christmas. I've only played through it a few times at home—a Beethoven concerto that I don't know nearly well enough to play up to speed. I play it about half tempo, but when I'm finished, there's an enthusiastic round of applause from my small audience.

"How was your Christmas, Emma?" Mrs. Bates walks over and asks me as I'm gathering up my things to leave.

"It was nice," I say. "My older sister's home from college for a few weeks. How was yours? And where's Mr. Bates today?"

Her face falls as soon as I mention Mr. Bates, and her eyes well with tears. And then I know I've said the wrong thing, again. "He's been under the weather. First the flu right after Thanksgiving, and now he has pneumonia. He's been in the hospital since the day after Christmas." Her voice breaks, and she stops talking, shakes her head, like for a minute she doesn't have the words to continue. "I want to stay there with him around the clock, but I can't. My kids tell me I'm too old for that." She grimaces, like she doesn't agree. "But I don't even drive anymore, so I have to count on the nice van driver here to take me over to the hospital every morning during ICU visiting hours."

"Oh, I didn't know he was sick," I say. If I had, I certainly wouldn't have brought it up, like this. I can't imagine having to go to the hospital every day for weeks and having to worry about the person you love being there. I feel terrible for her. "I'm so sorry."

"I know, honey." She grabs my hand and pats it gently. "He hasn't been himself these past few years, but at least he was still right here with me every day. I've loved that man since I was nineteen years old, and I don't even know how I'm supposed to exist without him."

"I'm sure he'll get better soon and he'll be back here with you." But even as I say it, I'm *not* sure, and I can't stop my voice from faltering a little. He's old, and being in the ICU doesn't sound great.

"I hope you're right, Emma," she says. "I hope you're right."

I'm quiet back in the car with Izzy. She's telling me how she went and got her nails done today, and I know she's wanting me to compliment her on the color, a bright sparkly purple. But I'm still thinking about poor Mrs. Bates. What would it be like to live almost your entire life loving the same person, and then reach eighty-six years old and not even know how to be apart? I always thought Mr. Bates was a burden to her. I assumed she was stuck in the Villages with him, when she could've been off still doing something exciting with her life. But after talking with her today, I don't know that I ever really understood her at all.

"Em," Iz is saying. "Did you hear what I said?"

"Your nails," I murmur. "They look great."

She frowns. "No, I was talking about dinner tonight. We should stop at the store and get something healthy to make for Dad, now that he's back working so hard. We have to make sure he's still eating well. You'll need to do that when I'm back in LA, too…" Her voice trails off, like maybe she's asking a question or she's feeling unsure I can handle it.

"Of course," I say. "You don't have to worry. I'll make sure Dad eats healthy when you're gone."

But I close my eyes for a minute, and I think about Mrs. Bates, and then about Dad, and how he loved Mom once for her eyes, and how he lost her when they were still so young. And how next year, when Izzy and I are both gone, Dad will still be here, really and truly all alone. Will he even know how to exist anymore without us?

to both gather more specific data before states and take the app to the next level for our presentation for the judges. We can talk about how we're actually doing good with it, too."

Matching people already is doing good, isn't it? But George sounds so eager I keep my mouth shut and nod. Besides, only a few people have come up to me at lunch this week, asking for a download. Maybe if we are offering something specific—a date to the dance—it'll give us a whole new surge of interest. And our school does have a policy that students can only bring other registered students to the dance as dates, so what better way to do that than to use our app?

And George is right—we need more data. As far as we can tell, so far we have only forty-eight couples dating as a result of our app (and three others who were, but then broke up over the break). There are four hundred people in our high school, so we have room to make more matches between now and the middle of February.

After the meeting ends, Jane offers to drive Sam home and the two of them walk out together—Sam laughing at something Jane says. Ben is waiting to give Robert and Hannah (who lives right near him) a ride.

I let Izzy take the car again, her last day at home, as she said she had some shopping to do before she flew back to LA, and George and I walk out to the parking lot to look for her. We don't see her, so we sit down on the curb and I text her.

Be there in 5, she texts back.

It's chilly outside, and I shiver and zip my parka up higher.

CHAPTER 25

"I had an idea," George says on Friday after school, the first meeting of coding club since the winter break. My mind is only partly here, as mostly I'm thinking about the fact that Izzy goes back to California tomorrow, and how quiet the house is going to be again without her. And how I'll miss her, but also, it might be nice to get my life back again, the way it was last fall. And my car. Getting my car back will be nice, too.

"We have about six weeks until states." George is still talking. "And when I looked at the calendar, I realized the competition is right before the Valentine's Day formal. So what if we offer to match couples for the dance with a five-dollar donation to the Environmental Defense Fund? That gives us a way

"You want my hat?" George offers, pulling it from the pocket of his parka.

"Nah, I'm okay. Iz says she'll be here in five minutes."

"Are you sad for them to go back?" George asks. "I mean, obviously you'll be happy to have your car back. But other than that?"

I shrug, remembering how George sounded bitter the first morning they were home, calling John *the prodigal son*. "Are you?"

"No…yes…maybe a little?" He shrugs, too. "High school will be over for us soon and next year we'll both be off… somewhere." I let his words settle a little. George is sitting right next to me on the curb, so close; the puffy shoulders of our parkas are touching. I've seen and talked to him almost every day this year. It's hard to imagine that next year we'll be living completely different lives, far apart. Even the thought of that makes me feel sad now. "Sometimes it just feels like everything is changing so fast, you know?" George says. I nod. I do know. "But these past few weeks with John back home, everything sort of felt the way it always was, the way it always used to be. And that was kind of nice, too."

"George?" I say softly. "We'll still be friends next year, right?"

"Emma." He puts his hand on my arm, and even through my parka I can feel the warmth of his fingers. "I want…"

"What?" I think about that ridiculous thing Izzy said, which she based on the way he looked at me. He's looking at me in a strange way now, frowning a little. "What do you want?" I say softly.

Before he can answer, the sound of a car honking makes us both jump up. Izzy has pulled up while we were talking and we haven't noticed her.

"I'm freezing," George says, changing the subject. "Let's get in the car."

John is in the passenger seat, so George and I both slide in the back. I stare at him, wondering what he was about to say, what he *wants*. I want to ask him again. But then John turns around to talk to us. "How was nerd club, kids?"

"John." Izzy elbows him, before driving out of the parking lot. "Be nice."

"What?" John says, leaning over to kiss Izzy's shoulder affectionately. "I am nice. George is proud of his nerd status, aren't you, George?"

George shrugs and shoots me a little grin, as if to say he'd way rather be us than be John, who, according to Izzy, struggled with his classes last semester. Then George actually answers John's question and tells him what we were just doing in coding club. How we're going to use our app to match couples for the Valentine's dance next month and also ask for donations for the Environmental Defense Fund to get matches.

Izzy stops at a light, turns her head and rolls her eyes at John, like she forgets we are sitting behind her and we can see her. Or maybe she just doesn't care. The light changes and she weirdly turns off Highbury Pike, instead of going straight, toward John and George's house.

"Hey, where are we going?" I ask her.

"It's our last night," she says vaguely. "And we wanted to do something fun."

I get that old familiar aching feeling in my stomach, like I've swallowed something heavy: dread. Every Friday night last year, Izzy would try and drag me somewhere, insisting I needed *to have fun*! But really, fun for me is staying at home, working on code in my pajamas. In fact, I was already thinking about what I could work on tonight, how I'd upload it to GitHub, and maybe FaceTime Jane, who would probably be checking database stats at the same time. And Sam, too, who had promised before we left our meeting to text Mara and Liz about spreading the word about dance dates.

"Can you take me home first?" I say to Izzy, but she ignores me, or pretends she doesn't hear me, and she keeps on driving, getting on 95. She exits near Dad's office in Princeton, and then I realize she's heading toward the train station. They want to go into the city.

I hate going into the city. Hate the crowds and the noise, and the overwhelming smells of garbage and diesel on the streets. I cannot think of anything I'd want to do less on a Friday night than take the train into the city. The city is worse than the mall.

Izzy pulls into the train station parking lot, parks, and she and John get out of the car. But George and I stay in the back seat, unmoving for another few seconds. "Do you want to go to the city with them?" I say to George.

He sighs. "Not really. But do we have a choice?"

Last year, I would've agreed with him. How many times did I go along with Izzy, listen to Izzy, do what Izzy said I should want to do? Because Izzy is Izzy, my sister and my friend and my protector. It never mattered if what she wanted made me feel uncomfortable or if I just didn't find it fun. Because I always felt like I was supposed to be doing what Izzy was doing. Izzy is the sparkly normal sister who understands social situations. I'm the awkward math nerd. But this year I've kind of embraced being the math nerd, and really, why is it bad if I want to do math nerd things on a Friday night?

I get out of the car now and George slides out behind me. I walk up to Izzy and hold out my hand. "Give me the keys, Iz. George and I are going to go home. You two go have fun. I can come back and pick you guys up here later. You can text me when you're on the train back."

"What?" She frowns, her face turning in surprise. Her cheeks are pink from the cold, and she blows on her bare hands. She must've forgotten, or lost, her gloves again. "But we have dinner reservations," she protests.

"You and John go and enjoy them. It's your last night home and you should go have fun. But I don't want to go."

"Em," she protests again. "Come on."

"Look, I am a nerd. And I don't like the city. And I don't want to go out to dinner. I want to go home and work on code in my pajamas, and that's going to make me happy. That's who I am, okay? So stop trying to change me." I'm breathless and talking louder than I mean. Izzy stares at me, confused, or maybe hurt? So I feel like I've explained myself all wrong. But then she drops the car keys in my hand without another word.

"George, you coming with us?" John asks.

George looks at me, then back at John and shakes his head.

John shrugs and grabs Izzy's hand, and the two of them walk toward the train station building in front of us.

George and I get back in the car, in the front seat this time, and my hands are shaking. I feel a little bad that Izzy is probably mad at me now. But mostly, I feel relief, knowing I don't have to do what Izzy wants. I'm going to do what I want.

"Nerds rule," George finally says after a few minutes, and it breaks the tension a little, and we both chuckle. Then he says, "Hey, why don't we go to my house and order a pizza? I swear I won't even make fun of your gross mushrooms and olives."

"So not gross," I say.

"Agree to disagree, Emma," he says, and we both smile. "Come on," George says. "We can work on some code together. Then I can drive back with you later to pick them up so you don't have to go by yourself if it's late."

I consider it for a moment. Pizza and coding with George sounds like the perfect Friday night. But then I suddenly remember: Hannah. She and George were talking about dinner tonight in coding club earlier. "Didn't you make plans with Hannah?"

He makes a face, like he forgot. "Oh, yeah. I did…but I'll…invite her to come over, too. We can all work on code together."

Being the third wheel with the two of them, even if we are coding, sounds almost more painful than spending the evening in Manhattan. "Nah," I say, pulling into his driveway but not turning off the car. "You and Hannah go out and have fun. I can send my dad to pick them up later if it's too late."

George frowns, and doesn't get out of the car for a moment. "Emma," he says. He turns and stares at me, and his eyes are so intense. And I kind of want to tell him I do want to spend the evening with him, and maybe he could cancel his plans with Hannah.

But the thought of saying any of that makes my cheeks burn hot. I look away, stare really hard at the steering wheel instead. "You don't want to be late for Hannah," I say, more to the steering wheel than to him.

I hear him breathing next to me for a minute, and I wonder if he's going to finish what he was saying to me earlier, on the curb. *What do you really want, George?* But then all he says is, "Have a good night."

He gets out of the car and closes the door hard enough that the whole car shakes a little as he walks away.

CHAPTER 26

Izzy's flight is early the next morning, and I've been restless all night, worrying I'll oversleep and miss saying goodbye to her. Dad offered to go pick them up at the train station last night when I told him where Izzy and John went, but I left out the part about how I threw a fit and refused to go with them. And I'd fallen asleep before Dad got back with them. I then woke up every hour starting at two a.m., checking the clock.

I finally get out of bed at five, go into the kitchen and brew one of my mochas for Izzy, putting it in a travel mug for the road. Since Dad picked her and John up from Newark a few weeks ago, Mr. Knightley is coming by around five thirty to pick her up to drive them both back to the airport.

"Hey," Izzy says. I look up and she stands at the entryway

to the kitchen now, dressed in black leggings and a big gray UCLA sweatshirt, her hair pulled back into a messy ponytail. "You're up early."

"I made you this." I hold out the mocha, a peace offering.

She walks into the kitchen, smiles and takes it from me. "Thanks, Em. You didn't have to get up."

"I wanted to," I say. "I feel really bad about yesterday. I didn't want you to go 2,764 miles away and still be mad at me."

"I'm not mad," she says gently, taking the lid off the travel mug and blowing on my mocha, before taking a sip.

"I should've just gone to the city with you last night. I'm sorry." It's what I was thinking all night long, every restless hour I woke up. Why did I have to make a *thing* of it? It was Izzy's last night home until May. I could've just done what she wanted. Next Friday I'll be here all alone, and that thought makes me sad all over again, the way it did when Izzy first left me, last August.

Izzy shakes her head. "No. You shouldn't have gone to the city if you didn't want to go. You need to do you, Em. You've changed so much this year. I'm proud of you."

I shake my head. "I haven't changed at all." I've never liked the city. Never liked going out on Friday nights. I've always been a math nerd, and I will always be a math nerd.

"Yes, you have changed," she insists. "You have your own friends now. That girl…with the lab coat."

"Jane," I say, wanting Iz to know her name. I don't like the thought of Jane being reduced to her lab coat now that I know who she is underneath it.

"Right, Jane," she says brightly. "And Hannah, and George. And that cute guy who just moved here."

"Sam," I say.

She nods. "And even though I think your dating app is kind of ridiculous, Jessi says it's making you…*popular* at school. All the theater kids are super into it."

Now I remember which one Jessi is. Izzy's friend in my grade, who does musical theater. Have we matched her yet? We've done so many now, I'm not even sure.

"The app's not ridiculous," I say, not sure why I feel the need to defend it again now. But I do. For whatever reason I want Izzy to understand that it's actually a really amazing thing to be able to match people mathematically. "We've matched one hundred people. They're all dating…and happy." Well, most of them are still happy: 95.7 percent of them, anyway.

"Math is one thing," Izzy says. "Love is another."

The doorbell rings, and I hear Dad's footsteps on the stairs. Izzy grabs her suitcase from the hallway and then she comes to me and wraps me in a giant hug. "Everything can't be solved with an equation, Em. If you feel something…just let yourself feel it, okay?"

And then, just like that, Izzy is gone again, leaving me all alone in the kitchen, wondering what the heck she means.

CHAPTER 27

Interest picks up in our app again by the middle of January, and George totally believes it's because people care about the environment. But Jane and I agree, when she comes to sleep over and look through the data with me one Saturday night—we're getting more interest now because we're offering our app as a way for people to find dates for the dance next month. Sure, people are now paying us five dollars to give to the Environmental Defense Fund in exchange for an invite to download the app. But I have to wonder how many of them even know or care what the five dollars are for. People want dates for the Valentine's Day formal, plain and simple.

"It's less commitment," Jane says. "Maybe some people didn't want matches, or to date exclusively, or to fall in love. But people do want to find someone to go to the dance with."

She sounds a little wistful when she says it, and she's been checking her phone all night, like she's waiting for something important.

"Do you want a match for the dance, Jane?" I ask her. We both have the latest beta version of our app on our phones, and it would be easy enough for her to create her own log-in, put in her own name, answer the few survey questions, get a match and then for her to text him—or her—through the app to see if that person would want to go to the dance with her. As long as she's willing to cough up five dollars for George's charity for him to give her a code to get past the opening survey. And even if she's not, I can still run her match through the simulator on my laptop. George wouldn't care.

She shakes her head. "No, no. I think we should all go to the dance together actually," she says. "Coding club, I mean. It'll be the day after states, so we can celebrate our win and see all the couples we matched together."

I think about the disaster of the last dance I went to with her and George. But now our app is different. As Izzy even noticed, *I'm different*. "You really think we'll win?" I ask Jane.

"I hope so," she says. "But either way, I'm really glad we got this far, that you and I got to work together and became friends this year, Emma."

"Me, too," I say. "And honestly, I'm glad you don't want a match for the dance, either. It's nice to have a friend who actually thinks like me."

Jane nods, and then glances again at her phone. And I have this weird feeling I said something wrong, but I have no idea what.

★★★

At lunch the next week, Mara walks over and joins our table after we've all sat down and started eating. Sam and Laura are talking to each other, involved in some boring conversation about choir music that I'm only half listening to, catching words about song choices and solos here and there. Mara ignores them and starts talking to me.

"I want to update you on all our team's matches," she says. Their season is over, but it's a tight-knit team and they are friends all year long, she tells me, so she knows what's going on with everyone. "Liz and I are doing great," she says with a huge smile. Then she starts talking about four other girls, still dating their original matches, and my attention drifts back to Sam and Laura.

"Emma," Mara says, nudging me gently with her elbow. "Are you even listening?"

"Yeah, sorry. I'm listening." The truth is, I was half listening, half staring at Sam and Laura, wondering what's going on with them. They finished talking about choir, and now Sam is concentrating very hard on his sandwich, which appears to be peanut butter and jelly on wheat. He's methodically eating each crust before he tackles the center. Laura is focusing very hard on her soup.

"I was saying Alyssa and Garrett broke up," Mara is saying now. "And Alyssa wants to try the app again, find another match for the dance. How does she do that?"

I shake my head. "There isn't another match," I say. "Garret is her best match in the school."

"But what if she doesn't want to date her best match?" Mara asks.

I turn to her and frown. "Why wouldn't someone want to date her best match? Plus, Garrett is a really nice guy."

"Maybe Garrett just isn't for her?" Mara shrugs, and it feels like she's missing the point.

"Mathematically, she matches with Garrett. Or our whole algorithm is wrong. And I don't think it's wrong. It's working for almost everyone else. It worked for you," I remind her.

"What if we add a feature so you can block certain matches, E?" Sam speaks up, surprising me. He's put his sandwich down, and has his full attention focused on me and Mara. "What if we could get the database to exclude people you've dated in the past or people you haven't quite connected with who you have matched." Laura frowns at him, like somehow this is an insult to her.

"Yeah," Mara says. "Exactly. Can we do that, Emma?" She stares at me, waiting for an answer.

"I'll see what Jane and George think," I say. "And then I'll text you later and let you know what we come up with."

"Cool." Mara stands up, slaps the table gently with her hands and smiles at me. "You guys are so smart. Seriously. I love that you figured this whole love algorithmic thingy out."

"Algorithmic thingy," Sam says quietly after she walks away. "That's kind of catchy."

And suddenly Laura looks up from her soup and laughs and then so do I and so does Sam. And maybe our table is, as John referred to us in the car, *nerd club*. But it's kind of nice to feel like I'm not in it alone.

★ ★ ★

"Plan B," George says during our coding club meeting, the last Friday in January. He opens the simulator on his laptop, with a brand-new app screen. I'd told him about what Mara asked earlier in the week, and apparently Liz had come to him at his lunch with the same request. I've seen on GitHub he's been updating and changing code all week. "I designed one more screen we can add," he's saying now. "A page to go to only if your first match doesn't work out. It'll cancel the first name out of the database and rematch you with your second highest match."

"Isn't Plan B like a pill you take if you think you're accidentally pregnant?" Hannah asks.

Redness creeps up George's neck, quickly flushing his cheeks. I look from him to Hannah, who doesn't seem to be embarrassed in the least. *Are the two of them…?* I close my eyes, hating that thought. For whatever reason, right up until this moment, I didn't picture them actually doing anything more than holding hands. Hannah's only a freshman, after all. But that was stupid of me, wasn't it? They've been dating for a while now. Of course they're doing more than holding hands. I don't want to think about it. I shake the thought away. *Why do I even care?* But also, ugh. "Okay," George is saying. "So it needs a better name. But consider the idea."

I close my eyes for a second, push myself to focus, to stop thinking about George and Hannah like that. Together. But now I can't get the awful image out of my head. *Plan B. Focus. Focus.* "Mathematically how does that make sense? And the competition is a little over two weeks away," I add. "I don't know if we should change anything at this point…"

"Second chance," Robert offers. We all look at him, surprised because he still barely speaks up at these meetings. "That would be a way better name than Plan B. We can have a *second chance* screen for people whose first match didn't work out for whatever reason."

"Yes," Hannah agrees with him. "I like that. And what if one person is a 96 percent match and someone else is a 95.4 percent match? That would almost be statistically equal, right Emma? Jane?"

I hold up my hands, and give Jane a look, like she should try and convince everyone because I don't think I can convince them to listen to me over George on this. "I agree with Emma," Jane says. "I just don't think we should reinvent the wheel this close to states."

"Only one new screen," George says quickly. "I already have the bugs mostly worked out. So we're really not reinventing anything."

"I'm with George," Sam finally speaks up. He offers me and Jane an apologetic smile.

"I'm still worried this will hurt us more than help us," I say, one final plea. "It almost feels like we're betting against our own hypothesis, saying our math is wrong."

But no one is still listening to me but Jane, who offers me a shrug, as if to say, *What can we do? We're outvoted.* Everyone else is commenting on the design of the new screen, brainstorming ideas for how to integrate George's animated hearts. I guess we're moving ahead to states with a "second chance" screen in place.

CHAPTER 28

Dad always likes to say that *hindsight is 20/20*.

Izzy used to make fun of him because he would say it so much when we were little, any time one of us would talk about something that upset us, or that we wished we'd done differently. *Hindsight is 20/20*, Dad said with a shrug. He still says it from time to time.

Dad, Izzy would always say, *if you pay attention, you know things way before hindsight.*

But for people like Dad, and me, people who don't always pay attention, or even understand how to pay attention, I guess Dad's expression makes a lot of sense.

It's snowing when George and I walk out to the parking lot after coding club the first Friday in February. We finished adding the second chance screen to the app earlier this week. George animated it with two upside-down hearts holding hands, which I do think looks cute despite my reservations about the change. And we now have the latest beta version running on 187 students' phones. So far, according to Jane, Alyssa is the first and only one to make a match with the second chance screen. And now she's going to the Valentine's Day dance with Anderson Adams, whom she matches at only ninety-one percent but whom she describes, when Jane asks her, as *so, so nice*.

All in all, I'm feeling pretty good about things as we walk out of the meeting. States is next week, but we're close to ready other than working out the last-minute presentation and technical details, and I don't think the second chance screen data will mess us up too much if only one person has used it.

The snow is already dusting the parking lot, making the world around us white and blinding. Flakes swirl in the air, hit our faces as we walk toward my car. George sticks out his tongue to catch one, and I laugh and remind him about what we learned in chemistry last year about acid snow.

"Oh, shoot," George suddenly says, and I think he's responding to my comment about the snow until he continues, adding, "I forgot my PE clothes in my PE locker. I want to wash them over the weekend. Do you mind if I go over there really quick?"

I nod. I don't mind. There's actually something weirdly nice about walking through the parking lot with George, in the snow. We turn and walk toward the side entrance of the school, to the gym, heading around the north side of the parking lot. The flakes start to fall harder, swirling in front of our eyes.

"Here." George takes his hat out of his pocket and puts it on my head. "It's my fault you're still out in this. The least I can do is keep you warm."

He tugs the hat down a little too far, so it covers my ears but then it almost covers my eyes, too, and between that and the swirl of snow, everything around me is obscure, light and ethereal and unreal. So when I first see them there together, back up against the brick wall by the gym, I blink, sure I'm seeing things wrong.

And then the second thing I think is, *Hindsight is 20/20.*

"Hey…is that Sam and Jane?" George says, catching sight of them through the blur of snowflakes about ten seconds after I do.

I don't answer him, because I'm already running toward them, my feet slipping through the slush, sliding. Neither Jane nor Sam notices me coming, because their faces are too close together, their eyes only on each other. Their lips are connected in a long drawn-out kiss.

"What are you doing?" I say to them when I'm close enough. I'm breathless, and a little numb with shock. They'd walked out of coding club together. Jane was going to drive Sam home, but why are they here—*kissing*? What are they doing? Sam is dating Laura and Jane hates love. I half expect them to both burst out laughing and explain their joke to me. Because it must be a joke. Nothing else makes sense.

Neither of them say anything for a minute—they're weirdly frozen there, holding on to each other. But neither one of them is laughing, either. Jane pulls away first, looks at Sam, horrified. Then turns to me. "Emma…it's not what it looks like."

Sam looks at her, shakes his head, takes her hand and then looks at me. "I'm sorry, E. It is exactly what it looks like."

"What does it look like?" I'm still confused.

George has caught up by now, and waves. "Hey, guys…" He sounds out of breath.

"I like her," Sam says to me, ignoring George.

She takes his hand. "And I like him," Jane says, biting her lip a little, refusing to meet my eyes, so it suddenly feels like she lied to me about everything.

"E…" Sam says gently.

"Don't call me E," I spit at him. "You're cheating on Laura. And you…" I turn to Jane. "You're ruining everything we worked so hard for with our app. And what about all those things you said about not wanting a match, not having time for a boyfriend. *Love is the worst.*"

"E," Sam says again. I glare at him. "I mean…Emma. Look, I tried the second chance match, and I still don't match Janie. We have nothing in common other than our hair color and we took that out of the algorithm months ago. We're never going to match in our app. But that doesn't change the way I feel about her." He looks at her, smiles at her. She turns and smiles back at him.

States is next week and they're ruining everything we've worked for. If they don't believe in our app, in the code we wrote for love, then who will?

But worse is the feeling of betrayal. It washes over me, thick and blinding, and then settles as a wave of nausea pushes up my stomach to my throat. Sam, who didn't want to kiss me last fall, because he said he matched with Laura in the app. But I guess the truth really was, he just never *liked* me. And Jane. *Jane.* She slept over at my house multiple times, and I thought she was actually my friend. She told me she *didn't want a match*. She was lying to me, too. I feel bile rushing up my throat, and it's hard to breathe.

"Emma." Jane steps forward and reaches for my arm. I pull back roughly and her lab coat slips up. For a second I catch a glimpse of her scars, and I remember how she showed me once, who she really was. How she protects herself. Now her face falls, like I've wounded her. "Come on," Jane says. "I know you want our app to win, but what about how we feel? What about our friendship?"

I think about what Izzy said before she left: *If you feel something...just let yourself feel.*

But all I *feel* now is anger. And without another word to either of them, I turn and storm off toward my car.

"Emma!" George is calling my name and running after me when I glance back. He's holding his hands out trying not to slip. He's forgotten all about his PE clothes now. But I'm not going to remind him. There's no way I'm turning back in the direction of the gym, where I assume Jane and Sam are still kissing.

George catches up to me right when I reach my car. I get in and start the engine, and he lets himself in the passenger side. "Emma, stop." He puts his hand on my arm. "Just calm down a minute before you drive, okay? The roads might be slippery."

He's right, and besides, I'm also freezing. I turn up the heat, warm my hands in front of the vents. George does the same on his side of the car. Finally, when I'm warmer and can breathe a little bit again, I drive out of the parking lot.

The snow is starting to stick on Highbury Pike, and it really does take all my focus to drive. And to breathe. I inhale and exhale, in and out. Foot on the accelerator; foot on the brake. I creep down Highbury Pike at twenty-five miles an hour, until finally we make it to George's driveway and I release my tight grip from the steering wheel and exhale.

"Why don't you come in for a little bit? Drive home later," George says kindly. "The snow's supposed to stop soon, and it's not cold enough out to stick for very long."

George is right, the weather is forecasted to improve. And I don't really feel like going to my big empty house all alone right now, or enduring the scary last mile of driving. But I hesitate, not sure I'm up for conversation, either, not even with George.

"Come on," George prods. "I'll make you some hot chocolate. We have marshmallows."

"I mean, if there's marshmallows..." I smile a little, in spite of all the anger I still feel swelling in my chest for Jane and Sam.

"And besides." George turns, and his eyes glimmer a little so I know he's teasing me now. "You owe me a rematch in Ping-Pong."

★★★

Ping-Pong is all about the ball. Never taking my eye off it. Back and forth and back and forth, and I don't lose sight of it. There's no hindsight in Ping-Pong.

I beat George again—this time by two points instead of one. I raise my paddle in victory, feeling sweat pool under my sweater.

George laughs and collapses in a bean bag, and I put my paddle down and collapse on one next to him. We both need to catch our breaths. Our hot chocolate has cooled on the end table while we were playing, and I pick mine up and take a little sip.

"It's not that bad," George says after a few minutes. "Is it?"

"What? Your hot chocolate? Or the fact that I beat you at Ping-Pong every time?"

He smiles and shakes his head. "My hot chocolate is delicious, and maybe I let you win." I burst out laughing, and so does he for a minute, but then his face turns more serious. "So Sam and Jane like each other," he says, his voice a little softer. "So what?"

"So, Sam matches Laura…and Jane didn't even try to make a match. She told me she didn't want to date anyone. She never liked my app idea, and now she's ruining the whole thing. Maybe that was her plan the whole time?" I'm breathing hard, and my words tumble out fast and angry, and I know they're ridiculous, that I don't really mean them, even as I say them. Jane wants to win next week. Jane said she believes we can win. But she also said she didn't want a match or a boyfriend.

George gives me a look like he thinks I sound crazy. "Emma." He shakes his head. "Jane wouldn't do that."

I bite my lip. It feels impossible to even talk rationally about Jane or Sam right now without this blinding, furious heat rising up inside of me. "Who's going to believe in The Code for Love if even the club members don't?" I say.

George nods, like he gets what I'm saying now. "We made a good app. And we should be proud of the coding we did. I'm proud of it. I think we have a real chance of winning the state competition. And I know Jane and Sam believe that, too. But come on, Emma, you don't really believe that math should tell you who to love, do you?"

I think of what Izzy said: *Math is one thing. Love is another.* But Izzy doesn't understand the algorithm the way I do, the way George does. "I do believe that," I say. "Why don't you, George?"

He shakes his head. "What if you just feel something for someone? What if there's no mathematical sequence to it at all, but you *feel* something for her deep in your gut, that's different than the way you've ever felt about anyone else?" He stares at me, his eyes so intensely focused on my face that my cheeks turn hot, and I have to look away. I look down at my sneakers.

"So what are you saying, George? Sam is with Jane because…of a feeling in his stomach?" I tilt my head back up to look at him, and he's still staring at me, his green eyes wide and a little glassy.

He shrugs, opens his mouth, then closes it, like he's not sure he should say more. "I don't know," he finally says. "I don't know what Sam and Jane feel. But what about you, Emma? Haven't you ever felt something that can't be quantified?" he asks softly.

He meets my eyes again, and holds on to them, like he's challenging me to say more, to say something else. Maybe he wants me to tell him that I don't think he and Hannah are a good match, or that I agree with him that it's possible math can't always figure out love, no matter how perfect our code is. Or maybe he wants me to say that sometimes I feel something unexplainable deep in my gut when I'm around him. But so what? Even if I do, it doesn't mean anything.

Instead, I say, "Math matched eighty-seven happy couples for the dance next weekend. And then, there's Sam and Jane."

"Sam's supposed to take Laura to the dance," George says quietly. Then he adds, "And taking someone to a dance doesn't mean you love her. Doesn't mean she's the one you're supposed to *be* with." His eyes refuse to let go of mine, and I feel my cheeks growing hot again. It's unnerving.

Finally, I look away first. I glance toward the window, and the sky is turning purple and blue with the oncoming night. "I think the snow stopped," I say. "I should get home."

CHAPTER 29

I ignore Sam at lunch on Monday, choosing to sit at a table across the room, by myself, instead. I'm far enough away that I can't tell if he's still sitting with Laura today, or not. I crane my neck to try and see, wondering if Laura knows about Sam and Jane, if Sam's betrayal runs deeper than just lying to me. Poor Laura. I was actually starting to like her.

Mara spots me, a minute or two after I sit down by myself. "Emma!" she calls, motioning me to her table. "Come sit with us."

I don't really want to sit with a group of girls I don't know. But Mara's still motioning and calling for me, like she thinks I didn't notice her the first time, and I'm pretty sure she won't stop until I go over there. So I stand and walk to her table, which is her and five other girls who I think are either on the track or volleyball teams. I think we've matched all of them in the app.

"Guys, you all know Emma, right?" Mara says. I offer an awkward wave and they all stare back at me, unsure. "She made the Love Code app."

"The Code for Love," I correct, but none of them notice because they're all talking at once and gushing about how much they *love* the app, and by extension it kind of feels like they like me, too. I think about how Izzy says I've changed, and it occurs to me for the first time that maybe she's right. No one knew who I was last year, much less wanted me to sit at their lunch table or talk to me.

Mara moves over, pats the bench next to her and I sit down. I start eating my sandwich, listening as they all talk about their dates for the dance and how cool they think my app is. Conversation turns into what they're all wearing to the dance, and then one girl, Olivia (I think?), turns to me and says brightly, "Who are you going with, Emma?"

"Oh," I say, putting my sandwich down. "I'm not… The coding club is planning on going together, as a group." But I remember this was Jane's idea, and that I'm mad at Jane now, too. So maybe we won't still go as a group. "Or," I add, "I might not even go at all."

"You didn't do your own match?" another red-haired girl whose name I can't remember asks, looking incredulous. I shake my head. "Why not?"

"I don't want a match," I say.

"But aren't you just a little bit curious who you're supposed to be with?" Olivia asks now, pressing me.

I think of what George said, that taking someone to a dance doesn't mean *you're supposed to be with her.* Olivia and Mara and the rest of these girls clearly feel differently.

"Emma doesn't have time to date," Mara interjects, saving me from explaining more. "She's going to be our class valedictorian." It hasn't officially been declared yet, but I'm also pretty sure it's going to be me, as I currently have an A in Spanish while George has an A-.

I shoot Mara a grateful smile. "Exactly," I finally say. "And besides, I'm too busy working on code so you can all have dates."

And it turns out that was the right thing to say for once, because they all laugh like they think I'm funny, and maybe, they even like me.

Coding club planned to meet Tuesday, Wednesday and Thursday this week after school to practice our presentations and make finishing touches to all our data charts, tracking data up until the very last minute. On Friday, we'll all take a bus to Newark, missing the day of school to compete in the state tournament.

I know I won't be able to avoid Jane and Sam, and skipping it isn't an option after school on Tuesday, either. There's still work to be done before the competition, and I'll already have to leave early, by four, to get to the Villages to get my volunteer hour in. I have to go to the meeting.

When I walk in, Jane and Sam each look up from opposite

sides of the room and wave at me, but I refuse to acknowledge them. Instead of sitting next to Jane at the meeting, as I've been doing now for months, I walk to the other side of the room and pull up a chair next to Hannah. Ms. Taylor takes the whole thing in and frowns, but she bites her lip, not saying anything at all.

"Hey, Emma," Hannah says, her face curling up into a surprised smile. I haven't spent as much time with her since she started dating George, and the truth is, I'm not really sure what's going on with her at the moment or how she's feeling about everything. She looks kind of nervous—she has a strand of hair twisted around her finger, which she then untwists and settles against her shoulders.

"I thought you and I could work together today on writing up the mechanical for the judges," I say to her. She nods and smiles and stops playing with her hair. Part of our entry for states is writing out an explanation and justification of all our code. Really, Jane would be more suited to do this with me than Hannah, since she took the lead on coding the database, but I'll write up what I can and Jane can do the rest on her own tomorrow.

Out of the corner of my eye, I see Jane holding on to her laptop, walking over to where Sam is sitting. They both look at her screen, and start working together on what I assume is editing Jane's data chart. Robert is working alone in the corner on perfecting the trifold board. George has an environmental club meeting and will be here a little late.

The truth is, I don't really want Hannah to help me now. I definitely don't *need* her to help me. I can work quicker on my own. But I also want to make it look like I'm engaging her in conversation so I don't have to say anything to Jane or Sam. So when she first starts talking in hushed tones about George, I smile and nod, and murmur, "That's great." But then she just won't stop talking about George.

George is so sweet…

And did I tell you what George texted me last night?

And did I tell you what he said to me last week?

George, George, George, George, George…

I think of George, handing me a cup of hot chocolate overflowing with marshmallows. George saying to me, *What about you, Emma? Haven't you ever felt something that can't be quantified?*

"Hannah, stop!" I snap at her. My words fall out angry and loud, and weirdly feel out of my control. "George doesn't even really believe that math can predict love, okay?" I say. "And he's not talking about you like this. You're embarrassing yourself."

I'm not sure when he walks in exactly, but as soon as I'm done with my outburst, I look up, and there George is, standing in the doorway, frowning. He stares at me: hurt, or disappointed, or just angry. I don't want to look at him. *I can't look at him.* So I turn away, back to Hannah.

Her face is bright red, and she scrunches up her cheeks like she's trying not to cry. Everything I said to her rattles around in my brain and feels like a punch in my stomach, and then I want to cry, too. "Hannah," I say softly. "I didn't—"

"I don't know why you have to be so mean, Emma," she cuts me off. She stands up, grabs her backpack. "I'm going home. I have a lot of homework, and you don't need my help, anyway."

"Hannah," I protest. "Wait. I'm sorry. Come on. We're working on the mechanical together."

"No," she says. "*You're* working on the mechanical. You won't even let me touch it."

She has to walk past George to leave, and out of the corner of my eye I see him give her a hug, say something to her in a hushed tone. But I won't let myself look over there; I won't stare. I continue to work on the mechanical, concentrating very hard on the app screen on my phone, on the codebase running on my laptop, on typing out my justification for each line of code. If I concentrate on the code, I won't cry. *I can't cry.*

"Jeez, Emma." George sits down in the chair next to me, where Hannah just left. His voice is soft, but he's clearly annoyed. "What's wrong with you?"

"Nothing's wrong with me." I snap at him, too. Though it feels like everything is wrong with me. My stomach still hurts and I'm starting to get a headache, and I still can't look at George, see the way he's hating me right now, because then I really will cry. I shouldn't have snapped at Hannah like that, and I shouldn't be snapping at George now, but I can't stop myself, either. "We have work to do," I finally say. "And I'm trying to focus. Everyone just…needs to focus."

"You're supposed to be mentoring her," George says softly. "That's our job as presidents. If we don't help the underclassmen learn, what will the club be next year when we're gone?"

"It won't be our problem next year, will it?" I don't really feel this way, of course. I want the club to do well next year because we've made it good this year, but I bite my lip, not willing to agree with George out loud right now, even if he is right.

He stands, looks around the room. "We're supposed to be a team," he says, quietly enough at first so only I can hear him. Then he raises his voice, says it again: "We are supposed to be a team!"

Robert looks up from what he's doing, his focus on George. Sam and Jane glance at each other, then look back at what they were working on, like neither one of them wants to make eye contact with George.

Ms. Taylor pulls her glasses down the bridge of her nose, casts us all a worried look. "Maybe we all just need a little break," she says. "Let's go home, take a breath and we can finish what we need for the competition tomorrow."

But it feels impossible to take a breath, and I can't stop replaying what just happened in my head as I drive to the Villages. Even as I'm playing piano, I can't relax into the music the way I usually do, instead letting the memorized patterns fall from my fingers by rote, my mind still spinning. I keep hearing George's angry voice in my head: *Jeez, Emma. What's wrong with you?* And the more I hear it, over and over and over again, the more it makes me want to cry. I don't even *want* to be social like Izzy, and I don't *need* friends like she does. But *George.* George is different. I need George. He can't be mad at me.

"Emma!" A smiling Mrs. Bates walks up to me when I'm

finished playing and am gathering up my things. "Guess what? Good news! Jack is coming home from the hospital tooo-morrow." She touches my arm with her manicured red nails as she talks, drumming her fingers against my forearm, and I can feel her excitement in the jingle of her bracelets.

"I'm so happy he's doing better," I say, smiling back at her. I'm really not in any mood to chat today, but I am honestly happy for her that he's better, that he can leave the hospital. Dad was in the hospital for one night and I felt sick over it. Mr. Bates has been there for weeks at this point.

She keeps her hand on my arm. "How's your school project coming?" she asks kindly.

I shrug, unwilling to tell her that it's kind of a disaster, that Jane and I are no longer speaking to one another, and Sam and I aren't eating lunch together. I was mean to Hannah, and now even George is mad at me. The competition is only a few days away, and I feel nauseous even thinking about how we're all going to work together.

She searches my face with her eyes. "That bad, huh?" I haven't said anything out loud, so I guess my expression is that transparent. "There wasn't any room for it in your survey, so I didn't ever get to tell you how Jack and I fell in love, did I?" I shake my head. "You know I played piano once, but maybe you didn't know that I went to Julliard?"

"Julliard? No, I didn't know that." So Mrs. Bates didn't just *play piano once*, she must've been amazing at it.

She nods. "Jack was there, too, and the first three months we knew each other, we didn't even speak. We were in the same classes, and he was a little miffed that a woman was getting all the accolades." She chuckles a little, like she's caught up in the memory. "Then our teacher assigned us to do a duet together at the winter recital, and we still didn't speak. Not with words, anyway. We'd show up to practice together, sit down and get to work. But I'll tell you, Emma, I fell in love with him that first time we played that duet together. The passion that he put into his playing." She smiles and shakes her head a little, like she can still feel that *passion*, all these years later. "Well…I just knew he would have that same passion in the rest of his life."

"Common interest," I say. "That's what we ranked highest from the survey results."

"Yes, perhaps… But how to explain on your survey that I had classes with other men who played the piano…and none of them were Jack?"

"There are other variables, too," I say. I suppose she and Mr. Bates had other things in common, that there are other ways to quantify their connection.

"But passion," she says. "How do you count passion, Emma?"

I shake my head. I don't know the answer to that.

"Anyway." She waves her hand in the air and her bracelets jangle. "You looked upset so I thought you needed a pick-me-up. What I was trying to say was, thank you for coming to play for us every week. It means a lot to me, and it means a lot to Jack, too. His mind isn't what it used to be, but the piano still makes both of us remember our passion. Makes us remember what it was like to fall in love all over again."

Is passion quantifiable? Should I have figured out a way

to include that in my algorithm? Is my algorithm wrong? "I feel like I messed everything up," I say quietly. "Everyone hates me right now."

She grabs me and holds on to me tightly in a hug. "Chin up, Emma. Chin up," she says. "You're a beautiful, smart, kind and talented girl. How could anyone possibly hate you?"

CHAPTER 30

As we're all boarding the bus to Newark a few days later, I can still hear Mrs. Bates's wobbly voice in my head reassuring me that no one could possibly hate me. Maybe I can just get on the bus, and put my *chin up* like Mrs. Bates says. I'm the co-president of the club. I can make a speech, and then we can all calm down and figure out a way to work together at the competition.

But what to say exactly…? I'm still mad that Jane and Sam don't believe in our project and went behind my back. Could I ignore that for the day and give the team some kind of pep talk? I try to work out some words as I walk on the bus, staring at my feet. *Chin up*, I hear Mrs. Bates say again. And I look up just in time to see Jane, who is carrying our trifold, bump it into a seat as she walks down the aisle of the bus.

"Careful," I say to her. My reaction is instinct—I'm trying to warn her, not reprimand her.

But she turns and glares at me, and I press my lips tightly together and I wish I'd just kept looking down and hadn't said anything at all. Sam stands in front of her, and he doesn't even turn around and meet my eyes when I speak.

I sigh and take a seat by myself near the front. I was wrong. I have no words to fix any of this, and I'd really like to keep my chin down. I go to put on my headphones as the bus gets ready to pull out of the parking lot, and then I realize I have done something insanely stupid: I'm supposed to be in charge of bringing the mechanical, and I don't have it with me. It's not on the seat next to me, not in my backpack. I took it home to work on it last night, but I'm sure I brought it with me this morning. *Didn't I?*

"Ms. Taylor!" I stand up quickly and shout her name, telling her I don't have it.

She checks her watch, and looks back at me, her eyes wide with worry. "Emma, we don't have time to wait for you to go and search for it."

"It's back in the classroom." George suddenly stands up, two rows behind me. "I saw it there but thought you were grabbing it on the way out, Emma. I'll run and go get it. Five minutes, Ms. Taylor." He jogs off the bus before I can think to say I'll do it. Hannah frowns at me from across the aisle and back two rows. Her eyes are blue-green daggers, and I sink lower in my seat, my heart pounding in my throat, worrying that it's not back in the classroom at all but still in my bedroom.

George is back a few minutes later, breathless, sweating. He stops at my seat, hands me the binder with the mechanical. I exhale with relief. He pauses for another few seconds to catch his breath and I think he might sit down here with me, too. I wish he would, because really, we should talk and make sure everything is prepared for our oral presentation. But he doesn't. He walks back a few rows to sit with Hannah.

"All right," Ms. Taylor says, clearing her throat. "Now, do we have everything?"

She calls off our checklist, and we respond one by one. Then I put my headphones on and try to concentrate on nothing but Beethoven for the seventy-three-minute ride to Newark. But even with the headphones on, it's impossible to relax. It feels like everything is about to implode, and it makes my stomach ache. I wish George were sitting here next to me, because I know he would say something to calm me down. I think about the way he reminded me to breathe when Dad was in the hospital, and I cast a glance back toward where he's sitting now. But he and Hannah are deep in conversation, and neither one of them seem to notice that I'm even here, on the bus, just a few rows in front of them.

There is a component to the all-state competition that is not a part of the regional tournament called the teamwork challenge. The whole team has to go into a room, and three judges do something to mess with our codebase, then give us thirty minutes to figure out a way to fix it and get our code running again. It counts as one-fifth of the final score, and is supposed to emphasize the *club* part of coding club, more than the coding part. Last year, we excelled at this challenge, but this year we have it at 9:25 a.m., first on our schedule for the tournament. We haven't uttered a single word to one another since we've gotten off the bus and gathered in the cafeteria at the host school.

As we're walking toward the judging room, Ms. Taylor gives us all a warning look, and tells us quietly to "Get it together." She stares right at me as she says it, like she thinks this is all my fault. Which really isn't completely fair, because it feels like Jane and Sam started this. Except her withering look reminds me of how I yelled at Hannah the other day and I feel bad all over again. I consider grabbing Hannah and apologizing quickly before we walk in the room, but she's walking ten paces ahead of me, holding on to George's arm, and even if I catch up to them, I'll still be annoyed that she and George are walking in as a team rather than me and him, as co-presidents.

But we all walk into the judging room, and then paste eager looks on our faces. And we do manage to *get it together.* George smiles at the judges and talks up how great our app is. And Sam spots the problem with the codebase as soon as the judges hand it over to us. Jane and I fix it within ten minutes. The judges check our work and tell us we did a great job.

"Wow," George says to Sam as we finish. "That was impressive."

"Photographic memory." Sam shrugs, like it's no big deal how fast he spotted the problem. But it kind of is. Finding the issue is always the hardest part in this challenge.

As we all leave the room we should be on this high because we totally just kicked ass in that challenge, finishing in seventeen minutes instead of thirty, but instead, as soon as we walk back toward the cafeteria, we stop talking again. Jane and Sam walk together in front of the rest of us, and then Hannah and George walk ahead of me, ignoring me, and only Robert hangs back, walking beside me.

"So far so good, right?" he asks me.

"Yeah," I say, my eyes focusing on Jane and Sam ahead, noticing that they are now holding hands. It feels like they're doing it just to annoy me.

"Then why does everyone look so upset?" Robert asks.

"I'm not upset," I say quickly. "Are you upset?" He shakes his head. "Great," I say. "Then we're all happy. We're all really happy."

Somehow we push through and keep it together all day, doing what we need to do in the moment, ignoring each other in the in-between times. Our last event of the tournament is the oral presentation George and I have to make for the judges. We sit on the floor in the hallway outside the presentation room, just the two of us, waiting for them to call us in. George hasn't said a word to me, and instead is reviewing his notes. But I remember my speech word for word from the regional competition, and I put my notecards down.

"Are you going to stay mad at me forever?" I ask him.

George puts his notecards in his lap, turns to me. "Who says I'm mad at you?"

"You're sure acting like you're mad at me."

He closes his eyes for a second, leans his head back against the wall, then opens them again. "Let's just get through this, okay? And then maybe we can talk tonight."

Before I can say anything else, the judges call us in. George jumps up, puts a huge smile on his face, and I stand and follow him inside the room.

George's presentation is first, and I see why he was reviewing his notecards. He's changed his speech from the regional tournament, putting a personal spin on why our matching app has been so successful at school, including how it has matched him to Hannah. How it's the first time he's *ever had a girlfriend*, and how wonderful it is to connect with a person *at your school who you really, truly match with mathematically*. For some reason, I think about what Mrs. Bates said about how she fell in love with her husband when she played piano with him at Julliard. How his music was life and passion. Is that how George feels about Hannah, too? It sure sounds like it now.

Last week when we were playing Ping-Pong, he said he didn't really believe that math can predict love, but clearly, he's changed his mind since then. Because now he's telling the judges all about how math did predict love, and how it's played out spectacularly in his own life. The judges smile at him, and I have to work really hard not to frown.

When he's finished talking, and it's my turn, I stumble for a second because it's hard to breathe, hard to remember what I'm supposed to say, and what I know. My mind is swimming in everything George just said—*drowning*. But George stares at me, gives me a nod of encouragement, and then I take a deep breath and recite the words I already know by heart, talking about how we came up with the algorithm, how we coded it. How our app is both social and quantifiable.

When we're finished, we walk out together, back toward the auditorium, where the rest of the team will be waiting, as they're supposed to announce the winners in there in twenty minutes.

George drops the smile from his face almost immediately. He runs his hand through his hair, messing it up, and he just looks like…George again. "So, will you come over tonight and we can talk?" He speaks quietly now, with none of the eagerness or confidence he just displayed for the judges.

"It's Friday night," I say quickly. "I'm sure you have plans with your *girlfriend*." It's the way he referred to Hannah repeatedly in his speech to the judges, and it grated on me, each time. I know they are dating, of course, but I've never heard George call her that before, and it feels so weird, so unlike George, that it bothers me.

"I'm not doing anything with Hannah," George says. "And we really should talk, Emma."

"I guess if we win…we will have to make plans for nationals…" I'm thinking out loud. The national competition is in Michigan in June, and it's not something we've ever been to before. In my previous years of high school, coding club only made it this far. Only first place gets to go on to nationals, and the closest we came was last year, coming in third. But in spite of the fact we all currently hate each other, our day has gone pretty well. I really believe we have a chance to come in first this year.

"Not about nationals," George is saying now. But we've

reached the auditorium, and Ms. Taylor is waving at us from near the front. We reach her before George and I can finish our conversation.

"Well," she says. "How did the oral presentation go?"

"Good," George says. "I think the judges liked us."

"Yeah," I say. "George really wowed them when he talked about his *girlfriend*." I realize as the words come out of my mouth that Hannah is sitting right in front of me. Her cheeks turn as red as her hair, and I feel bad about my mocking tone. What did George say the other day? I'm supposed to be mentoring her? I clear my throat. "I mean…George just did a really good job at putting a personal spin on why our project is so special."

Ms. Taylor smiles and George looks away, refusing to meet my eyes now. I go and take the last seat at the end of the row, right next to Ms. Taylor, and George goes and sits on the other side of her with Hannah and Robert. Jane and Sam are in the row behind us.

"Whatever happens," Ms. Taylor leans over and says to me. "You should be really proud, Emma."

"I'll be proud if we win," I say.

"You should be proud no matter what. You did this. You had this idea, and you made everyone else believe. No matter what happens with this competition, or where you end up going to college, you're going to be very successful in life. I just know it."

I feel tears stinging in my eyes, and it's partly her nice words but mostly that I feel I haven't really earned any of them, and the club is a mess right now.

The head judge walks up on the stage, ready to announce the awards, and I blink back my tears and turn my attention to him. Ms. Taylor pats my hand, excited. We have to wait a few agonizing minutes as he talks about all the amazing effort everyone put into their code and *blah, blah, blah*. And then, finally, he gets to the awards.

I can't help myself—I glance down the row at George, and I'm surprised to see he's already looking at me. He gives me a little shrug, and a smile, and I wish I were sitting next to him because I know I'd feel better if I were, if somehow it felt like we were still in this together. *Co-presidents.*

"In third place," the judge says. "Elizabeth High with their project: Recoding Space." An all-boy team jumps up, and goes up to the stage to claim their trophy.

"In second place," he says. "Highbury High with their project: The Code for Love."

"That's us," Ms. Taylor says, clapping her hands together. And it doesn't quite sink in that it's us until she says it. *Second place.* We haven't won. "Go on." Ms. Taylor gives me a gentle push on my shoulder. "Emma, go up with the others and accept your trophy." It's not until she says that, that I realize they've all already stood, that they're walking up toward the stage without me, and I have no choice but to stand and go up there with them.

My head is buzzing and the lights on the stage are too bright, and I feel weirdly like I'm walking through fog as I take my trophy and shake the judges' hands and go take my place up onstage with the rest of my team. I stand next to

Robert, who looks happy, and then look down at my sneakers, unwilling to meet George's disappointed eyes.

"And first place," the judge says. "New Haddenfield High with their project: Recode and Recycle." The word *recycle* bounces around in my head, and I think about George's animated Karma Can.

"Recycling," Jane says pointedly to me as she walks by me to get off the stage when the ceremony is over, and she might as well be saying that she *hates* me. That she's sorry she was ever friends with me. That I've made a mess of everything. That we won't be going to nationals, and it truly is all my fault.

CHAPTER 31

Ms. Taylor tries to give us a pep talk when we board the bus, saying how we should all be so proud and second place in the entire state of New Jersey, out of forty-seven teams, is nothing to sneeze at. And she points out the fact that if we had gone with the recycling app we may have scored even lower, as we definitely scored points for originality with The Code for Love. But no one says anything in response, and she gives up and sits down in the front as the bus driver pulls out of the parking lot. I put my headphones back on, and the ride down I-95 feels interminable. Seventy-three minutes might as well be seventy-three days.

I'm sitting near the front, so I'm the first one off, and I don't even say bye to Ms. Taylor before walking briskly through the parking lot to my car. "Emma, wait!" George calls after me, and it's only then that I remember I'm supposed to drive him home. I really, really don't feel like talking to him right now. Or hearing his blame, his *I told you so*. I don't care what Ms. Taylor said about recycling; this is my fault. But I'm not going to just leave him stranded in the school parking lot, either.

I sigh and get in the car and unlock the doors. He gets in the passenger seat. "Emma—" he says.

"I know," I cut him off. "And I don't want to hear it, all right? Let's just not say anything right now." I drive out of the parking lot and turn onto Highbury Pike, hoping traffic is light and I can get to George's house to drop him off fast. If I move the wrong way I feel like I might just spontaneously erupt into tears, and I don't want to do that in front of George.

"What do you think I'm going to say that you don't want to hear?" George says softly. I glance at him out of the corner of my eye and he's frowning.

"You know…*recycling*." I repeat the word the way it sounded in Jane's voice, like it's something sacred.

"I wasn't going to say anything about recycling. And besides, Ms. Taylor's right. Your idea really was more original." George shrugs, and I'm surprised he's not mad, like Jane. "What I was going to say was, that I guess coding club is over for us. Forever. And that now we can forget all about The Code for Love."

It's funny the way this project consumed us all year, and now, just like that, it's over. We'll never be in coding club again. There are no years left, no more projects to work on together. "Yeah," I say. It all hits me hard, and I feel even more like I'm about to cry. I bite my lip. "But I guess we don't have to talk about nationals at all. You and Hannah can go out tonight."

"I told you," George says, an edge to his voice like he's annoyed with me. "Hannah and I don't have plans tonight."

"Well, you should make some plans," I say as I finally pull into his driveway. "She's your girlfriend, isn't she? At least our app wasn't a total loss."

"Emma." He says my name again, softer this time. I can feel his eyes on me but I don't turn, just look straight ahead and hope he'll get out of the car quickly before I can't hold back my tears any longer. "Why do you have to be so...?"

"What?" I finally do turn, and instead of the anger in his eyes that I'm expecting, I see something else. There's an intensity in the way he's looking at me that makes it hard to breathe. And I can't even remember what I was about to say or how I was just feeling. We stare at each other for a few minutes, until finally I say, "You're right. Coding club is over now. Forever. What else could we possibly have to talk about?" It's the wrong thing to say, and I know that as soon as the words fall out of my mouth.

Because George doesn't say another word. He gets out of the car and slams the door too hard behind him.

I watch him walk toward his front door. My stomach aches, and I think about getting out of the car, going after him. But I'm not sure what I would say next. And then he's inside his house, and what else is there for me to do but go home?

I'm shocked to see Dad's car in the garage when I get to my house. It's only a little before six, and he never comes home this early. I'm worried that it's his heart again, and I run into the house.

"What's wrong?" I ask him when I find him sitting at the kitchen table. "Is your heart okay?"

He shakes his head. "Nothing's wrong, Em." I notice he's dressed in his weekend attire, jeans and a plaid shirt, and he's drinking a cup of herbal tea. He looks perfectly normal, relaxed even.

"But you're home," I blurt out, confused.

He laughs. "I came home early because I thought I could take you to dinner to celebrate your competition. We can bring the rest of your coding friends if you want, too? Anywhere you want," Dad says. "My treat."

I drop my backpack on the floor, sit down next to him and lay my head down on the cool wood of the kitchen table. I'm so relieved that Dad's heart is fine, but my own heart feels like it's breaking in my chest. And though I know that is physically impossible, scientifically inaccurate, I feel an overwhelming crushing heaviness. It's hard to breathe. The tears I held back in the car with George are running down my face. "We didn't win," I say, pressing my lips against the cool wood, but I don't think that's why I'm crying. What George said in the car hits me again: it's all over, for good. The entire club hates me. "And I have no friends," I say to Dad. My voice breaks on the word *friends*.

"Oh, honey." Dad reaches his hand over and rubs my back, the way he used to do when I was little. He hasn't done it in so long that I suddenly remember what it was like to be six years old again, to have him and Izzy here, hovering and protecting me and helping me. And look what I've done, all on my own this year. I've ruined everything. "Do you want to tell me what happened?" Dad asks gently. "Did you guys mess up your presentation?"

I bite my lip, because there is so much to say. I don't know how to be social. I don't know how to have friends. Izzy was right. I was crazy to tell people who to date, and Jane and George were right, too. People care more about recycling. "We didn't mess up," I finally say. "We came in second. We just weren't good enough. My idea just wasn't good enough."

"Second!" Dad exclaims in a way that makes me wish I hadn't told him. "That's great, Em! Why don't we still go to dinner to celebrate?" Dad's voice takes on a hopeful lilt. "Your choice."

"Do you mind if we do it another time?" I feel bad, knowing he came home early for once, for me. But I don't have the energy to go sit in a restaurant and talk right now, even if it is just with Dad. "It's been a long day, and I'm exhausted, and I kind of just want to have a bowl of cereal and get into bed and wallow."

Dad stands up, goes to the cabinet and pulls out a bowl. Then he heads to the pantry. "Cinnamon Toast Crunch or my very heart-healthy bran?" he asks. "Never mind, silly question." He pulls the Cinnamon Toast Crunch out and pours a huge bowl, fills it with milk and brings it over to me with a spoon.

I move the cereal around with my spoon, not hungry at all, but Dad is staring at me, and I take a few small bites just to mollify him.

"You know," Dad says. "Whatever happened with your friends, I'm sure it's not as bad you think. And you're almost done with high school. Next year you'll be off at college, in the big leagues, Em." I roll my eyes. Dad and his baseball metaphors. "Everything will be better for you there," he adds.

He says it with such confidence that I almost believe him that college will be something else, something amazing, a place where I can be a math nerd and where my terrible social skills won't be a problem at all. Sitting here now, feeling completely broken, it's hard to even fathom that there's any such place that exists, much less how far away I might have to travel from Dad to find it. "I don't want to leave you alone next year," I finally say in response.

"I'm gonna miss you, too, kiddo." Dad reaches across the table and rubs my back again. "But I'm going to be just fine here alone. And you're finally going to have a place to soar. I'm so excited for you, honey. I really can't wait to watch you fly."

But what if I don't want to fly? What if I'm not ready? If I can't even keep things together here in Highbury, with coding club, how am I ever going to keep it together at college?

CHAPTER 32

Sometimes I dream in code.

When I work on it a lot for a project, or right before bed, my subconscious is still there, filled with lines of code, and my dreams are laced with numbers and sequences. I often wake up with the new ability to solve a problem that was bothering me in the code the night before, my mind having worked it out somehow while I slept.

But the night after states, all the code I dream of makes me sad, and I keep waking up all night, restless and bothered, hour after hour. There are no more problems to solve, no solutions. It doesn't matter now what the app does, or how well it works, or if there are bugs, or if the code is flawless. The competition is over. We've lost.

I finally get out of bed around noon the next morning, feeling anxious and still exhausted. I go get my calculus homework, hoping it'll make me feel better. Numbers always soothe and calm me, and if I can get my mind off the stupid code, I can move on, figure out a new problem. But I can't concentrate on these numbers, either. Every time I try to focus and work out an equation, I keep seeing the look on Sam's face when I yelled at him, like he was wounded. And the sound of Jane's voice as she said *recycling*. And Hannah asking me why I had to be so mean. And *George*, and that way he was looking at me in the car yesterday, the way he slammed the door, and couldn't get away from me fast enough. My eyes start to prick with tears again. I put my calculus book down.

If math won't help, maybe piano will? I walk over to my keyboard, and run my fingers across the keys, playing my way through the minor triads, patterned and dark, fitting for my mood. But my hands are shaking, my heart beating way too fast in my chest.

Everything is ruined, everything is broken, and even numbers and piano can't soothe me.

My phone chimes with a FaceTime from Izzy, and I hesitate before I answer, not ready to face her. But I suppose I shouldn't be surprised, either. It's after three now; I haven't gone downstairs all day. Dad must've put her up to this.

I reluctantly accept her call. "Hey, Iz."

"What's going on with your hair?" she says right away. I reach my hand up, pull my hair into an awkward ponytail in my fist. "Are you still in bed?"

I ignore her questions. "What's going on? How are you?"

"What's going on with you?" she says. "I called to see how your app competition was yesterday."

"We came in second," I say. "So we don't get to move on to nationals."

She shrugs. "Bummer, Em. But second is good! And you still have the dance tonight. Are you excited?"

I forgot I'd told her a few weeks ago that coding club was all going as a group. I haven't talked to her in over a week, so I haven't updated her on the fact that the whole club hates me now. "I'm not going," I say.

"What?" she squeals. "Why not?"

I reluctantly tell her what's happened, starting with how I freaked out when I saw Jane and Sam kissing and ending with how we lost yesterday and George stormed out of my car. "This is all your fault, you know," I say. My voice shakes by the time I get to this part, and I feel so angry with her I can't control my tone. Or maybe, it's that I'm angry with myself, for listening to her.

"Me?" She widens her eyes, confused.

"You were the one who told me *to code a boyfriend* before you left for school. You gave me the idea for this whole thing. You told me to be more social this year without you."

She frowns and rubs her forehead. "Oh, Em," she says. "That's not what I meant at all."

"Great. So, now I'm back where I started," I tell her. "No friends." Actually, it feels much worse than where I started, because now that I've had friends, it feels harder *not* to have them again. I have this dull ache of loneliness in my chest.

I've always been fine keeping to myself, being alone, and now I'm not so sure. I feel weirdly empty.

Izzy shakes her head. "So…you were a little mean. Go apologize. That's what friends do. Sometimes they fight, but then they make up. You can fix this, Em."

"*Me?* But what about Jane and Sam?"

"You're mad at them…because they like each other?" Izzy frowns.

"They're not supposed to like each other, mathematically. It's like they were sabotaging everything we worked for with our app."

"But your competition is over now, right?" Izzy asks. I nod. "So who cares what the app says? Jeez, Em, go take a shower, get a dress from my closet and go to that dance and apologize to your friends."

She makes it sound so easy, like I can fix everything. But what she said is at least partly right. *The competition is over.* We lost. And it's almost the end of my senior year. Coding club is done for me, forever. That's what George was trying to say to me yesterday in the car, isn't it?

Numbers are still better than people. Some people. But not Izzy, never Izzy. And not Jane. Or Sam. Or Hannah. Or George. Definitely not George.

"I don't know, Iz," I finally say. "What if they won't forgive me? Especially George. He looked really mad when he got out of the car yesterday."

"Em." Izzy sighs so loud it's almost like I'm hearing her from 2,764 miles away, her frustration bouncing across all those miles and not just coming through the speaker in my phone. "George will forgive you."

I remember what she'd said about George over Christmas break. That she'd based her assumption on this ridiculous idea that she could tell his feelings simply by the way he looked at me. "He's dating Hannah," I remind her.

"He might be dating Hannah, but only because of the silly app you guys made," Izzy says.

But I think about the way they were holding hands at the competition yesterday, the way George convinced the judges how great our app was by using her as an example, and I tell Izzy she's wrong. That with all the miles between us, she really doesn't see what's going on the way I do.

"Oh, Em," she says. "Just go take a shower and go to the dance."

After Izzy and I hang up, I do get out of bed and take a shower. I let the water run over my face, wishing for it to bring me clarity, help me decide what to do next. Izzy got me into this mess with her stupid offhand comment in the first place. But Izzy also understands people in a way I never will. Should I take her advice now? I don't really want to go to the dance, much less alone. And besides, what if I go and I try to apologize and no one accepts my apology? Then I'll feel even worse.

I get out of the shower, put my sweats on and go downstairs to make a mocha. Dad must've gone out or into work because the house is dark and quiet. I grab my calculus homework again, and sit with it at the table, determined to focus on the numbers. This has to make me feel better, help me think everything through. It always does.

But I'm just staring at the page, the numbers still swimming in front of my eyes. I keep thinking about Jane, about the way she showed me her armor and then let me in behind it, and how you don't just do that and then decide to hate a person forever—do you? Maybe Izzy's right. I have to go apologize to her. To all of them. At least I have to try.

It's five o'clock by now and the dance starts at six. I shut my calculus book and go upstairs to Izzy's room. I turn on the light, and walk inside the closet and thumb through her dresses.

She left the dress she wore to this very same Valentine's Day dance last year, or maybe it was the year before. It's red and strapless, and it hits midcalf, and it's not something I would ever normally wear.

But I try it on, and look at myself in the full-length mirror. I pull my hair back, and hold it on top of my head with my hand, and suddenly I can see the weird resemblance between Izzy and me that everyone would always say was there when we were younger but that I have never been able to see myself. Standing in Izzy's room, in Izzy's dress, I wonder if maybe I can channel Izzy's good ways with people. If I really can fix everything I've ruined.

CHAPTER 33

I sit in my car in the school parking lot for a good twenty minutes, trying to work up the courage to go inside to the dance by myself. I even text Izzy and tell her I'm wavering on going in. I don't expect her to text right back because I know she and John have Valentine's Day plans. But then she surprises me.

Em, get out of the car and go inside. Now!

I don't want to, I text back.

Get over yourself!!

My face turns hot, aware she is yelling at me across all these miles and over text no less. But then she adds, Love you, with three different-colored heart emojis. The last one is yellow, and that makes me think of George and his animated yellow hearts in our app, and I feel so sick to my stomach and sad and nervous that I know I couldn't stand it if he stays mad at me forever. I have to go find him and apologize. So I take a deep breath and force myself to get out of the car.

It's loud inside the school, and as I walk in, the hallway floor is thumping with bass. There are couples outside the gym, taking a breather, and when I get closer, I see Mara and Liz are among them, holding hands. They're standing next to Alyssa and Anderson, who are kissing. Looks like their *second chance* might have worked out? I'm so busy staring at Alyssa and Anderson that I almost walk right into Brianna and Ian walking out of the gym before I notice them. I guess they got back together? "Oh, hey, Emma," Brianna says. "Cute dress."

"It's…I…" I feel like I should explain that it's Izzy's dress, and that inside of it I feel nothing like myself. I'm impersonating Izzy, trying to channel Izzy's social skills. But instead I just say, "Um…thanks."

Mara has noticed me now, too. "Emma, you look great!" she exclaims, and she lets go of Liz's hand to walk over and give me a hug.

It's weird because, in my head, everyone in the entire school is mad at me. But clearly none of these people are mad. *Why would they be?* They're all happy because I helped them get matches for this dance. We might've lost the competition yesterday. But they're all standing here together now, because of me. Well, because of me and George, Jane, Sam, Hannah and Robert. And even though we didn't win, everything isn't all terrible, is it?

"Hey, have you guys seen the rest of coding club?" I ask.

"I just saw Jane in there." Liz points her thumb to the gym. "She's wearing black. A long-sleeved dress." Liz wrinkles up her nose a little, but picturing Jane in a long-sleeved ugly black dress makes me smile because it's so...Jane.

I thank Liz, and walk inside the gym. There are so many people, and everyone's moving, a swirl of colors: reds, and blues, and blacks. A lot of girls are wearing black. It's going to be impossible to spot Jane. I consider turning around, walking out. But then I think about what Izzy texted me, to *get over myself*. And I take a breath and push my way into the crowd, scanning for a familiar face.

I see Robert first. He's dancing with someone—Ben, I think. Yes, I get a better look. Definitely Ben. They're both laughing, and they're not mad at me, so I make my way toward them. As I get closer, I see the red of Hannah's hair. She's dancing with them also. And not too far from them, I spot the black lace sleeves of Jane's dress, and then there's Sam with her, dressed in a gray suit with a pink tie. None of them see me yet, and I could still turn around and run out, but my legs keep moving. I want to go to them, want to be with them. I force myself to breathe, to keep walking.

When I'm a few feet away, Jane looks up and sees me. She gets a weird look on her face and I can't tell if it's surprise, or annoyance, or anger. I stop walking, bite my lip, unsure exactly what to do next, or what to say. Finally, I raise my hand

and wave. And then she slowly raises her hand, waves back. So I keep walking until I'm right next to them.

"Hey guys," I say, shouting so they can hear me over the music.

Sam turns, and I expect him to smile at me the way he usually does, but instead he frowns, looks down at his feet for a second and then back up at me. "If you're here to yell at us for dancing—"

"I'm not," I cut him off. "I'm here to apologize. I'm really, really sorry. For everything. I shouldn't have gotten mad at you guys for liking each other. And I shouldn't have even come up with this stupid app in the first place. It's my fault we lost the competition, and I'm sorry for that, too." They stare at me for a minute, not saying anything. Tears prick my eyes as I think that Izzy really was wrong, and they're never going to forgive me.

But then Jane lets go of Sam's hand, and grabs mine instead. "I'm sorry, too," she says. "I should've been honest and just told you how I felt about Sam. I mean…I guess I was trying to on New Year's Eve but I was scared you'd get mad."

"I probably would've." I laugh. "And I'm sorry for that, too."

Sam grabs my other hand. "E, our app is freaking awesome. Don't be sorry for that. Look around us. Jane and I were just counting how many people are here together because of us."

I do what he says, look around, and there are a lot of familiar faces, people who came to me at lunch to ask for a download. "But the two of you prove the app doesn't really work," I say. "You *match* Laura."

Sam shakes his head. "Laura tried the second chance and she's here with Garrett. They're a much better match than we were."

Jane shrugs. "And if we had more time, maybe we just needed to perfect the algorithm? Or maybe I'm the one who's the anomaly? It wouldn't be the first time in my life."

As we've been talking, Hannah and Robert and Ben have danced in closer, and now Hannah is standing on the other side of me. "I'm really sorry," I say to her, too. "I shouldn't have snapped at you. I want to be your friend, and I'll teach you more about coding before I graduate—if you want."

She's still dancing, her red curls cascading down her back, away from her face, so all her features are visible. Her eyes are bright green and catch the revolving lights in the gym, and I'm staring at them, thinking I would deserve it if she hates me forever after the way I yelled at her about George. So it catches me off guard when she swoops in and gives me a hug instead. "I'm so glad we became friends this year, Emma. I'm going to get better at coding next year and make you proud."

"And I'm glad the app worked for you and that you and George are happy. I really am." Even as I'm saying it, I'm working extra hard to try and make myself sound convincing. The truth is, even now that coding club is over, I still hate the thought of her and George together. Because I hate the thought of George with anyone. And now that I've admitted that to myself, in my own mind, somehow it's easier not to feel mad at Hannah anymore, because this has nothing to do with her.

"Emma, no, George and I—"

And then I realize George isn't here with everyone else. "Hey, where is George?" I ask. I really need to apologize to him, too. More than anyone else, George is George, and I don't want to spend the rest of our senior year not talking to each other.

"That's what I'm trying to tell you," Hannah says. "I don't know where he is. George and I talked last night, and we both agreed we don't want to date. We never really wanted to date. We just want to be friends. We were only going along with the whole dating thing because…well, we both really wanted our app to win. But now the competition is over." She sounds weirdly relieved.

They don't want to date? But what about all that stuff she said to me in coding club last week? "But you said he's such a great guy," I protest.

"He is a great guy. But we're not in love with each other." She shrugs, like it's really no big deal.

What about what George said to the judges yesterday about his girlfriend? Maybe he feels differently than Hannah? Or was that all just George making stuff up to try really hard to win?

"So, he's not here?" I look around again, still not able to process what she's telling me. But I don't see him nearby, and I can't imagine who else George would be dancing with, other than coding club. George isn't here.

"I haven't seen him," Hannah says.

"Neither have I," Jane says, and Sam shakes his head.

"I texted him," Robert offers. "And he said he needed to stay home to finish a project."

"A project...?" We don't have anything due in any of our classes. And George is so...George. It's not like him to skip out on going to the dance with coding club as planned just because we lost, or even because he's mad at me.

"I'm going to go out in the hallway and text him," I shout as the DJ switches the song and something loud with a fast beat shakes the floor again.

I make my way out into the hallway and sit on the bench in front of the trophy case. I think about that last dance in the fall, when I sat here. When George tried to convince me what he heard outside the bathroom with Phillip and his friends, and I refused to listen. And all along, George was doing everything he could to help us win, wasn't he? Even going along with his match to Hannah, making the judges believe, making *me* believe.

Haven't you ever felt something that can't be quantified? George asked me once. My stomach aches now, and my phone shakes in my hands as I consider what to text him. Is this what George meant?

I type out a few things in a text, then delete them. Then finally settle on: I'm really sorry for everything. Where are you? I'm at the dance and I want to talk to you in person.

Three dots pop up right away, and my heartbeat quickens. He's not so mad that he's not going to respond. He's here, on the other end of my phone.

I've been working on fixing our code all day. Download the newest version of the app. And log in as you.

I don't have a user log-in, as I've always been working on code as an admin.

I don't even have an account, and my computer is at home.

I made you an account!

George...the competition is over. We lost.

Please, Emma, just look at the changes I made. Log-in is EmmaW. And password is your favorite pizza toppings, CamelCase. Please, just try it.

I don't see the point, but George seems like he's not going to leave it alone until I agree. Fine. But will you come to the dance so I can apologize and we can talk?

He sends me a thumbs-up, and I click on the update and settle into my seat in front of the trophy case, waiting for the newest version of the app to upload with the very bad cell signal we get at school.

Finally, it does, and I open it and log in as George told me, my name and "mushroomsAndOlives" for the password. The first screen is the same, with George's two yellow hearts, holding on to the words *The Code for Love* in between them. If I want to get to the next screen, to see whatever changes he's made, I'm going to have to click to take the survey. Which I haven't done yet myself, and definitely don't want to do now. But George really wants me to see his changes, and somehow I feel like I've messed up so badly I owe him at least this much. So I sigh and click on the survey.

Instead of the survey, though, something entirely different pops up: an animated version of a guy with messy blond hair and glasses, wearing the same gray Converse George always wears. Is this supposed to be George?

Animated George walks across my phone screen and holds up a sign that says: *Emma, click for the real code for love.* Wait… what is this? Did George put in an Easter egg for my account?

I touch the sign with my fingertip, and animated George walks to the next screen.

When you can't stop staring at the way she chews on her pencil in calc…

An animation of a girl with blond hair and a navy blue sweatshirt, chewing on her pencil, comes on my screen. I chew on my pencil like that when I'm thinking. Wait, *is that my Wednesday sweatshirt*? Is this supposed to be me?

I tap the screen, and on the next one, it says, *The way her eyes light up when she solves an equation.*

It goes on, screen after screen…

The way her voice sounds when she says your name, and it makes you feel like you're someone special.

The way whenever you're with her, you feel happier than you ever do.

And when you're not…you miss her the second she's gone.

The way she smiles when she beats you at Ping-Pong, and you want her to beat you again just to see her smile. An animated Ping-Pong ball goes back and forth across the screen, and I feel warm just thinking about playing with George.

I'm smiling as I click on the Ping-Pong ball, and on the next screen, animated George and animated me are dancing together. I remember the way I felt, dancing with him for real in the fall, the way I leaned into him, and he smelled and felt and sounded just right and comfortable, and how for a few seconds we held on to one another and everything felt perfect.

What if you just feel something for someone…deep in your gut, that's different than the way you've ever felt about anyone else? George said once. Is this what he meant?

"Emma." I hear George's voice, and I think it's coming from the app. Until he says it again, louder. "Emma!"

I look up, and he's running down the hallway, breathing hard. He's not dressed for the dance—he's wearing jeans and a plaid shirt and his Converse—like he hadn't planned on coming at all until I texted him. "Did you see the app?" he says, breathless.

I turn off the screen of my phone and put it back in Izzy's clutch. Then I stand and walk toward him, only stopping when I'm right in front of him, when we are standing face-to-face, eyes to eyes. George touches my arm, my body warms, and all the stress and worry of the past few days falls away. "I saw it," I say.

"Did you like it?" he whispers, still breathless, or maybe terrified of what I'll say next.

"I loved it," I say quickly. "I mean…I don't know about the accuracy of your algorithm in this version, but that was some pretty impressive animation."

"Yeah?" He smiles, his whole face relaxing, and he's the George I met in sixth grade again, challenging me to an equation during math Olympiad, the George driving my car too fast to the hospital, promising me that Dad was going to be fine. The George ordering me mushroom and olive pizza in his kitchen and teasing me about how gross it is. The George lobbing a Ping-Pong ball across the table at me, trying so hard to get me to miss. "What was your favorite part?" he asks now.

I put my arms gently around his neck. "I liked when you had them dance, at the end."

He wraps his arms around my waist, and the music is close enough that we can hear it but far enough away that we can hear each other breathing, too. And we sway back and forth for a few minutes, saying nothing. Inside the gym, the slow song stops, and something fast comes on. But neither one of us move apart. Instead, we just stand there, still slow-dancing, still holding on to one another.

I put my head on George's chest and listen to the sound of his heart beating against my ear. And I think about what everyone said: Dad fell in love with Mom's eyes. Izzy likes that John makes her laugh. Mrs. Bates says there's no way to quantify *passion*. And Izzy says she can see how George feels about me, just by the way he looks at me.

I like George because he understands me, because we understand each other. Because he's smart and so easy to talk to, and because when I'm upset he makes me feel better. Being with him, I'm comfortable and happy and safe. And maybe there is no math, no numbers, that can predict any of that, or especially not the way I am feeling right now, right in this very moment, leaning into his heartbeat in my ear.

"I wanted to tell you how I felt for so long, but I just didn't have the words, Emma," George says into my hair.

I move in closer to him, hold on tighter. "Who needs words when you have code?" I finally say.

"And this." George wraps his arms tighter around me, and I think what he means is what he feels, what we both feel. There are no words, no math, no code. Just the two of us, here, together. Maybe this is what Izzy meant when she told me, *If you feel something...just let yourself feel.*

George puts his hand on my chin, and tilts my face toward his gently. We stare at each other, and I know he's about to kiss me. For the first time in my life, I am certain I want to kiss someone, and I'm certain he wants to kiss me back. I *really* want to kiss him. I want to know what George's lips feel like on mine and how he tastes. I want us to breathe together, for a moment.

And then I don't want to wait for him to do it, either.

I stand up on my toes, lean in just an inch closer to him and I kiss him first. The music and the sounds of the gym and all the other couples we matched with our code all fade away.

There is just me and George.

Kissing him is better than beating him at Ping-Pong or at math, and I already know, when Izzy asks me later, I won't be able to explain why. Except that I am warm and light. Really, really happy. Whatever is happening now is completely unquantifiable. It is passion and music. And there are no words, no numbers, to describe it.

For once, I don't care. I'm not thinking about numbers at all. I'm only thinking about George, and the feel of his lips on mine. And I don't want to ever stop kissing him.

SIX MONTHS LATER

"Em!" Izzy shouts my name from downstairs. "George is here."

I'm in my bedroom organizing my suitcases, taking out some winter clothes in order to fit all my coding books. I'll be back to visit Dad for a weekend before it gets too cold and I can always bring warmer clothes back to Pittsburgh with me then. I sit on the final suitcase to get it to close, then run down the steps.

George is sitting at the kitchen table talking to Izzy, but when I walk in, he stops talking, looks at me and smiles. We've been together since the night of the Valentine's Day dance, but still, every time I see him, I feel the same unexplainable way I felt seeing him walk into the school that night.

My heartbeat speeds up and my face grows warm. And it's silly because he's George, and I have seen him thousands of times in my life. But now that I understand the way he feels about me, and the way I feel about him, everything is different.

"Have fun, you two," Izzy says. Her hair is up in twisty rollers. She and John have a date planned in the city tonight, before they head back to LA on the weekend. Dad is driving with me to Pittsburgh tomorrow, but he'll fly back and be home in time to take Izzy to the airport to fly to LA on Sunday.

Numbers don't lie, and George and I ended up tying for valedictorian, as we both had the same exact 3.99 GPA, in all the same honors and AP classes. Mr. Dodge called us into his office in May and said he wanted to find a way to break the tie. But I stood up and told him I thought George and I should be co-valedictorians. We were co-presidents of coding club, after all. Co-everything by the end of the year. It didn't seem fair we had both worked so hard, both landed at number one in our class, only to have one of us be pushed to number two in some kind of random tiebreaker. It took some convincing—Mr. Dodge called it *unconventional*—but in the end, George and I gave the valedictorian speech together.

Still, Ms. Taylor was right that my statistical chances of getting into Stanford were low. In the end, I guess I was just another math brain in a sea of math brains—at least to Stanford. But I did get into Carnegie Mellon, *and* I got the scholarship Ms. Taylor found for me, for women in tech. When you do the math, CMU is just below Stanford in rankings for coding, and with the scholarship, I'll be going there almost for free. Plus, Pittsburgh is only a five-hour car ride; I'm taking my car, and I'll be able to come back and check on Dad on the weekend a few times a semester.

George got into the animation program both at CMU and at USC, and I thought for sure he'd go to LA with John and Izzy. But ultimately, he said LA was just too far for him. Whether he meant too far from Highbury, or from me, he didn't clarify. But I'm so happy we're both going to Pittsburgh together. I couldn't imagine having to say goodbye to him, not seeing him every day, or only being able to FaceTime with him from across the country. Izzy keeps telling me that college is this big, amazing and overwhelming new world, and I'm glad I'll have George there with me to navigate it.

"Emma." George says my name again now. "You ready to go?" We're supposed to meet Jane, Sam, Robert and Hannah at the diner for dinner to say goodbye before George and I are off to Pittsburgh tomorrow. Hannah has been away at camp all summer, and Sam was in Phoenix with his dad. So we haven't all been together since the last weekend in May, when they came to watch me come in first place in my piano competition, and then we all went out to celebrate after.

"Yeah. I'm ready," I say. Izzy grabs me for a quick hug, and I hug her back. After spending the whole summer with her, it's not going to be any easier to say goodbye again tomorrow than it was last year. But I'll see her again one more time in the morning before I leave. So I let her go now, and walk outside with George. I'm taking my car to Pittsburgh, and it's partially packed, so George had offered to borrow his mom's car and drive us to dinner.

"Hey," George says once we're out in the driveway, alone. He takes my hand and squeezes it. "I missed you."

I laugh. "We saw each other last night." George's mom had a going-away party for him and John at their house, and George and I had another Ping-Pong rematch. I won again. And I'll admit, it's still satisfying to beat George, even now that we're dating. But maybe not as satisfying as after I beat him, when we turned off the lights, shared a bean bag chair and lay next to each other, kissing for a long time. Until his mom noticed we were missing from the party and called up to ask where we were.

I smile again now, thinking about lying there with him, his lips on mine, and I stand up on my toes and give him another kiss. I feel his smile against my lips as he kisses me back. "We should go," he says. "We're going to be late." But neither one of us moves.

Instead, George kisses me again. I kiss him back, and everything else disappears.

There's no numbers, no math, no time. There's only me and George, and this unquantifiable, beautiful feeling between us.

★★★★★

ACKNOWLEDGMENTS

I'm so grateful to everyone at Inkyard who championed this book and saw it through to publication. Thank you to Lauren Smulski for falling in love in the very early stages and helping me make Emma shine, and to Bess Braswell, Natashya Wilson and Connolly Bottum for seeing this book through production and into the hands of readers. Thank you also to Kate Studer for her thoughtful editorial insights.

An enormous thank-you to my agent, Jessica Regel, who always encourages me even when I call her to tell her about a crazy new idea I've had. Your belief in me means everything! Thank you also to the wonderful team at Foundry: especially Sarah Lewis, Sara DeNobrega, Mike Nardullo and Claire Harris.

Thank you to Gregg, for love and support always, and also for explaining how coding an app would work. (All errors, unintentional or otherwise, are mine, not his.) And to my kids, who've been asking and encouraging me to write a book for them for years—thank you for being the wonderful people (and readers!) you are. Thank you also for all the robotics competitions you've participated in over the years, which were useful in modeling the coding club competitions.

Thank you to my friends for encouragement and support, especially Maureen Leurck and Tammy Greenwood for helping me stay sane daily. And a huge thank-you to Brenda Janowitz for the early read and encouragement! Thank you to Andrea Katz, huge champion of my books and also supportive friend. And to my friends on the home front for the love, support and mahj—you make my writing and my life infinitely better.